MORE BAD BLOOD

Eva Carmichael

Best Wishes

Eva Carmichael

Published in paperback, 2020 in association with:
JV Publishing
Tel: 07860213358
jvpublishing@yahoo.com

ISBN: 9798577787288

Acknowledgements

Thank you to John and Vicky (JV Publishing) without whose expert help and constant encouragement this novel would not have been possible.

Thank you also to my faithful beta readers, Nicola, Maureen and Margaret. I really do appreciate your comments.

Last, but by no means least, a big thank you to Billy and Judy for allowing me to successfully promote my first book *'Bad Blood Rising'* on Redcar Market in 2020. It really was an enormous help. I look forward to promoting *'More Bad Blood'* throughout 2021.

1

The white Bedford van was parked discreetly on waste ground just off the M40 outside Dover. Two men sat in the front of the vehicle.

"Bloody hell, George, if you must smoke that stuff do it outside. You're making the van stink."

"Chill out for Christ's sake, it's only weed. Want some?"

"No, I don't." Luke spat indignantly. "The boss will go ape if he knows you've been smoking that shit."

"Fuck him," George sneered. "Nobody tells me what I can and can't do. I'll tell him that too if I ever get to meet him."

"That's never going to happen. You know the rules."

George glared at his companion as he ran a large, calloused hand through his bushy red beard. "How come you're the only one who knows the main man anyway? If you ask me—"

"Nobody is asking you. If you don't like the way things are run, you can always go back to being a doorman. Risk getting your head kicked in at some grotty club for minimum wage."

"No, mate, that's not what I'm saying. I just think it's odd that I've never met this guy, that's all. We take all the risks."

"You get well paid, don't you? I don't see the problem."

George shrugged his massive shoulders and opened the van door. "I'm going for a piss," he said, climbing out of the van and making his way into the undergrowth. "I won't be long."

"You'd better not," Luke said. "It's turned ten. The lorry should be here any minute." He checked his appearance in the van's mirror. It was a handsome face that stared back at him with just a hint of his African ancestry. At twenty-six, Luke Jarvis was two decades younger than his companion. His hair was black and professionally styled. His eyes were dark brown, almost black. They were not kind eyes, however, but cold and hard, almost menacing. "Hurry up," he yelled, catching sight of the approaching lorry. "They're coming."

George grunted as he climbed back into the front seat of the van. "All right, keep your hair on."

4

"Remember what I've said. Leave the talking to me. You just do as you're told. Got it?"

George scowled at his companion but remained silent.

The twenty-four-wheeler pulled up behind the van. '*Delaney's Logistics*' emblazoned in large green letters on the side of the vehicle. '*Transporters across the Globe*'. George smirked in the knowledge that the valuable part of the lorry's cargo was only destined as far as Birmingham. He watched as Luke got out of the van and approached the driver, Albi, a large, bald-headed man with a swarthy complexion. Albi jumped from his cab and lit a cigarette.

There was a brief exchange of words before Luke returned to the van. "Open up the doors," he said, "and hurry up, we haven't got all night."

George got out of the van and went to the side of the vehicle. Swiftly, he slid open the doors as Luke and Albi opened up the back of the lorry. He watched as Luke grabbed one girl by the arm and dragged her from the lorry, forcing her into the van. This was soon followed by a second girl, then a third.

Five had been put into the vehicle when Luke pulled the last girl from the lorry and steered her towards the van. The girl was no more than sixteen, slim and pretty, with long, black hair styled in two braids tied with red ribbon. She was crying. Her left cheek bruised and swollen. Like the others, she appeared drugged and barely able to stand.

Albi sneered. "Make sure you watch that one. She fights like a tiger. Look what the bitch did." He held up his left hand bound in a blood-stained handkerchief. "She bit me."

Luke frowned. "Why would she bite you? What did you do to her?"

Albi grinned and shrugged his shoulders. "I just wanted to make her feel welcome if you know what I mean?" He winked and laughed coarsely. "Next thing, she's kicking and biting like a wild animal. I had to hit her to calm her down."

"You shouldn't have done that. You know the rules. You're not supposed to harm any of the girls."

"It's a perk of the job, mate. Don't tell me you haven't helped yourself before now?"

"When the boss finds out he'll—"

Albi threw down his half-smoked cigarette. "What will he do? Find another courier? Good luck with that. I get through customs without being stopped because my cousins work for port security. Safe delivery is almost guaranteed." Albi walked over to Luke and put out his right hand. "Now, where's my money?"

Luke glared at him before handing over a brown package. "The boss will be in touch when he has another delivery."

Albi sneered. "I'll be waiting." He climbed back into his cab. "See you next time."

Luke watched as the lorry roared into life and headed back to the motorway. "If the boss has any sense, he'll find another courier," he muttered. "That bloke's a liability."

"He's got a point though," George said. "He always gets through the port without any hassle."

"He's still an arsehole," Luke said, climbing into the van. "Now put your foot down we're going to be late."

2

They had been travelling for about an hour when George glanced at Luke and sighed. "I don't like it when we're moving women. I prefer moving drugs or booze. It's a lot less trouble."

"It's not as profitable."

"What do you mean? The drugs we've collected have been worth thousands, tens of thousands probably."

"Yeah, but when they're gone, they're gone. With a woman, she can be sold again and again. It's like having your own ATM machine."

George chuckled. "I never thought of it like that. That's very true."

Luke groaned, holding his stomach. "I need the loo. That bloody vindaloo, it feels like my gut's on fire."

"There's a service station up ahead. I'll pull in there."

Five minutes later, George drove to the services and pulled up abruptly. He watched as Luke disappeared into the building and parked the van between two high-sided lorries in a dimly-lit area of the car park. He climbed from the cab and lit a cigarette. It was then he heard shouting and screaming from inside the vehicle. He crept around to the rear doors. "Be quiet in there," he hissed.

"Help, please open the doors. Nadia's ill, she's having a fit."

"I said, be quiet. I won't tell you again."

"She's unconscious," screamed one of the girls. "I think she's dying."

No, this can't be happening, George whispered to himself, clenching and unclenching his fists. *Where the fuck is Luke?* He scanned the car park, but there was no sign of him. Unsure what to do, George paced nervously around the vehicle. He could feel the sweat running down the back of his neck and his heart, wildly pounding, in his chest.

"Please open the doors," the voice pleaded. "You must help her or she will die."

Panicking now, George rushed to the side of the vehicle. The girls were still wailing, louder and more insistent this time. "Oh, fuck it," George muttered, as he slid back the bolts. Immediately the door opened, all six girls rushed forward causing George to fall back onto the tarmac.

"Run," cried one girl. "All of you run."

George sprang to his feet and grabbed two of the girls. Pushing them back into the van, he locked the door and gave chase, catching a further two. They struggled, but they were no match for the powerfully built man as he roughly shoved them back into the vehicle.

It was then Luke approached, half carrying, half dragging one of the girls. "What the fuck's going on?" he yelled, pushing the girl into the van. "I found this one heading for the services. What did I tell you about messing with them?"

"I didn't," George said. "They were screaming that one of them was ill. I only opened the door to—"

"Have you rounded them all up?"

George shrugged. "I think so."

Luke opened the doors and looked inside. "Shit, there's one missing."

"I'll find her," George said, rushing into the undergrowth. "She can't have gone far."

Both men searched furiously for the missing girl. A driver of a red Nissan drove up to the van and wound down his window. "Is everything all right, mate? Have you lost something?"

"My phone," Luke answered, "but it's all right, I've found it now, thanks."

Satisfied, the driver pulled away. There was a rustling amongst the shrubbery as George pushed his way through. "She's not in there," he said breathlessly. "Well, not anymore, she isn't." He held up a red hair ribbon. "I found this in the bushes, but there's no sign of her."

Luke shook his head in despair. "Christ, the boss is going to do his nut."

"It wasn't my fault," George said. "I was only trying to

help."

"You stay in the van. I'll let him know what's happened."

George climbed back into the cab. He was angry that the girls had tricked him, but Luke shouldn't have left him on his own with a cargo of six, he reasoned. Luke was supposed to be the experienced one in this sort of thing, not him. He'd tell the boss that too if he ever got to meet him.

The van door opened, and Luke climbed into his seat.

"What did he say?" George asked quietly.

Luke turned angrily to face George. "What do you think he said? Let's get this lot over to Birmingham now."

"What about the one who's still out there?"

"There's nothing we can do about it. She'll be well gone. Anyway, the boss has another job for us when we get rid of this lot. He wants us over in Leeds."

George frowned. "I fucking hate Leeds. What sort of job is it anyway?"

Luke snarled. "The sort that pays your wages. Let's get moving. We don't want to be late. We're in enough trouble as it is."

3

It had been two years since Karl had been shot. He grimaced as he stretched for the bottle of painkillers.

Lisa reached out and gently placed her hand on her husband's arm. "Is your leg hurting, love?" she said.

Karl merely grunted by way of response.

"Why don't we do something nice today?" Lisa continued, handing him a glass of water. She picked up the newspaper and turned to the 'What's on' page. "It's been ages since we went anywhere together. What about the cinema, or maybe the theatre? There's that new Alan Bennett on at the Alhambra."

"You go," Karl snapped. "I have to work." He picked up the telephone and dialled a number. "The business doesn't run itself."

"Darling, you have to rest more. You know what the doctor said."

"And you know what I think about doctors. They're … Alex, is that you?"

"Good morning," Alex answered sleepily. "You're early this morning. Is everything all right?"

"Why shouldn't it be?" Karl said.

"Well, it is Sunday. The club doesn't open until later."

"I need you over at the Emerald right away to help Peter. He's expecting a delivery from Charlie this morning."

"Not another load of dodgy booze? You do know what will happen if we get caught?"

"I've been doing this for years, and I haven't been caught yet. Now get your arse over there and give Peter a hand."

Karl slammed down the receiver and turned to his wife. "He's an idle bastard."

"Alex is a good boy," Lisa said. "You've got to remember that working in a night club is still a new thing for him. Give the boy time to adjust."

"He's had two years to adjust. That boy is lazy. He'd rather spend money than earn it."

Lisa sighed. "I hope you're not bringing up his gambling again. He's over that now."

"He'd better be." Karl banged his fist down hard on the table. "I was the one who paid off his debts, remember? Forty grand it cost me. And do I get any gratitude?"

Lisa flung the newspaper down and walked over to Karl. "Alex is paying you that money back. He's worked so hard trying to please you. He even changed his surname from Sutton back to Maddox."

"You'd no business calling him Sutton in the first place," Karl said. "Those two were born a Maddox."

The kitchen door opened, and Christina came into the room.

"Is everything all right?" she asked, walking over to her mother and kissing her on the cheek. "I hope you two aren't arguing again?"

Lisa smiled. "Of course we're not, darling,"

"What time did you get in last night?" Karl snapped. "You weren't home at two this morning when I got back from the club."

Christina sighed and poured herself a coffee. "Dad, I am twenty-eight. If you must know, I went to a party with friends over in Sheffield."

Karl furrowed his brow. "What friends?"

"Nobody you know. Now, if you don't mind, I'm going to take my coffee upstairs and finish reading my book." Smiling, she turned and left the room.

"Do you know who she was with last night?" Karl asked, turning to face Lisa. "You don't think she's—"

"Think she's what? Selling herself to men?"

"No, that's not what I meant. I just think it's best if we know what she's up to, that's all."

"For goodness sake, our daughter got involved with the wrong crowd. That was years ago. She's learnt her lesson."

Karl frowned. "I still think we should know who she's seeing. Christina is vulnerable."

"Don't be ridiculous."

"I don't see how you can say that after what happened," Karl said.

"Karl, I think I know our daughter better than you."

"And whose fault is that?"

Lisa groaned. "Please, don't start raking up the past. I did wrong not telling you I was pregnant when I left you, but we both know the reason for that." She poured herself a coffee before turning to her husband. "If we're going to make this work, we have to be more tolerant of each other. Alex is doing his best to help you run the clubs, you know he is."

"Well, maybe his best isn't good enough."

"Rubbish. He gave up his medical career to work with you."

"Let's not kid ourselves, Lisa. Alex left medicine before he got thrown out. We both know he was stealing drugs from the hospital to pay off his gambling debts."

"That was because of his addiction. His life was spiralling out of control, but he's over that now. He's stopped gambling. He needs a new challenge, more responsibility. A chance to show you what he can do."

"What are you saying? You think I should let him run a club?"

"Why not? You're opening a new one in Manchester soon. Why not let Alex manage it for you? You know he's more than capable."

Karl was silent for a moment. "I'll think about it," he said, "but no promises. I still think he's an idle bastard. I just wish he was more like Christina."

"You're spoiling that girl, Karl."

"What do you mean? You think I've made it too easy for her?"

"I do."

"Christina's had it hard, having to sell herself on the streets because of that bastard Guido Rosso."

"I know her life's not been easy, but to buy her that beauty salon was—"

"She's my daughter, and I will do anything I can to help

her."

Lisa shrugged and went over to the sink with her empty cup. "Karl, there's something you should know about Christina."

"What's that?"

"Christina, she... she tells lies."

"Tells lies?"

Lisa turned to face her husband. Still a handsome man, she thought, looking into his dark-brown eyes. Karl walked over to the sink and pulled her roughly towards him.

"Well?" he demanded. "Explain what you mean about Christina."

"Ever since Christina was a little girl, she's told lies. I was quite worried about her at one time."

"All kids tell lies, everybody knows that."

"Yes, but Christina's not a kid any more. I know she's my daughter, and I love her very much, but the truth is, Karl, our daughter is a compulsive liar."

Christina stood in the hallway outside the kitchen door which was slightly ajar. She clenched her fists tightly as scowling, she made her way silently up the stairs to her room.

Sarah yawned, propping herself up on her elbows. "Who's that ringing at this hour?"

Alex climbed out of bed and made his way to the bathroom. "Karl, of course. Who else would ring at seven-thirty on a Sunday morning?"

"Doesn't that man ever sleep? What did he want?"

"He wants me down at the Emerald right away."

"Why? Can't it wait?"

"You know what Karl's like. Everything has to be done straight away or else."

Sarah snuggled back under the duvet. "He's a damned nuisance. I don't know why you let him get away with it. He treats you like his personal dogsbody."

"That's not true," Alex said. "I'm learning the business."

"What is there to learn about running a sleazy pole dancing

club? It's sordid. You're a trained doctor, Alex. You should be working in medicine, not at Karl's beck and call at the Emerald."

"You won't be saying that when I get my own club."

"Why would you want to run one of Karl's seedy clubs anyway?" she said. "I thought we were going to start a family?"

"We are, but not yet. There's plenty of time for kids later."

"That's what you keep saying."

"For God's sake, woman, stop complaining. I don't have time for this."

Alex walked into the bathroom and turned on the shower, slamming the door behind him. When he emerged ten minutes later, Sarah was sleeping. Quietly, he made his way down the stairs and out into the street.

4

Rachel stretched her elegant limbs and yawned. The bedside clock showed eight-thirty. Slowly, she threw back the covers and made her way to the bathroom.

The four days she had spent in Paris with Greg had been exhausting. Her life was becoming exhausting. Still, she had a few days at home before she went to Dubai with Damian. Maybe she'd stay on and relax in the sun after the week's booking.

Rachel quickly showered and slipped into her designer leggings and top, before going into the kitchen for a glass of juice. She was surprised to hear the doorbell ring. She didn't usually have visitors so early on a Sunday morning. Walking over to the intercom, she could see the visitor was her younger sister, April.

"Come up," she invited, pressing the button and releasing the outer door.

April rushed into the flat and threw her arms around her sister's neck. Rachel looked at April's pretty face, streaked with tears, her pale-grey eyes red and swollen.

"Darling, what's the matter?" she asked, leading her sister into the lounge. "What's happened?"

April began sobbing uncontrollably as she tightly clung on to her sister. It was some minutes before she regained her composure. "It's… it's Alfie," she said at last.

"What about Alfie? Is he all right?"

"He's gone. He's left me."

"What… what happened? Did you have a row?"

"No, it was nothing like that," April said, shaking her head emphatically. "We both went to work yesterday as usual, and everything seemed fine. Then, when I came home, I found he'd packed all his stuff and… and left."

"But he must have had a reason. Have you tried ringing him?"

"Yes, of course I have, but it just goes to voicemail."

"And you have no idea where he's gone or why?"

April was silent for a moment. She began twisting her hair between her fingers, a habit she did when she was nervous. "I think he left because… because of the baby."

Rachel gasped in surprise. "What baby?"

"I did a pregnancy test a couple of days ago, and it was positive. I thought he'd be pleased we were going to have a child together."

"Do you want the baby?"

"I don't know. We hadn't planned it but… what am I going to do, Sis?"

Rachel handed April a tissue. "Maybe it's just the shock. Men do react strangely at the thought of being a dad. Once he comes to terms with it, I'm sure he'll be back."

"But what if he doesn't? I can't have a baby on my own, I won't."

Rachel took her sister's hands in hers. "Don't worry, I know someone who can help."

"I can't go to some backstreet abortionist. It wouldn't be right."

"I'm not suggesting you do that. I know a doctor, well he used to be. He can make things right if that's what you want?"

April shrugged and lowered her head into her hands. "I don't know," she said quietly. "I'll have to think about it."

"Well, there's plenty of time to decide what you want to do. I'm going to make some coffee. Would you like one?" April nodded.

Rachel brought two mugs into the lounge and handed one to her sister.

"This person you know," April said. "You said he was a doctor?"

"Yes, that's right. His name's Alex. He doesn't practice medicine anymore though."

"And you say he can help me?"

"I'm sure he can."

April sipped the coffee in silence for a few minutes, looking admiringly around the spacious room. "I love what you've done to this place," she said at last. "You always did have good taste with décor."

"Glad you like it. Black and grey isn't for everyone."

"It looks stylish and very expensive. I take it you're still err … working?"

Rachel nodded. "I'm still escorting if that's what you mean."

"Aren't you frightened of being with men you don't know? It can be dangerous."

"Not if you're careful. My clients are all wealthy men who just want a little naughty fun sometimes." She leant over and placed her arm around April's shoulders. "Don't worry. I always vet clients before I arrange a meet. Anyway, enough about me. How's your job going? Are you still at the same salon?"

April sighed. "I am until the end of the month. Laura is cutting back on staff. She says there's too much competition from that new salon that's opened up on the Headrow."

"You're being made redundant?"

"Yes, me and two other stylists."

Rachel smiled. "Maybe I can help there. My friend runs that salon. I'll call her later and see if they've any vacancies." There was a shrill ringing sound. "Who's that at this hour?" She frowned as she picked up her mobile.

"Hello... Jacqui, you're an early bird. Is everything all right?" Rachel walked through into the kitchen, closing the door behind her. She returned to the lounge a few minutes later.

"Sorry about that, Sis. That was Jacqui, a friend of mine. She wants me to cover for her tonight at the Belmont."

April frowned. "I don't understand."

"Jacqui's an escort. The agency she works for have taken a deposit for a booking, and it's tonight."

"So, what's the problem?"

"One of Jacqui's private clients wants to meet her, so she's asked me to take the booking for her."

"Why doesn't she just tell the agency she's not available?"

Rachel huffed. "Jacqui works for Cupid's Angels. That's

the one owned by Karl Maddox. If the agency even suspect Jacqui's moonlighting—"

"But won't the client know you're not Jacqui?"

"How could he? He's never met her. The client is expecting a twenty-something blonde, and that's what he'll get." She began to laugh. "Stop worrying. Girls stand in for each other all the time."

"But isn't it dangerous? You don't know anything about this man."

"Cupid's Angels always vet their clients. They'll have taken his Visa details for the deposit so stop worrying, it's perfectly safe. You'll be okay on your own tonight, won't you? I'll only be a couple of hours."

April nodded. "Of course I will. Anyway, being on my own will give me time to think."

"Well, if you're sure…?"

April smiled. "I thought you were going out for a jog? Or is that the new loungewear?"

"I suppose I'd better. You can join me if you want. I have more sportswear in the bedroom."

"No thanks. Exercise was never my thing. I'll go back to my flat and collect some of my stuff if you don't mind me staying here for a few days."

"You're welcome to stay as long as you want." Rachel opened a drawer and removed a key. "Here, take the spare key. I'll only be an hour, and then we can have a proper talk."

"Thanks, Sis." April smiled as she watched Rachel leave the flat.

5

It was nine o'clock when Rachel entered the lobby of the Belmont Hotel. Her smart appearance and confident manner ensured that she would not be challenged by hotel security. She made her way to the lift and ascended the three floors to where the client was waiting. She knocked lightly on the door of room 366.

"The door's open," a husky male voice said from inside the room.

Rachel pushed against the door and entered. The room was dimly lit. A bedside radio was playing, and soft music filled the air.

Stefan Finch was laid on top of the bed. He was naked save for the large, white bath towel that he had wrapped around his ample waist. She pouted seductively as she sauntered towards him. Stefan was in his early fifties. She could see he had recently been in the shower as his grey hair was still damp and pushed back from his face. A friendly face, she thought, with a ruddy complexion and dark-brown eyes.

He smiled. "You must be Jacqui," he said, not attempting to move from his position on the bed. "You're very beautiful."

Rachel lowered her head coyly. "Thank you," she said and blushed in her much-rehearsed manner. "You're very kind, Mr Finch."

"That's very formal. You must call me Stefan."

She grinned. "You're very kind, Stefan," she said, bending over and kissing him lightly on the cheek.

Stefan smiled again. "First things first. Your fee is over there on the dresser."

She reached over and placed the brown envelope in her bag. "Thank you."

"Would you like something from the mini bar, Jacqui?"

"Mm, what a good idea," she purred.

"You'll find a couple of glasses and a bottle of champagne in the fridge."

Rachel poured two glasses of champagne and handed one

19

to Stefan. She noticed that his left hand, bearing a gold band on his ring finger, was trembling slightly as he took the glass.

"Cheers," he said, holding the glass to his lips and sipping its contents.

"Bottoms up," she whispered seductively and took a drink of the liquid before placing the empty glass on the bedside table.

Almost robotically, Rachel began to sway to the rhythm of the music. Moving to the bottom of the bed, she unzipped her dark-blue mini dress. Experience had taught her that back zips can be clumsy to unfasten, so she always made sure her clothes had side fastenings. She soon wriggled out of her dress, revealing pretty black underwear and lacy top stockings. Making her way to the side of the bed, Rachel adeptly unfastened her bra. Teasingly, she leant over Stefan holding the bra closely to her. He grabbed it, and threw it onto the pillow next to him. He then reached out for her, cupping her firm breasts in his hands. His breathing became laboured and erratic, and Rachel could see sweat beginning to run down his face.

"Not so fast tiger," she purred, pulling away from him. "I've got more to show you."

She began to sway once more to the music as she made her way slowly to the bottom of the bed. She turned her back to Stefan as she unfastened the side strings of her panties, swivelling her hips to the music. Stefan groaned as she removed them and let them fall to the floor. '*I don't think he's going to last the two hours he's booked.*' She smiled to herself as, placing her hands on her hips, she slowly turned around to face him.

"Oh, no," she gasped in terror at the sight before her. "Don't do this to me, Stefan. Don't you fucking dare do this to me."

Stefan's head lolled to one side, his eyes bulging, and his mouth open. She knew at once he was dead.

Rachel rushed to the side of the bed and began to shake him, gently at first and then more violently, causing him to roll over sideways into the middle of the bed. She sat on the edge, staring in disbelief at his lifeless body. She felt confused. Her heart was racing. Her first thought was to ring for help. Maybe a doctor could revive him, could breathe life into his dead body. But no, it was too late. Stefan Finch was beyond help. Anyone could see that. And what would become of her if she summoned someone? There would be questions, accusations. No, she could do without the hassle.

Hastily, Rachel put on her dress and panties. Her immediate thought was to get out of the room as quickly as she could. It was then she noticed the leather wallet on the bedside cabinet – a wallet bulging with notes. Next to the wallet was a blue leather box containing a gold Rolex. Overcome with temptation, she reached out and swiftly removed the cash and put it into her bag, along with the watch. After all, she reasoned, Stefan had no use for it now.

She was halfway towards the door before she saw the briefcase. A large, expensive-looking brown leather briefcase with the distinctive gold lettering 'SPF' in the top right-hand corner propped on a chair. Without hesitation, Rachel picked it up and hurried out of the room into the hotel corridor. The lift was ascending to her floor. Quickly, she turned and ran to the stairwell leading directly to the foyer. Soon she was outside, swallowed up in the busy street.

6

The lift doors opened, and four people exited. An elderly couple turned left along the hotel corridor. The other two occupants turned right.

"What room number did the boss say he was in?" George asked.

"366," Luke replied. "And don't forget what I said. Keep schtum and let me do the talking."

George shrugged. "What's this bloke supposed to have done anyway?"

"He's taken something that doesn't belong to him. Now shut the fuck up."

George grabbed Luke by the arm, pushing him against the wall. "Don't talk to me like I'm some moron. I've asked you a question. What does the boss want with this bloke?"

Luke glared at his companion and attempted to release his grip without success. "Look, mate, all I know is that he stole something that doesn't belong to him and we're here to get it back."

George tightened his grip on Luke's arm. "What sort of something?"

"A briefcase. We have to get back a briefcase. Happy now?"

George frowned. "What's so special about the briefcase?"

"How the hell do I know? The boss just said to get it back. Now, are you going to let go of me or are we going to spend the night out here?"

George gave one last defiant glare at his companion before releasing his hold.

Both men hurried along the corridor until they reached their destination. Luke was surprised to see that the room's door was slightly ajar. He looked up and down the corridor, and satisfied that it was deserted, entered the room, followed closely by George.

Luke gasped at the sight before him. Stefan Finch's naked, lifeless body was slumped across the bed. He rushed over and lifted the man's head. Stefan's eyes wide open and spittle drooled over his lips and chin.

"Bloody hell, the bastard's gone and croaked," George said almost in a whisper. "We'd better get out of here fast." He turned towards the door.

"Not before we get what we came for," Luke said, looking anxiously around the room. On the bedside table, he saw a small box with 'Rolex' printed in gold. The box was empty. Two empty glasses, one with a distinctive pink lipstick impression around the rim lay next to it. A brown, leather wallet was lying on the floor next to the bed. Carefully, he picked it up and looked inside. Stefan's driving licence was in a front compartment and behind this, several bank cards. Photographs of a middle-aged woman and two teenage boys occupied other compartments in the wallet. Luke rubbed his chin. "There's no money," he said. "The wallet has no money." He looked closely at Stefan's limp body lying on the bed. "The watch has gone too. You can see he wore a watch from the tan line on his wrist. That's probably on its way to a pawn shop."

George looked over at his companion and shrugged but remained silent.

Luke leant over Stefan and picked up a black lacy bra lying on the pillow. "It looks like he didn't die alone."

"Lucky sod," George smirked. "That's how I want to go when the time comes."

Luke glared at him. "Have you found the briefcase? That's what we're here for, remember?"

George shook his head. "There's no sign of it. The hooker probably took that too."

"Then we have to find her and fast."

"How the hell are we going to do that? Do you have any idea how many whores there are in Leeds?"

Before Luke could reply, there was a shrill ringing sound. "What's that noise?"

"It's coming from the wardrobe," George said. He opened the door and removed the mobile phone from the pocket of a jacket. He looked at the screen. "It's his wife ringing. Poor cow doesn't know she's a widow." George was about to put the mobile back when Luke stepped forward.

Luke snatched the phone from George. "Give me that," he said. "I want to try something."

Luke scrolled the caller list. "He only made two calls today," he said. "Let's see who he spoke to." He dialled the first number.

"Ace Star Taxis," a bored voice said. "How can I help?"

"Sorry, mate, wrong number," Luke answered. He dialled the second number.

"Good evening, Cupid's Angels," a husky female voice said. "What can we do for you this evening?"

Luke quickly hung up. "Well, at least we know who supplied the totty," he said. "All we have to do now is find her."

George sighed heavily. "Oh, yeah? How are we going to do that? These agencies have hundreds of tarts on their books."

"Don't worry, we'll find her. I'll have to check in with the boss first though and see how he wants me to handle it."

7

Rachel was relieved to find April asleep when she got back to her apartment. Putting down the briefcase and bag, she walked over to the cabinet and poured herself a large vodka. Her body trembled from the shock of what she had witnessed in the hotel. She swallowed her drink in one gulp and got up to pour herself another. *I should ring someone, she thought. I should tell someone about Stefan. It's only right.* Hesitantly, she picked up the telephone and rang the hotel reception, making sure to withhold her number.

"Room 366," she said breathlessly. "I think the occupant is ill." Not waiting for a response from the receptionist she replaced the receiver. *There, I've done all I can,* she sighed. *I'm not to blame for the poor bastard dying.*

"Is that you, Sis?" April called, walking through into the lounge. "Is everything all right?"

"It's late. You should be asleep."

"Oh, I can't sleep. My head's spinning with wondering what to do."

"Can we talk tomorrow, April?" Rachel sighed. "I'm exhausted."

"Okay. Goodnight," she said as she headed back to her room.

Left alone, Rachel went into the hall and picked up her bag and the briefcase, taking them into the lounge. She began to count the notes she had taken from Stefan's wallet. There was almost five hundred pounds. Then she examined the Rolex. It bore the inscription *To Stefan, All My Love Letitia'.* Rachel frowned. She knew a pawnbroker in town who didn't ask too many questions. Maybe she'd ask April to pawn the watch for her while she was in Dubai.

She studied the briefcase, which had a sturdy combination lock. Rachel gently shook the case and could hear something inside, something quite heavy. Frowning, she walked to the back of the room and lifted up the thick black rug covering the shiny granite tiled floor. Carefully, she pressed the corner of one of the large tiles and it moved sideways to reveal a cavity below. Placing the briefcase inside the safe, she returned the tile pulling the rug over the top. "I'll deal with that when I get back from Dubai," she yawned. "Right now, I need to sleep."

8

Christina had been surprised to receive the call so early in the morning from Sophia, one of her senior beauticians. Sophia, looking anxious and distressed, was already at the salon when she arrived.

"Christina," she sobbed, rushing towards her. "I need your help."

"What on earth's the matter?" Christina asked, putting her arm around Sophia's trembling shoulders. "Calm down and tell me what's wrong."

"She's in here," Sophia spoke in a whisper as she opened the door to one of the treatment rooms. "I didn't know what else to do so... so I brought her here."

The room was small, with white painted walls. The only furniture was a treatment bed and a trolley full of cosmetics. A girl of about sixteen was cowering by the only window in the room. Her face tearstained and bruised. Her long, black hair tangled.

"This is Nadia," Sophia said, walking over to the girl and taking her hand. "Nadia is my sister."

"Why is she here?"

"Nadia was trafficked to England."

"What do you mean, trafficked? I don't understand."

"She was drugged and put into a lorry with half a dozen other girls. She managed to escape and came here to be with me."

Christina gasped. "Have you reported what happened to the police?"

Sophia shook her head violently. "No police. They will send her back to Romania. I want my sister to stay with me where she'll be safe."

"But Sophia, you can't—"

"Please, I'm begging you. Let Nadia stay and work here with me. I can teach her how to do nails. She can keep the salon clean and—"

Christina held up her hands. "We can't do that. You know

we can't."

"Are you saying that we should give her back to the traffickers?"

"Of course not. But if we go to the authorities and report what has happened, they can make sure she gets home safely."

"No, no, we can't do that. You don't understand. Nadia will never be safe at home now. She must stay here with me."

Christina sighed and walked over to the girl. She gently took her hand and helped her to her feet. "Has she told you anything about the men who took her?"

"She told me she was raped by the man driving the lorry. When they got over the Channel, she was put into a van. When it stopped, she managed to get away."

"The poor kid," Christina said, pushing the girl's dark hair back from her face. "Has she seen a doctor?"

"No, no doctor. A doctor would report what has happened."

"Not the doctor I'm thinking of," Christina said, turning to Sophia. "But how is it that you work legally in England, but not your sister?"

"We have different fathers," Sophia said quietly. "My father was from Scotland. He was a relief worker in my country. He died when I was six, and Mother married a local man."

"So, you have a British passport, and Nadia doesn't?"

"Yes. I could come to England, no problem, but Nadia… Well, the whole thing is crazy."

"I think it's best if you take your sister home," Christina said gently. "I'll call round later with my friend, the doctor, to make sure she's okay."

"And no police?"

"No police, I promise."

"Thanks, Christina." Sophia smiled and hugged her friend tightly. "I knew I could rely on you to help."

When Sophia and Nadia left the salon, Christina picked up the phone and dialled a number.

"Hello… Alex, it's me. I need you to do something for me."

9

Jacqui entered the foyer of the Monarch Hotel just before nine o'clock that evening. The Agency had told her the booking was on a personal recommendation from another client.

The Monarch was one of the swankiest hotels in the city. She got into the smoked-glass lift and pressed for the fifth floor. Room 502 was where her client was waiting. She knocked lightly, and it was opened almost immediately. The room's occupant, a man in his thirties, was tall and muscular, she noted, with a light-olive complexion and short, dark hair. He was dressed casually in grey trousers and a pale-blue sweatshirt.

"Ah, you must be Jacqui," he greeted as he gently steered her into the room by her arm. "I'm Luke."

"Hi," Jacqui smiled, "it's very nice to meet you."

The room, lavishly furnished, had pale lilac walls with an iridescent sheen, and a thick purple carpet covered the floor. At the far side of the room were French doors, slightly ajar, leading out onto a small balcony with panoramic views of the city.

"What a beautiful room," Jacqui said. "It's the first time I've been to the Monarch. It really is impressive."

Luke smiled as he gently placed his arms around her trim waist. "Would you like something to drink, Jacqui?" he asked. "Wine or champagne, perhaps?" He began to run his fingers seductively up her spine, resting on her slim shoulders.

"No, thank you," Jacqui purred, enjoying the touch of his caress. "I never drink alcohol."

"Is that right?" Luke's tone became harsh as he put both hands around her neck. "You had a drink the other night with Stefan at the Belmont, didn't you? You do remember Stefan? The man you robbed and left to die."

"I don't know what you're talking about," she cried. "You have the wrong girl. I haven't been to the Belmont in months." Frantically, Jacqui struggled to free herself from Luke's grasp.

"Liar," he yelled, slapping her hard across the face. "What have you done with the briefcase you stole, you thieving little whore? I want it back, do you understand?" He began to shake her violently. "You give it back, and you can keep the rest of the stuff, but I want that briefcase."

"I don't know anything about a briefcase. Please, Luke, you're hurting me."

The bathroom door opened, and George came into the room. Surprised by the newcomer's sudden appearance, Luke released his grip and Jacqui ran towards the open French doors and out onto the balcony.

The balcony was narrower than she had realised. Unable to stop the momentum, Jacqui plummeted over the top of the smoked-glass screen and fell screaming into the night's blackness.

"What the fuck have you done, you stupid bastard?" Luke yelled at George. "I told you to stay in the bathroom."

"I just came out to …" George blustered. "I didn't know she'd throw herself over the edge, the silly cow."

Luke rushed towards the door. "We'd better get out of here quick."

Both men left the room and hurried along the corridor to the waiting lift. It wasn't until they were outside on the street, walking away from the hotel, that Luke stopped and turned to George. "There's something not right. I think we had the wrong girl."

"What do you mean? You asked Cupid's Angels for the same escort who had visited Finch, at the Belmont, and they said it was Jacqui."

"I know, but I don't think that girl tonight is the one who nicked the briefcase."

George looked puzzled. "You mean there are two Jacqui's? I don't think the agency would allow that."

"I'm telling you, she's not the one who visited Stefan Finch at the Belmont. I'm sure of it."

"What makes you say that? You can't believe a word these whores tell you."

"For one thing, she refused the champagne I offered. She said she didn't drink alcohol. When have you ever known a tart refuse a free drink? The girl that visited Finch certainly drank. There were lipstick marks on the glass, remember?"

George shrugged. "Maybe she was driving," he said unconvincingly. "Or maybe she couldn't drink because she was on some medication or—"

"Or maybe she just didn't drink. Then there was the bra she left behind in the room."

"Yeah, she must have been in too much of a hurry she forgot to put it back on."

"The bra left at the Belmont was far too big to have belonged to that girl tonight."

George smirked. "I never realised you were an expert on women's tits. I think—"

"I couldn't care less what you think. I know I'm right."

"So, what do you suggest we do now? We've no way of finding who she was."

Luke was quiet for a moment. "There's the watch," he said at last. "There can't be that many Rolex watches being pawned. We can visit pawnbrokers in Leeds. It's bound to turn up."

George moaned. "Can we do that tomorrow? I'm starving. I haven't eaten since breakfast."

Luke glowered at him. "I've got to ring the boss and tell him what's happened. He's not going to be happy. I can tell you that."

George shrugged. "It's not my fault. It was an accident."

"Let's hope he sees it that way." Luke sighed as he climbed into the van.

10

Alex lit a cigarette and slowly surveyed the Emerald Club. He knew that if he played his cards right, one day, this would all be his. All he had to do was impress his father.

Peter Borowicz, Karl's right-hand man, walked into the room. "What time are you expecting Karl?" he asked. "I need to speak to him urgently."

"What's the problem? Maybe I can help."

"Thanks, but I'll wait for Karl."

"I'm in charge in Karl's absence," Alex said. "If there's a problem, I need to know. Now, what is it?"

The door opened, and Karl entered the room. "Is everything okay?" he said, addressing Peter.

"No, boss," Peter answered sternly. "I need to speak to you urgently. It's important."

"You'd better come through to the office."

Karl turned to his son. "Alex, can you fetch up a coffee? I left without one this morning."

Peter saw the look of anger on Alex's face before he followed Karl through the foyer and ascended the stairs. On entering the office, Karl sat behind his desk and indicated for Peter to sit in the chair opposite.

"Well?" he said coldly. "What's up?"

"It's Jacqui, boss. One of the girls from the agency."

"What's she been up to? Don't tell me she's been picked up by the police?"

"No, it's nothing like that. I've just heard Jacqui's dead."

Karl stiffened. "How? When?"

"She fell from a hotel balcony last night."

"How the hell did that happen? You don't just fall from a balcony. You either jump, or you're pushed. Which hotel was it?"

"The Monarch."

"Who was the client?" Karl said.

"He said his name was John Smith. He paid for the booking in cash."

"Bookings should never be made with cash. They should be made through a credit card. What went wrong?"

Peter shrugged. "I don't know, boss."

"What about the hotel's register? Surely they'll have his details."

"All I know is that Jacqui visited a client at the Monarch and fell over the balcony."

Karl narrowed his eyes and drummed his fingers on the desk. "Ask Paul to come up, will you? We'll see what he can find out."

Peter nodded and opened the office door to leave. As he did so, Alex almost fell into the room, spilling coffee onto the carpet.

"Shit!" he spluttered, glaring at Peter. "Look what you made me do, you clumsy bastard."

Peter rushed from the office as Alex walked over to his father's desk with the half-filled coffee cup. "Sorry," he said, placing the cup on the desk. "It wasn't my fault."

"Never mind about that," Karl said, "there's something I want to talk to you about. Take a seat."

Alex sat across from his father. "What is it?"

"It's about the club I've bought in Manchester."

"What about it?"

"How would you feel about running it for me, on a trial basis of course?"

Alex grinned. "Do you mean it? Run my own club? That's fantastic. I… I don't know what to say. I promise I won't let you down."

Karl scowled. "You'd better not. The Amethyst will be open for business in a couple of weeks. It'll mean you and Sarah moving over to Manchester, of course."

"Oh, I don't mind that. I'm ready for a change of scenery anyway. Where in Manchester is it?"

"It's not far from your old stomping ground," Karl said, fixing Alex with a stare. "But I'm sure you've learnt by your mistakes, eh, son? There'll be no more visits to the Lucky Ace Casino?"

"I don't gamble anymore, Karl, you know that," Alex said indignantly.

"Make sure you don't, or you know what will happen."

There was a knock on the door, and Paul Borowicz, Peter's brother, entered the room. Whilst Peter had the brawn, his brother Paul had the brains. He had a knack for finding things out and, right now, Karl needed to find out all he could about Jacqui's punter.

Karl waved a dismissive hand to Alex. "We'll speak later, son. Right now, I have pressing business to take care of."

11

"There's no need to be nervous," Rachel said to her sister, as they walked into the salon. "You'll like Christina, she's very friendly."

"Rachel, how lovely to see you, it's been ages," Christina greeted warmly, kissing Rachel on the cheek. She turned to face the younger woman. "And you must be April? Rachel tells me you're looking for a job."

"Yes… yes," April said. "I'm being made redundant soon."

"How long have you been qualified?"

"Just over twelve months."

"That's good," Christina said, smiling. "I've asked one of the girls to give you a trial this morning. If everything goes well, you could start working here next week."

Christina signalled to one of the stylists. "Victoria. A word?"

The young woman who had been arranging equipment at her work station came over to the group. "Yes, Christina?"

"This is April. Could you take her through the usual trial?"

Victoria nodded. "This way," she said. April followed Victoria into the staff quarters.

Christina showed Rachel into her private office. "We can wait in here," she said. "April will only be half an hour."

Rachel sat on the couch. "You've done wonders with this place, Chris," she said. "It's beautiful."

Christina smiled. "It is, isn't it? Dad's been very generous. Actually, I don't know what I'd have done without his help." She walked over to the sideboard. "How about a coffee until April's done?" Not waiting for a reply, Christina poured two cups from the cafetiere and handed one to Rachel. "So tell me, what are you up to these days? Are you still working?"

"Yes. I'm busier than ever, not that I'm complaining. I'm off to Dubai tomorrow for a week."

"Dubai? That sounds exciting. I've never been there. You must tell me all about it when you get back."

"I must say, Chris, when I heard you'd given up escorting to run a salon, I couldn't quite believe it."

"Well, all things come to an end, some time or another."

"Don't you miss it, though?"

Christina frowned. "No, I don't, not one little bit. By the way, nobody here knows about my past."

Rachel grinned. "Don't worry. Your secret's safe with me."

"Tell me about April. You said she's staying with you?"

Rachel sighed deeply. "She's just broken up with her boyfriend, Alfie. The poor kid told him she was pregnant, and he didn't want to know, the selfish bastard."

"April's pregnant?"

"She thought she was, but it turned out the pregnancy kit had given a false reading."

"Lucky escape, eh? April's a pretty girl."

Rachel smiled. "She's talented too. She cut my hair the other day. What do you think?"

"It looks lovely. She obviously knows what she's doing."

The two women chatted happily for twenty minutes before there was a soft rap on the door.

"Come in," Christina said. A nervous-looking, young woman, with long black hair and a pale complexion came into the room. "Christina," the girl spoke softly with a thick accent, "Victoria said she has finished now, and could you come down, please?"

"Thank you, Nadia."

Both women left the office and joined Victoria. "Well, how did she do?"

"Absolutely fine," Victoria smiled. "April is an excellent stylist."

"Does this mean I have a job?" April asked, turning to Christina.

"I don't see why not. Be here on Monday at half-past eight."

"Really? Oh, thank you, thank you," she squealed with excitement. "You won't regret it, I promise. I'll go and tell that old bat what she can do with her job."

Before Christina could respond, April had rushed through the door and was heading down the street.

"Thanks, Chris." Rachel smiled, hugging her friend. "I really appreciate it. I'm sure April won't let you down."

"I'm sure she won't. Now, promise me when you get back from Dubai you'll ring me, and we can get together and have a proper catch-up."

"I will, I promise, and thanks again. I owe you."

12

When Paul left Karl in the Emerald Club, he drove straight to Cupid's Angels, the largest escort agency in the north of England. It was a small, prefabricated building on the edge of an industrial estate in Leeds. Immediately inside the building was a small reception desk with a computer and telephone. Wendy, the receptionist, was just finishing a call when Paul entered.

"Good morning, Paul," she greeted pleasantly.

Paul nodded by way of an acknowledgement as he sat on the chair at the other side of the desk. He reached over and turned the computer round to face him. "Did you make Jacqui's appointment at the Monarch Hotel last night?" he asked.

Wendy frowned. "Yes. I can't believe she's dead."

Paul brought up Jacqui's assignments on the screen. "It says here that the client paid in cash. Why was that? You know the rules. Bookings should always be made using a card."

"Mostly they are," Wendy said, "but sometimes a punter insists on paying in cash, so there's no trail."

"Didn't you try to persuade him?"

"Well yes… but he said his friend had recommended Jacqui a couple of days earlier, so I thought it would be all right."

"His friend?"

"Stefan Finch. He had booked an appointment with Jacqui a few days earlier at the Belmont."

"Stefan Finch?" Paul said. "Where have I heard that name before?"

Wendy picked up a newspaper and handed it to Paul. "He's in here. He had a heart attack and died, poor man."

Paul studied the paper and read the article about how Stefan Finch had been found dead in the Belmont Hotel, while on a business trip to Leeds. After a couple of minutes, he turned and walked towards the door. "In future, you do not take cash from a punter. There are to be no exceptions. Is that understood?"

"But, Paul, I—"

"Don't argue, Wendy," Paul said, a stern look on his handsome face. "Just do what I say."

Half an hour later, Paul telephoned Karl. "Karl, I'm going to London to check out a possible lead," he said. "I should be back later tonight."

"Is there something I should know?" Karl asked.

"I'm not sure yet. I'll call in the club first thing tomorrow and fill you in."

"What's going on?"

"Sorry, Karl, I can't talk now, my train's just pulled into the station."

Before Karl could respond, Paul hopped nimbly onto the London train and took his seat.

13

The journey to London took just under two hours. Paul got a taxi and arrived at the small stationery company owned by Stefan Finch. The offices were modern, and according to the newspaper article, employed eight staff. He walked up to the front desk and smiled at the young receptionist. She was a pretty girl, with almond-shaped brown eyes and a healthy complexion. The girl's dark hair was swept off her face and tied back with a scrunchy.

"Hello," Paul said, "I'm here to see Mr Finch. I'm afraid I don't have an appointment—"

The girl burst into tears and retrieving a tissue from the top drawer of her desk, proceeded to blow her nose loudly.

"Is everything all right?" Paul asked as the girl sobbed uncontrollably.

"Jenny, go into the staffroom and get a cup of tea, dear," said a middle-aged woman putting her arm around the girl's shoulders. "I'll deal with this."

"Yes, Mrs Winters," the girl said, getting up from her seat and hurrying through a door to the left of her desk.

"Can I help you?" the woman addressed Paul.

"I came hoping to have a word with Stefan, I mean Mr Finch. Is he available?"

"Are you a friend of his?"

Paul smiled. "More an acquaintance. We met a couple of months ago."

Mrs Winters leant closer. "I'm afraid I have some bad news," she said softly. "Mr Finch died. He had a heart attack a few days ago. It was all very sudden."

"I'm sorry to hear that," Paul said, feigning surprise. "He seemed a decent sort of chap."

"Oh, he was," Mrs Winters said. "A very decent man. He played the organ at church most Sundays you know, and he helped out at the amateur dramatics. Very good he was too." She took out a handkerchief and dabbed her eyes. "He was a pillar of society, poor Mr Finch."

Paul gave a sympathetic sigh. "It's always the good ones that go first. Life can be so unfair." Mrs Winters nodded in agreement. "Where did this happen?" Paul asked innocently. "Not in the office, I hope."

"Oh, no, thank goodness. That would have been too dreadful. Mr Finch died in a hotel in Leeds, poor man." She blew her nose loudly before continuing. "He'd been up to Edinburgh on business and stayed at the family's hotel."

"Stefan never mentioned owning a hotel," Paul said.

"Well, it's his wife's family's business really. The staff at The Five Pipers said he showed no sign at all of being unwell during his stay."

"You say he died in Leeds?"

"That's right. He stopped off to meet some clients. He had the heart attack in the hotel he was staying at."

"His wife must be devastated."

"She is. We all are," Mrs Winters said, clasping a gold locket around her neck. "But what makes it worse is poor Mr Finch was robbed."

"That's terrible."

"Apparently, after he died, someone got into his room and stole his wallet and his Rolex."

Paul shook his head. "What is the world coming to?"

"The watch was worth a lot of money. It was a birthday present from Letitia, his wife."

"Can't they trace a Rolex? Maybe the police will—"

Mrs Winters shook her head. "I doubt it," she said. "It did have an inscription on the back, but who looks there? No, I don't think it will ever see the light of day again."

"Well, let's hope you're wrong," Paul said comfortingly.

Mrs Winters dabbed her eyes again. "They took his briefcase too. Can you believe it?"

"What would anyone want with his briefcase? There weren't any valuables in it were there?"

"I wouldn't have thought so. It would have had half a dozen signed contracts, that's all. They'd be no use to anyone else."

"Then why steal it?"

"The briefcase was expensive. It was one of those fancy leather ones by Ralph Lauren. Mr Finch was very proud of it." She blew her nose loudly before continuing. "It bore his initials in gold, 'SPF', Stefan Peter Finch. His wife bought it for him last Christmas."

"Do the police have any idea who robbed him?"

"No, but I wouldn't be surprised if it isn't one of the hotel staff."

"Well, I'm very sorry to hear about Mr Finch," Paul smiled sympathetically. "Perhaps you'd pass on my condolences? Now, I really must be going. I have a train to catch."

"Can anyone else assist you?" Mrs Winters asked, adopting a professional manner. "Mr Lovell has taken over from Mr Finch temporarily. I'm sure he can help."

"That's very kind," Paul said, walking towards the door, "but I'm afraid my business was with Mr Finch."

Paul walked out of the building and hurried along the street.

14

"Are you sure I can't persuade you to stay a little longer, Joe?" Angie pouted. "You know how the kids love having their uncle around."

Joe smiled and walked towards his sister, arms outstretched. "Angie, it's been great staying with you and Josh these last few months. I don't know what I'd have done without you, but it's time for me to move on. I think we both know that." He hugged her, kissing her lightly on the cheek.

A tear trickled down her face, and she wiped it away with the back of her hand. "But where will you go? What will you do?"

"I'll be fine, stop worrying. I've had plenty of time to plan my future."

"But, Joe, you—"

"How about I take everyone out to dinner tonight before I leave?"

"Sorry, love, but Josh won't be back until late. They're short-staffed at the hospital."

Joe grinned. "Serves him right for being a doctor. So, it looks like it's just me, you and the kids."

Angie frowned. "Why don't we stay in and I'll cook something special instead?"

"I don't think so, dear sister," Joe said. "I've eaten your specials before. I think its best if we eat out."

She sighed, a faint smile crossing her lips. "Maybe you're right. Cooking was never my strong point." She reached out and gently took Joe's hands in hers. "But seriously, what are you going to do?"

Joe was silent for a moment as if searching for the right words. "I've decided to go back to Leeds," he said at last.

Angie gasped, her grip on Joe's hands tightening. "No, you can't do that. Not after what happened? You can't be serious?"

"I'm very serious," Joe said. "In fact, I've got a business meeting tomorrow afternoon."

"What sort of business?"

Joe grinned. "Did anyone ever tell you that you ask too many questions?"

"Don't be flippant. You know Karl Maddox still has his damned club in Leeds."

Joe put an arm around his sister and gently squeezed her. "Forget about Maddox. That's all water under the bridge."

"Is it? You ran off with his wife. You don't think he's ever going to forgive you for that, do you?"

"Erica's dead," Joe said softly. "Karl had twenty years with her and made her life hell. The eighteen months we were together was the best time of my life."

"I know, love, and it's all very sad that she died, but why Leeds of all places? There's nothing for you there only more trouble. Surely you can see that?"

Joe walked over to the window. "I have unfinished business, Angie," he said quietly. "Please, stop worrying about me. I can take care of myself." He turned to face the two boys who were watching television. "Well, boys," he asked cheerfully. "What do you fancy for dinner?"

"Burgers," they both chorused loudly.

"Can we go to McDonald's, please, Uncle Joe?" Nathan, the older of the two boys, pleaded. "Daddy never takes us there."

Joe looked enquiringly at his sister.

Angie smiled. "Oh, all right. I suppose so. Just this once. Upstairs both of you and get washed."

15

It was early the following morning when Paul Borowicz entered the office at the Emerald Club.

Karl sat behind his desk, working. "Good morning, Paul," he said, not raising his head from the paperwork on his desk. "I hope your mysterious trip paid dividends?"

Paul shrugged and sat facing Karl across the desk. "I'm not sure," he said. He outlined the conversation he had had with Mrs Winters the previous day.

Karl listened intently. "I can understand nicking the Rolex, but what would anyone want with a briefcase, especially if it were just business papers inside?" Karl scowled. "You say it's a stationery company?"

"That's right. I've done some checking, and that type of briefcase costs well over two thousand quid."

Karl gulped. "Two thousand pounds for an attaché case? I thought you said he ran a small company?"

"He does. It's his wife, Letitia, who has the big bucks. Her family own three hotels in Scotland."

"I don't suppose you found any trace of this John Smith bloke?"

"No, I'm afraid not. According to the hotel receptionist, he gave a fake address when he booked the room. She did give me a good description of him though, and she said he was with another bloke."

Karl sat bolt upright. "What, there were two of them?"

"It looks like it. I thought Jacqui had more sense than to go into a hotel room where there were two punters."

Karl frowned. "It's not the only thing that surprises me about her. I would never have thought her capable of stealing from a client, dead or alive."

Paul shrugged. "I'll write everything up, and then we can decide what to do next."

"You do that. I'm going to Manchester this morning to sort out the new club."

"I thought you were going to slow down and start taking

things easy?"

Karl grinned. "I am. I've decided to let Alex run the Amethyst. He's chomping on the bit to get more involved."

Paul frowned. "Are you sure he's ready for the responsibility?"

"I take it you don't?"

"It's your decision, boss, but can you trust Alex not to gamble again if he's left to his own devices?"

"Alex swears he hasn't been near a casino since that business with Jonny Dalton."

"And you believe him?"

Karl shrugged. "I'd like to. Maybe I should put someone in the Amethyst to keep an eye on him for a while?"

"That's up to you, but it won't do any harm to be on the safe side."

There was a sharp rap on the door. It was Alex. As always, his appearance was pristine.

"Come in, Alex," Karl invited. "We were just talking about you."

"The car's outside," Alex said. "We should be setting off now if you want to avoid the heavy traffic."

Karl turned to Paul. "I'll leave you to deal with what we discussed. I'll be back later today, so try and have the report ready for me, okay?"

"Sure, boss," Paul said and glanced at Alex, who was frowning at him from the doorway. "I'll see you later."

16

It was early evening before Karl and Alex arrived back at the Emerald. Walking into his office, Karl spotted a large brown envelope on the desk. "Ah, that'll be from Paul," he said, ripping the envelope open.

"Is there anything I can do?" Alex asked.

Karl shook his head and read Paul's report.

"Well, if there's nothing else?"

"No, you get off home. We're done for tonight. Go and make up with your wife. She looked pretty upset the last time I saw her. Take her some flowers or something."

"I don't know if I want to make up with the silly bitch."

But Karl was engrossed in the papers in front of him. Silently, Alex left the room.

It was a twenty-minute drive to the Raeburn Apartments, a swanky new development at the edge of town. Alex parked his Audi in one of the two reserved spaces for apartment 16 and made his way into the building. Using his own key, he entered the lavish apartment, throwing his coat over the back of a chair. "Katie? Katie, where are you?"

"Give me a minute, I'm in the shower," a female voice answered.

Grinning broadly, Alex removed his shirt and shoes and walked into the bathroom. "Don't rush," he said, removing the rest of his clothes. "I'm coming to join you."

Katie was in her early twenties. Her long black hair cascaded onto her slender shoulders and her eyes the colour of burnt amber.

Alex stepped into the shower and embraced her. "Mm, I've missed you," he murmured, as he ran his hands over her glistening black skin.

"I thought you were coming over this afternoon. What happened?"

"I had to go to Manchester with Karl. He's opening a club over there."

"Another one? How many is that he owns? Three?"

"Four," Alex said. "But guess what, Katie? I'm going to be running the club. What do you think about that?"

Katie put her arms around Alex's neck and smiled. "Darling, that's wonderful," she cooed. "But if you move to Manchester, when will I see you?"

"Don't worry about that. I'll sort a flat over there for you."

"Really? It will be great moving back there. That's where we first met, remember?"

He grinned. "How can I forget? You were the prettiest croupier at the Lucky Ace Casino."

Katie sighed. "It seems such a long time ago. You used to visit regularly back then."

"Yeah, but I visit your flat now, instead." He nuzzled her neck. "Now, I think we're both done with the shower. Let's go to bed."

"It's getting late, Alex, shouldn't you be leaving? You don't want your wife getting suspicious."

Alex lay next to Katie on the king-sized bed. He propped himself up onto his elbows and sighed. "Yes, I suppose you're right. I don't want that jealous bitch kicking off again."

He climbed out of bed and began putting on his clothes. "When I move over to Manchester things will be different."

"Won't Sarah be joining you?"

"No, she bloody won't," he said. "She wouldn't move to Manchester."

"Not even to be with you?"

"Especially not to be with me. When I'm in charge of the Amethyst Club things will be different. I'll dump that silly cow and you and I can—"

"Hey, not so fast," Katie said, slipping into her silk dressing gown. "This… this me and you… well, you do know it's just fun, right? I don't want to settle down or anything, Alex. You do know that?"

He scoffed. "I'm not proposing marriage, for Christ's sake," he said, fastening his shirt. "I only meant we would be free to have more fun together, that's all." He picked up his jacket and turned towards the door. "Oh, I nearly forgot," he said, reaching into his pocket and removing several notes. He threw them onto the dressing table. "Don't spend it all at once."

"Please, Alex, I—" But Alex had slammed the door and was already making his way down to the foyer.

Katie watched from the window as Alex climbed into his car and sped off into the night. Pouring herself a vodka, she picked up the telephone and dialled a number. It was answered immediately. "You were right," she said and sipped her drink. "Karl has bought the nightclub in Manchester and Alex is going to be running it."

17

Joe arrived for his meeting at eleven o'clock the following morning. Smartly dressed in a dark-blue suit and open-necked white shirt, his dark, handsome face gave no sign that he was in his early forties. He strode up to the large, imposing door of the house and pressed the bell. It was a few minutes before it was opened by a plump, middle-aged woman dressed in a smart floral tabard. In one hand she held a can of polish and in the other, a bright yellow duster.

"I'm Joe Stevens," he said. "I'm here to see Mr Glendenning."

"Right, love," she said in a broad Yorkshire accent. "He's expecting you. Follow me, please."

Joe was led into a spacious, elegantly furnished sitting room.

"Mr Stevens?" the occupier said, walking towards him with his hand outstretched.

Matthew Glendenning was a tall, handsome man in his late twenties. His hair almost white, his eyes a pale shade of blue. Joe's eyes widened, Matthew's resemblance to his late father, David, was striking.

Joe smiled, regaining his composure. "Thank you for seeing me," he said and proceeded to shake hands with Matthew.

"Please, take a seat," Matthew said, indicating for Joe to sit on one of the brocade armchairs. "Coffee?" he asked. Joe nodded. Matthew turned to the housekeeper. "If you don't mind, Ellen." Ellen nodded and left the room.

"I must admit I'm intrigued by your letter," Matthew began. "You say that we have a mutual acquaintance. Who might that be, may I ask?"

"Charlotte O'Connor, or Flynn as she is now."

Matthew's posture stiffened. "How do you know Charlotte?"

"It's a long story. I take it you haven't been in touch with her since—"

51

"No," Matthew said. "Everything was such a shock, what with my father and... How is Charlotte?"

"She's living in Ireland with her husband. I've tried to persuade her to come to England to visit, but after what happened with Karl Maddox."

"That bastard," Matthew said. "It's a pity my dad didn't finish him off when he had the chance instead of just shooting him in the leg."

"I was sorry to hear what happened to your father," Joe said.

Matthew balled his fists. "Don't be. He was no better than Maddox. He caused my mother's breakdown. She's in a nursing home now, and I don't know if she'll ever come out."

The two men remained quiet. The silence interrupted by Ellen entering the room with a tray of coffee.

"You haven't said what it is that you want," Matthew said once she had left the room.

Joe put the cup on the table and turned to his companion. "I have a score to settle with Karl Maddox. I think we both do. I thought that perhaps we could join forces."

Matthew held up his hand. "Before we go any further," he said, narrowing his eyes, "what has Karl Maddox done to you? You used to work for him, didn't you? His right-hand man, so I heard. Until you ran off with his wife, that is."

"That's right, but only so I could stay close to Erica, and make sure she was safe. You can't imagine how that man treated her."

"Where's Erica now? Are you two still together?"

Joe lowered his eyes. "Erica died six months ago. Cancer."

"I'm sorry to hear that."

Joe shrugged. "Nothing will bring her back," Joe said, "but that doesn't mean I can't avenge her for all the suffering Karl put her through."

Matthew leant forward. "What is it you plan to do? I take it you have a plan?"

Joe grinned. "Yes, I have a plan. I'm going to destroy Karl Maddox, but I'm going to need your help."

"You do know that I'm not a police officer anymore? I left the service shortly after Dad shot himself."

"Yes, I heard. It must have been very difficult for you."

"After what that bastard did, it was impossible. So tell me, how do you propose to get at Karl? You know he's always surrounded by those gorillas he employs."

Joe smirked. "Those gorillas can't protect him from what I have planned, but perhaps we could discuss it over lunch?"

Matthew shrugged. "Sure, I've nothing else on today."

18

Karl was in his office when Alex came into the room." You wanted to see me?" he asked.

"Yes, son. Come in and sit down."

Alex sat across the desk from his father. "What is it, Karl? Is everything all right?"

"I want to go through the final details," Karl said. "The Amethyst will be opening in a couple of weeks. Are you sure enough girls have been recruited?"

"Don't worry. I've got more than enough."

"What about security staff? How many minders have you got?"

"Six," Alex replied. "That should be plenty. I can easily get more if I think they're needed."

"I want Marco in charge of the doors," Karl said. "He's worked in all the big clubs around the country so his experience—"

"Marco? You can't be serious? He's nothing but a loud-mouthed thug. I don't want him in my club. He—"

Karl banged his fist down on the desk. "Actually, Alex, I think you'll find it's my club, at least for the moment. I'll decide who does what, and Marco is in. Understand?"

Alex shrugged. "If you say so," he muttered. "But I still think Marco is—"

"Enough!" Karl said. "Now tell me about the girls."

19

The Jubilee Restaurant was tucked away in a side street on the outskirts of Leeds. It was one of the city's hidden gems. Joe and Matthew arrived there at twelve-thirty.

"Good afternoon," greeted the bald, middle-aged waiter. "Do you have a reservation, sir?"

"Mr Stevens," Joe said, removing his coat and hanging it on a peg. "I booked a table for two yesterday."

"Ah yes, sir, that's right. This way please, gentlemen."

They followed the waiter to the far side of the room and took a seat at a table next to the window.

"Can I get you a drink, gentlemen?"

"A red wine, please," Matthew said.

"And you, sir?" he said, addressing Joe.

"I'll have the same, in fact, bring a bottle. What do you prefer Matthew, Shiraz or Merlot?"

Matthew smiled. "Shiraz, I think." He picked up the leather-bound menus and handed one to Joe.

"I've heard the steaks are very good here," Joe said after a few minutes.

"In that case, I'll have a sirloin, cooked rare."

Joe smiled. "Good choice. I think I'll have the same."

The food was delicious, and, having declined dessert, both men were relaxed, enjoying the freshly brewed coffee.

"Well, now we've got that out of the way," Matthew said, dabbing the corner of his mouth with the linen napkin, "perhaps you can explain to me exactly what I'm doing here?"

"How do you fancy being a partner in a small casino in Manchester?"

Matthew gasped. "A casino? You are joking, right? What on earth do I know about running a casino?"

"Probably not much, but I do."

"Joe, you're not making sense. Why would I want to own a casino?"

Joe fixed Matthew with a stare. "Because, Matthew, this

particular casino is only a few hundred yards from where Karl Maddox's new club is going to be based. A club that is going to be run by his son, Alex."

Matthew frowned. "You've lost me, I'm afraid,"

"Alex Maddox has a serious gambling problem. He got in over his head a couple of years ago, and Karl bailed him out. Karl thinks Alex has stopped gambling, but he's wrong."

"I still don't understand how this affects me."

"Karl is looking to put Alex into the driving seat soon and let him take over all of his clubs. If Alex is in hock to us, we could take Karl's kingdom from under his nose without him realising what's happening."

"That's all very well, Joe, but where exactly do I come in?"

Joe smiled. "Money. I don't have the capital needed to buy the licence to run a casino, but you do."

"Are you serious?"

"I've never been more serious. You do want revenge on the bastard that destroyed your family, don't you?"

Matthew stared at Joe, his fists tightly clenched. "Of course I want revenge, but I'm not convinced buying a casino is going to achieve that."

"Jonny Lomax owns the Lucky Ace Casino in Manchester. I know he's desperate to sell up and move on. I've already spoken to him about buying it. I know I can get it at a knock-down price."

"What if I decide not to go along with this crazy venture?"

"Matthew, this is the best chance you'll ever have to bring Karl down. Please think about it. We don't have much time." Joe signalled to the waiter to bring the bill. "I've got everything worked out down to the last detail," Joe said, handing Matthew a large brown envelope. "This is my business plan. Run it past your solicitors, I'm sure they'll tell you that it's sound. It's just cash that's needed. I have some, but not nearly enough to get a licence."

Matthew tapped his chin with his finger. "Give me a few days to think about it. It's a big commitment."

"We don't have a few days. We have to get in quick before

somebody else does."

"I won't be rushed," Matthew said. "I'll study your business plan and get back to you. That's the best I can do. Take it or leave it."

Joe sighed. "Okay, but don't leave it too long, or the chance will be gone."

After paying the bill, Joe and Matthew walked towards the exit.

"I was thinking of getting in touch with Charlotte," Matthew said as he approached his car. "You said you have her address?"

"I'll email it. I know Charlotte would love to hear from you."

Matthew smiled. "Thanks. I'll call you soon with my answer."

20

Shamus Flynn took a sip of the juice from the feeder that Charlotte was holding to his mouth. He smiled weakly and nodded his gratitude before sinking back onto the pillow.

"That's right, Shamus," she said, "try and get some rest."

The old man closed his eyes and Charlotte thought he was sleeping. She was surprised when he spoke. "I think you should do as your brother suggests and visit him in England," he said, almost in a whisper. "After all, apart from your grandmother, he's the only blood relation you have."

"I'll think about it," Charlotte said softly. "I haven't mentioned Matthew's invitation to Patrick yet. He might not want me to go back to England again, especially after all the trouble with Karl."

"It must be your decision," the old man said. "Matthew is your brother. It's only right that you should get to know each other properly."

"Yes, but Patrick's my husband. I need to speak to him before I agree to anything."

"Charlotte, you're a sweet girl, but please don't let my son dictate. He can be forceful at times, he always has been, but you must not allow him to bully you." Shamus' breathing became erratic, and he gripped Charlotte's hand tightly. It was a few minutes before he spoke. "Erica left you some money in her will, didn't she?"

"Yes. Twenty thousand pounds."

"What have you done with it?"

"I haven't touched it. It's in a high-interest bank account."

"That's very sensible. Keep something to one side for a rainy day. You never know when you might need it."

"What do you mean, Shamus? Patrick is very generous. He gives me everything I need."

As if on cue, the door opened, and Patrick Flynn came into the hospital room. He was tall and handsome, with an unmistakable air of authority. He walked over to his wife and lightly kissed her on the cheek. "What are you two plotting?"

he asked, smiling.

Charlotte glanced at Shamus. "Nothing, darling. I was just telling your father about Matthew."

"Matthew?"

"My brother, well half-brother. He's invited me over to England for a visit. You too, of course. He says he wants to get to know me better."

"Why would you want to have anything to do with him after all that trouble with his father?"

"That's unfair," Charlotte said. "Matthew can't be held responsible for what his father did."

"I think she should go," Shamus said. "It's important that she keeps in contact with him. After all, he is family."

Patrick turned abruptly to face the old man. "Shouldn't you be resting, Father? You don't want another attack, do you?"

Shamus lowered his head and remained silent.

"I think it's time we were leaving," Patrick said, taking Charlotte's coat from the hook and holding it up for her. "Is there anything you want, Father? I can bring it in for you tomorrow."

"No, I have everything I need, thank you."

Charlotte leant over and kissed the old man lightly on the cheek.

"Remember what I said," he whispered. "Go and see your brother. He'll keep you safe."

Charlotte furrowed her brow but she said nothing.

Once inside the Mercedes, Patrick turned sharply to face his wife. "What have I told you about visiting the old man without me? I've told you he's senile. His ramblings are disturbing."

"Patrick, your father's dying. He needs company. I don't understand why—"

He glared at her and tightened his grip on the steering wheel. "In future, you do as I say and keep away from him unless I am there too. Is that clear?"

Charlotte nodded as she fought back tears. They drove in silence for a few minutes.

"I suppose you'd better start packing if you're going to England," Patrick said at last.

"You mean I can go? You don't mind?"

"Why would I mind? Matthew's your half-brother after all. I think it will be good for you both to get to know each other."

"But what about your father? I can't just leave him."

"Don't worry about him. I'll take care of Shamus."

21

It was just after one o'clock when April arrived at the premises of Thomas Walker, a pawnbrokers' shop, tucked away at the back of Lower Briggate. She had been given the address by Rachel before she had left for Dubai. Rachel had told her exactly how much to ask for the Rolex. To her surprise, the proprietor, a tall, wiry man with darting grey eyes and a crop of blonde curly hair, did not haggle over the price. On the contrary, he seemed very keen to acquire the watch, even though it bore an inscription.

He grinned, revealing a mouth of broken, uneven teeth. "You'll be out spending all that cash up at the shops I expect. I know what you young girls are like once you've got some money in your pocket."

April huffed. "Actually, I'm going back to work."

"What sort of work will that be then, if you don't mind my asking?"

"I'm a hairdresser," April said. "I work at the new salon on the Headrow."

"Oh, very nice. If you'll just sign here," he said, handing her a piece of paper. "We've got to keep things legal."

April signed the receipt and hurried out of the shop, aware that the man was leering at her through the window.

As soon as she was out of sight, he picked up the telephone and made a call.

It took April half an hour to get back to the salon. Mrs Turner was already there for her two o'clock appointment.

April smiled. "I won't keep you a moment." She hurried into the staff room to take off her coat. Victoria, Sophia and Nadia were sat at the small dining table finishing their lunch.

"How are you enjoying working here?" Victoria asked. "Are they keeping you busy?"

"Very busy, but that's how I like it." April smiled. "It makes the day go quickly."

"Half a dozen of us are going out for a meal in a couple of weeks for Christina's birthday. Would you like to come too? It should be fun."

"I'd love to," April said as she put on her pink cotton smock. "But I really must hurry. I don't want to keep Mrs Turner waiting." She went through into the salon.

It was just before four o'clock when Luke and George parked on the Headrow. They got out of the van and walked towards the salon. "Remember what I told you," Luke said. "Keep your mouth shut. I'll do the talking."

George grunted. "All right. You've already told me twice."

"Good afternoon, gentlemen," said the receptionist, as the two men entered the salon. "Do you have an appointment?"

Luke smiled. "No, I was hoping you could fit me in for a trim. What about you, George? Do you fancy having that beard cut off?"

George growled by way of response.

"If you take a seat, Sally will be with you in a few moments."

Luke frowned. "I was hoping April could do it. I've heard she's very good."

"All of our stylists are very good, sir," the girl said. "Sally is available this afternoon for walk-ins. April is busy with appointments."

"That's a shame. In that case, I'll call back tomorrow when April is free."

"Her first available appointment tomorrow isn't until two o'clock. Is that convenient?"

Luke smiled. "That's fine." They walked towards the door, and Luke paused. "Which one is April, just so I know?"

"April is the stylist over there, sir," she said, pointing to the far side of the salon. "She's the one putting in the foils."

Christina was in the office at the rear of the salon when Sophia and Nadia burst into the room. Nadia was almost hysterical.

"What's the matter?" Christina asked. "What's upset her?"

"It's those men," Sophia said, "they've come looking for her."

"What men? I don't understand."

"The two men who came into the salon just now are the same two who were driving the van. They're the traffickers."

Christina held Nadia's shoulders firmly. "Are you sure about that, Nadia?"

Nadia nodded furiously. "I will never forget them," she sobbed. "I thought I'd be safe here with Sophia. How did they find me?"

"What did the men say?"

"I don't know," Sophia said. "They were talking to Marie in reception. Nadia was over by the sinks cleaning when they came in."

"Did they see her?"

"No. Nadia said she got down behind the chair until they left. Then she came to find me."

"You'd better take Nadia upstairs to work for the rest of the day. I'll speak to Marie and see what they wanted."

As the two women rushed upstairs, Christina went over to the reception desk. "The two men that came in earlier, what did they want?"

Marie hunched her shoulders. "One of them wanted a trim. He insisted it was done by April."

"April? Are you sure that's what he said?"

"Yes, of course. He said she had been recommended and he would call back tomorrow at two."

"He didn't mention anyone else?"

"No, just April. He asked me which girl she was, and I pointed her out. Then he left."

"Thanks, Marie. By the way, if either of them come back into the salon, I want to know straight away."

Marie frowned. "Okay," she said.

22

Karl was in his office at the Emerald when Christina came rushing into the room. "What's wrong?" he asked as his daughter ran towards him, arms outstretched. "What happened? Tell me."

"Dad, I'm sorry," Christina said breathlessly. "I know I should have told you earlier but—"

"Told me what? What's going on, Christina?"

"It's Nadia, one of the girls working at the salon. She was trafficked from Romania."

"What do you mean? Are you sure?"

"She was taken a few weeks ago and brought to England in a lorry."

"How has she ended up in your salon?"

"Her sister works for me. Nadia managed to escape and make her way to Leeds to be with her."

"And you say Nadia escaped from a lorry?"

"No, she was moved from the lorry at Dover and put into a van with half a dozen other girls. She escaped from the van."

"So, what's upset you so much?"

"The two men in the van turned up at my salon today. Nadia recognised them."

"They did what?" Karl clenched his hands into fists.

"One of the men wanted to make an appointment with April."

"Who's April?"

"She's one of my stylists. The man booked an appointment for tomorrow at two. I don't know what to do, Dad. I'm scared. I don't want to get mixed up with these people."

"Did they mention Nadia at all?"

"No, but it can't be a coincidence coming to the salon, can it? They must know Nadia's there."

"Where is she now?"

"She's gone home with her sister."

"Well, there's not much I can do about it tonight. I'll be over to the salon tomorrow and find out what the hell's going on."

"Thanks, Dad. I've told Nadia not to come to work tomorrow until it gets sorted."

"What about April? What do you know about her?"

"I don't know her that well, she's only been working for me for a few days but she seems a nice kid. I used to be good friends with her sister, Rachel. We worked together when…"

"So, Rachel's on the game, eh?"

"She's a high-class escort. She's with a client in Dubai at the moment."

"You don't think Rachel has anything to do with these traffickers?"

Christina shook her head. "No, I'm sure she hasn't."

"Let's hope not for her sake. You say Nadia's sister works for you?"

"Yes, Sophia has been with me for almost a year."

Karl frowned. "I'll call round to the salon tomorrow afternoon and find out exactly what's going on."

"Thanks, Dad, I knew you'd help." Christina made her way to the door. "Now, I must be off, I'm meeting a friend for dinner."

"What friend? Do I know him?"

Christina folded her arms. "Who said it's a he?"

"Do I know him?" Karl repeated.

"Goodnight, Dad. See you tomorrow."

23

April hated being late for work. She glanced anxiously at her watch as she approached the salon. Only five minutes late. That wasn't too bad, considering she had got up half an hour later than her usual time.

Christina was in the salon when she arrived. "Good morning," she said. "Mrs Calvert, your eight o'clock, is being shampooed."

April lowered her eyes. "Sorry, I'm a little late," she began. "I slept in this morning."

"Don't let it happen again," Christina said. "I don't like clients kept waiting."

April nodded and hurried to the staff room to remove her coat and put on her pink smock.

Christina followed her. "Have you heard from Rachel? She should be coming back any day now, shouldn't she?"

"She telephoned last night. She's decided to extend her stay in Dubai for another week."

Christina sighed. "Lucky her. I wish I was in Dubai right now."

"I thought she was never going to leave," George said, opening the van door and stepping onto the path. "It's bloody freezing in the van."

"Stop whining and let's get on with it," Luke said, heading towards the block of flats. "We have to find that briefcase."

Gaining access into the two bedroomed flat was easy, and within minutes both men were standing in the small hallway.

"You check the bedrooms," Luke said. "I'll search the rest of the flat."

Drawers and cupboards were opened, their contents scattered over the floor. Furniture was upturned, beds stripped and wardrobes emptied, but there was no sign of the missing briefcase.

"The thieving bitch has probably got rid of it already," George said as he pulled out the last of the dressing table drawers. "There's nothing here, Luke."

"It must be here. Keep looking."

George huffed. "It's not. The briefcase is not in this flat."

"That stupid bitch didn't have the brains to hide it anywhere clever."

"What about the salon? Could she have it hidden there?"

Luke glared at George before his expression softened into a faint smile. "Could be," he said. "Let's go and pay young April a visit."

It was just after ten-thirty. April was busy blow-drying a client's hair when Luke and George burst into the salon.

"Your appointment's not until two," Marie said, as the two men rushed past reception. "It's—"

Luke dragged April away from the basin and pushed her against the wall. "What have you done with the briefcase? Hand it over now, or else."

"What briefcase? I don't know what you're talking about."

George loomed over the girl. "We know you took it from the hotel," he said. "Give it back, you thieving bitch, before you get hurt."

"I don't know anything about a briefcase," she whimpered. "I swear I don't. Please, you're hurting me."

Luke shook her by the shoulders. "You stupid little tart," he hissed. "We know you pawned the Rolex yesterday. We don't care about that. We just want the briefcase. Where is it?"

Christina forced herself between Luke and April. "Let her go," she yelled, pushing Luke backwards against the wall. "Let her go now, you bastard. The police are on their way."

George glanced around the room. "Maybe we should go, Luke," he said. "We don't want to get mixed up in—"

Luke held his fist up to April. "You have twenty-four hours," he said. "If we haven't got the briefcase by then, we'll be back."

"Get out," Christina screamed. "Get out of here, you bastards."

Both men turned and walked towards the door. Christina

watched as they got into their van and drove away at speed, before rushing over to April's side. "What was all that about? Who are those men?"

April was crying and shook her head. "I don't know who they are," she said. "I've never seen them before."

"Victoria, take over will you? April, you'd better come with me."

April followed Christina to the office. "Christina, I swear, I don't—"

"Enough. I've heard enough. What's this briefcase they're talking about? Do you have it?"

"No. I don't know anything about it."

"And the Rolex? They said you pawned it yesterday. Is that right?"

April dabbed her eyes with a tissue before she answered. "Yes, I... I did pawn a Rolex yesterday."

"Where did you get it?"

"Rachel gave it me."

"When?"

"Before she went to Dubai she asked me to pawn the watch." Tears were running down April's cheeks, and Christina handed her another tissue.

"Where did Rachel get the watch from?"

"She said it was a gift from a client. She told me where to take it and how much to ask. She said she would share the money with me."

"Which pawnbroker did you use?"

"Thomas Walkers in Briggate."

Christina frowned. "I thought he'd been closed down?"

"I didn't like the man in the shop. He was weird. He kept asking questions."

"Like where you worked?"

April nodded.

"Are you absolutely certain Rachel didn't give you a briefcase to pawn?"

"Of course I'm certain. She gave me the watch, that's all. What's all this about?"

Christina grabbed her coat from the hook. "I have no idea, but I intend to find out. You clean yourself up and get back into the salon. I have to go out for a while."

24

Karl leant back in his chair and lit a cigar while Christina told him about the two men visiting the salon.

"And you're sure they are the same men that came earlier?"

"Of course I'm sure, Dad."

Paul had been listening intently to the conversation between Karl and his daughter. "Did you hear either of them use a name?" he asked.

"The big one with the ginger beard was called George," Christina said, "and I heard him call the younger one Luke."

Paul frowned. "What I don't understand is how Rachel came to have the Rolex. It was Jacqui who visited Finch in the Belmont."

"Maybe Jacqui was short of cash and sold the Rolex to Rachel?" Karl said. "She probably did the same with the briefcase."

Paul rubbed his chin. "It's possible, I suppose. But what I can't fathom is the connection between the traffickers and the briefcase."

"It's obvious," Karl said. "Finch must have been involved with the traffickers."

"No, I don't think so," Paul said.

Karl shrugged and turned to face his daughter. "I want to meet this girl who claims to have been trafficked."

"I'll bring her over after I close the salon. What about April? Do you want to speak to her too?"

"Not right now. Maybe later."

"Okay, Dad. I'd better get back to work, but I'll be back at six."

Christina walked over to her father and kissed him lightly on the cheek before leaving the office.

"I'll see what else I can find out about this Finch bloke," Paul said, walking towards the door.

"I thought you said Finch was clean? He seems to be involved in this up to his neck."

"I'm going to find out exactly what Stefan Finch was up to

before he got to the hotel in Leeds. His office said he'd been on business in Scotland."

"You're not going to Scotland?"

"I'll only be a couple of days. Finch was staying in Edinburgh at the family's hotel. I might pick something up there."

"Okay, if you think it will help, but don't be long. Things might start kicking off here pretty soon."

"Oh?"

"I've just remembered where I know this George from," Karl gave a malicious grin. "I thought he sounded familiar."

"What do you mean?"

"George was with a gang that tried muscling in on my business a few years back. It was when Victor was working for me, so it must be nearly twenty years ago."

"I remember Dad saying something about that." Paul smiled. "Uncle Jan and Uncle Erik got involved too, didn't they? What happened?"

"Let's say I'm surprised George is back in Leeds after the beating he got." A broad grin spread across Karl's face. "But then, George was all brawn and not very much brain."

"You think he's still with the same gang?"

"No. The Kennedy clan were sent down for murder and extortion. They won't see daylight for some time."

"George must have hooked up with another outfit?"

"Yeah. From what I saw, George was always a follower, never a leader."

"Well, I'd better get going," Paul said. "I'll be as quick as I can. When I get back from Scotland, I'll call in and have words with that pawnbroker. See who paid him to report on April."

"Good idea. Let me know if you need any help. Peter's itching to get some action."

Chuckling, Paul left the room.

25

Joe and Matthew signed the documents in the solicitor's office at three o'clock in the afternoon.

Mr Grundy smiled. "Congratulations. You gentlemen are now the owners of the Lucky Ace Casino."

Matthew picked up the papers and placed them in his briefcase. "I think the first thing we'll do is change the name of the casino. What do you think, Joe?"

"What do you suggest?"

He paused. "What about the Lady Luck Casino?"

Joe shrugged. "It's as good a name as any, I suppose," he said.

"Well, if that's settled." Matthew smiled as he got up from his chair and held out his hand to Mr Grundy. "Thank you for dealing with this sale so promptly. We do appreciate it. Isn't that right, Joe?"

Joe nodded. "Absolutely."

"It's a pleasure," Mr Grundy said. "I know Mr Dalton is anxious to get the business sold. He's planning to move to the continent once the matter is resolved."

Matthew grinned. "Well, he can get packing now."

The two men left the office and walked towards Matthew's car.

"I have somewhere to go first," Joe said. "I'll meet you at the casino this evening."

"Okay, but don't be too long. We need to decide on a few things before we open."

"Don't worry, I'll be there."

"Oh, by the way, Joe, I heard from Charlotte this morning," Matthew said. "She's coming to stay with Marion for a few days and wants to meet up."

"Good. It'll be great to see her again. Is Patrick coming too?"

"Not straight away. His dad's in hospital, so Patrick's staying in Ireland for a couple of days, but he's hoping to join her by the end of the week."

"From what I saw when I was over there for the wedding, Patrick's a bit of a workaholic. He doesn't seem to spend a great deal of time at home."

"Her husband is a solicitor, isn't he?"

"Yes, he works freelance," Joe said. "Charlotte says he travels all over the world."

"I'm glad she's making a life for herself, poor kid. It can't have been easy finding out her mother had been a prostitute."

Joe frowned. "Worse still to know she had been murdered by Karl Maddox."

"Well, that's all water under the bridge I suppose," Matthew said climbing into his car. He waved and drove off towards the town centre.

26

An hour after leaving Matthew, Joe arrived at a smart block of flats just off Leeds city centre. He placed his coins in the parking meter and made his way to Flat 11. The door was opened almost immediately by Marion Watson, Charlotte's grandmother. Marion was a tall, elegantly dressed woman in her early sixties with pale blue eyes and short auburn hair flecked with grey. She would have been attractive had it not been for the purple discolouration down the left side of her face – discolouration caused through an acid attack years earlier.

"Joe, how lovely to see you," she said and kissed him lightly on the cheek. "It's been ages. How have you been?"

"I'm fine," Joe said. "How are you? Charlotte said you haven't been too well."

Marion shrugged and led the way into the comfortable sitting room. "There's a problem with my blood pressure. The doctor says it's a bit high."

"But they can make it right, can't they? It's not life-threatening or anything like that?"

Marion smiled and sat on the couch next to Joe. "Don't worry about me. I'm going to be all right. I just have to be careful, that's all. How are you coping without Erica? It looks like you've lost weight since I last saw you."

Joe sighed deeply. "One day at a time, I suppose," he said quietly. "It just makes me angry that we had so little time together. When I think how that bastard stole those years, I—"

"I know, love," Marion said gently, patting Joe's knee. "But there's nothing you can do about it now. Erica's gone and Karl's carrying on as normal. Did you know he had a wife and two kids tucked away? They turned up a couple of years ago."

"Yes, I did hear something about it." Joe sat up straight and looked away.

Marion patted Joe's knee again. "So, what are your plans?" she asked. "You're not staying in Leeds are you, not with Karl still around?"

Joe turned to face Marion. "No, I'm working in Manchester."

"What are you doing over there?"

He grinned. "You'd better brace yourself, Marion. I'm part-owner of a casino. I've gone into business with Matthew Glendenning."

Marion shook her head slowly. "Why a casino of all things?"

Joe grinned again. "Why not a casino? There's lots of money to be made."

Marion shrugged. "Well, I suppose you know what you're doing," she said. "Did you know Charlotte's coming over to England next week? She wants to meet up with Matthew."

"Yes, he told me. He's really looking forward to getting to know her."

"I'm worried, Joe. That family have caused nothing but trouble. I don't think Charlotte should get involved with him. You neither for that matter."

"Don't worry. Matthew's nothing like his father. He's a decent bloke. You'll like him."

"What are you going to do about Karl? You know he'd kill you if he gets the chance."

"Not while he thinks I still have the knife he used to kill Paula."

"I can't see why you haven't handed that over to the police and got the bastard locked up after what he did."

"I can't do that, Marion. I don't have the knife anymore."

"What do you mean you don't have the knife?" she said. "It was the only thing that could prove Karl killed my daughter."

"I know, and I'm sorry, but Erica begged me to get rid of it."

"Why would she do that?"

"When Erica was dying, she pleaded with me not to expose Karl by using the knife. She knew that if I did, I would be in trouble for burying Paula's body. She didn't want me sent to prison."

"Joe, I think you've made a mistake. The knife was the only thing that could keep you safe."

"It still can, as long as Karl believes I have it." Both lapsed into an uneasy silence.

"I'll make some tea," Marion said, getting up from the couch.

"Not for me. I have to get over to Manchester. We're hoping to open the casino in a couple of weeks, so there's a lot to be done." Joe stood and walked towards the door.

Marion sighed. "I can't believe you're letting that bastard off the hook after what he did."

"Who said I was letting him off the hook? I'm just using different bait, that's all."

"I don't understand."

Joe smiled. "You will, Marion. Just watch this space."

27

Karl was in his office when Christina arrived at six-thirty that evening with the two sisters.

"This is Nadia," Christina said, "the girl I was telling you about."

Nadia smiled weakly but remained silent.

"So, you're the young woman who was trafficked, eh?" Karl said. "I want you to tell me exactly what happened, from the beginning."

Sophia held her sister's trembling hand. "It's all right, Nadia," she said softly. "There's nothing to be frightened of. Karl is going to help you."

Karl turned his gaze sharply to Sophia and scowled. "I never said that. I need to know why those bastards threatened my daughter in her place of business. That's all I'm interested in."

Christina put her arm protectively around Nadia's shoulders and guided her to the couch. "Sit down here," she said, "and tell Karl what you told me, okay?"

Nadia lowered her head and rocking slightly, stared at the carpet. It was a few seconds before she spoke. When she did, her voice was weak and quavering. "I worked in a hotel in Bucharest," she began, "the Hotel Superior. I cleaned rooms and sometimes I helped out in the kitchen. That's... that's where I met Ivan."

"Who's he?" Karl asked.

"Ivan was a porter in the hotel. He was kind, and I thought he was my friend." Tears ran down her cheeks, and Christina handed her a tissue.

"Come on, Nadia, be a brave girl," she said. "Tell Karl everything that happened."

Nadia regained her composure and lifted her head. "Ivan said he could help me get to England, but it would cost money. I told him I didn't have any money, well not much, but he said he would still help me, and I could pay him back when I started working here."

"How was he going to get you to England?" Karl asked.

"He said he had friends who owned a boat. They could hide me and—"

"Oh, Nadia," Sophia said, "why did you trust these men?"

"Ivan told me not to tell anyone about leaving. He said it could be dangerous if the authorities got to hear about it. I couldn't even tell my mother I was going. Ivan promised that he would tell her where I was once I was safe."

Karl slowly shook his head. "And you believed him?"

"All I could think about was getting to England to be with my sister. This seemed the only way."

Karl frowned. "So, what happened?"

"Ivan asked me to meet him that night when I finished my shift. He said he wanted to go over the final details. It was late, and I was cold. We sat in his van, and he offered me coffee from his flask. That's… that's the last I remember until I woke up in the cellar."

"Where was this cellar?" Karl asked.

"I didn't know where I was. It was cold and dark, and my wrists were chained. There were other girls in chains too."

"Where was Ivan?" Karl asked.

"I never saw him again."

"How long were you in the cellar?" Christina asked.

"Not long, just a few hours. Then men came and made us get into a lorry. They injected our arms and things were hazy after that."

"You said the driver attacked you?" Karl said. "When did this happen?"

"The lorry stopped at the side of the road, and the driver opened up the doors. That's when he grabbed me."

"Christina said he raped you. Is that right?"

Nadia nodded. "He flung me to the ground and raped me. I tried to struggle free. I bit his hand as hard as I could, but he kept punching me, so in the end, I just let him do what he wanted. I don't remember much else until we were in England."

Karl walked over to the cabinet and poured himself a

whisky. "You say you were moved from the lorry into a van?"

"Yes, two men were in the van, the same two that came to the salon."

"How did you manage to escape from them?"

"When the van stopped, we heard one of the men get out and walk away. We knew there was just one man in the cab, so we started yelling that one of us was ill. He shouted at us to be quiet, but we continued screaming for help. In the end, he opened the doors to see what was happening. As soon as the doors opened, we all threw ourselves out and ran."

Karl frowned. "You were the only one that managed to get away?"

"That's right. I hid in the bushes. I was so frightened. After a few minutes, the man called George reached down to grab me just as a car pulled up."

"So, what happened?" Karl asked.

"George was crouched down behind the bushes, and when the man in the car left, he turned to me and put his finger to his lips like this." Nadia copied the gesture. "Then he said 'good luck little one' and walked back to the van."

Karl raised his eyebrows. "You're saying George let you go?"

Nadia nodded.

"Show Karl what else those bastards did to you," Sophia said.

Nadia shuffled in her seat and fidgeted with her sweater sleeve. Reluctantly, she rolled up the left sleeve a couple of inches and turned her hand palm up. On her wrist was a bright green tattoo.

Karl moved closer and examined her wrist. "It looks like a clover leaf," he said.

"A three-leafed clover," Sophia spat. "That's not even meant to be lucky."

"All the girls had one," Nadia said quietly. "When we were in the cellar, a man came and did it."

"Why would they do that?" Christina asked.

Nadia sighed. "To make sure everyone knew who we

belonged to. They said we could never get away from them, they would always be able to find us."

Karl took a sip of his drink. "What do you know about April and a missing briefcase?"

"April works at the salon," Nadia replied. "She's kind. I like her."

"And the briefcase? Do you know anything about that?"

"No. I have never seen a briefcase."

"Oh sorry, Dad," Christina said, "that's my phone ringing." Christina removed her mobile from her bag. "It's April," she mouthed.

"Hello, April, is everything all right...? What...? How much damage is there...? I'll come right away. Stay calm and keep the door locked until I get there."

"What was that all about?" Karl asked.

"April's just arrived home to find the flat ransacked."

"Make sure she doesn't ring the police," Karl said. "The last thing we need is them sticking their noses in."

Christina nodded and walked towards the door. "Come on, Sophia, I'll drive you and Nadia home."

28

Twenty minutes later, Christina arrived at Rachel's flat. April, looking anxiously out of the window, ran outside as the car approached, and flung her arms around Christina's neck.

"Oh, Christina, thank you for coming," she said sobbing. "The flat's been ransacked. It's such a mess."

Christina patted her arm. "Never mind. We can tidy it up, as long as you are all right."

"They probably broke in after I left for work this morning. When they couldn't find the briefcase in the flat, they came to the salon."

"Don't worry about that now. You're safe, that's all that matters."

Christina followed April into the flat, and stared open-mouthed at the mess. Furniture had been upturned, lamps knocked over, and clothes scattered around the room. "They certainly made a thorough search," she said, striding over a pile of books lying on the carpet.

"It's just as bad in the bedroom," April said.

"We'll start tidying up in here first," Christina said. "There doesn't look to be anything broken, just stuff strewn about."

April sniffed. "They've thrown everything out of the wardrobe. All of Rachel's lovely clothes are in a heap on the floor."

"Don't worry about that," Christina said. "We can put everything back good as new."

"Do you think we should call the police and tell them about the two men?"

"Absolutely not," Christina said. "Karl will deal with this. We don't need the police."

"But—"

"April, I said no police. Now, help me get the couch and the chairs back where they belong, that's a good girl."

Half an hour later, the apartment was restored to its usual pristine appearance.

April smiled. "Thanks, Christina. I don't know what I'd have done without your help."

"That's all right. Rachel's my friend. It's the least I can do. When is she back, by the way?"

"She was a bit vague when I spoke to her this morning, but she should be back by the end of the week. She said she needed some time by herself to relax."

"Let's hope she knows something about this damned briefcase when she returns."

"I wish I could help, but Rachel never mentioned it."

"When did she give you the watch to pawn?"

"It was just before she left for Dubai. The day after she did that booking for her friend."

Christina frowned. "What friend?"

"Her name was Jacqui. She rang that morning and asked Rachel if she would do a booking for her at the Belmont. Jacqui said she couldn't do it because she was meeting someone else that night."

"You're sure Rachel went to the Belmont?"

"Of course I'm sure. She left at half-past eight."

"What time did she get back?"

"I'm not sure. I was asleep. When I woke up, she was in the lounge having a drink. That was about half-past eleven."

"Are you sure she didn't have anything with her?" Christina said. "A briefcase or—"

"I didn't see anything. She just said she was tired and was going to bed."

"And the next day she gave you the watch to pawn?"

"That's right. She told me to go to Thomas Walker, the pawnbroker on Briggate. I was to sell the watch, and we would share the money. I told your dad all about this."

Christina walked towards the door. "Do you want to come and stay with me for a couple of nights until Rachel gets back? I'm sure Dad wouldn't mind."

"Thanks, but I'd prefer to stay here."

"All right, if you're sure, but make sure you lock the door behind me. Don't open it for anyone."

April brought a hand to her mouth. "You don't think they'll come back, do you?"

"No, but you can't be too careful."

Christina waited until she was back in her car before she rang Karl. "Dad, you're not going to believe this…"

29

The Five Pipers Hotel was an attractive two-storey building on the outskirts of Edinburgh. Paul had pre-booked a room earlier that day. He quickly unpacked his overnight bag and made his way to the bar.

"Good evening," he greeted the young woman serving. "Shona, isn't it?"

"Good evening, sir." She smiled, automatically fingering the name badge on her blouse. "What can I get you?"

"A malt whisky," he said, "and whatever you're having."

"Thank you, but I'm not allowed to drink on duty."

"So, when are you off duty? Perhaps we can have a drink together then?"

The woman laughed and blushed. "I'm finished in another half-hour," she said. "I could join you then."

"Good, I'll take my whisky and sit over there." He nodded towards a small booth at the far side of the room. "Bring me another whisky and a drink for yourself when you're ready."

Half an hour later, Paul was joined by Shona. An attractive woman in her early thirties with sparkling blue eyes and shoulder-length auburn hair.

"Is this your first visit to Edinburgh?" she asked, playfully pulling on her hair.

"No, but it's the first time I've been to this hotel," he said. "How long have you been working here?"

She smiled. "This is my third year. I have my own room here."

"Do you like working in a hotel?"

"It's all right, I suppose. You get to meet all sorts of interesting people."

Paul winked. "People like me?"

She blushed again. "Are you here on business, Mr—?"

"Call me Paul. I'm just passing through. Perhaps you could join me for dinner later?"

"Oh, I don't think—"

"I promise I'll be on my best behaviour," he said, raising his hands in a mock gesture of surrender. "My intentions, as they say, are purely honourable." He winked again.

"Well, I… I suppose it'll be all right," she said. "Where do you want to eat?"

"This is your town, Shona. You decide. Perhaps we could go on to a club later?"

"Oh, Paul, I can't do that. My shift starts at six in the morning, so I have to be in bed by eleven."

Paul chuckled and drained his glass. "I'm sure we can manage that. Hurry up and finish your drink. I'm hungry."

Paul's liaison with Shona, although enjoyable, hadn't afforded him much information about Stefan Finch's recent visit. Shona knew who Finch was, of course. He and his wife were frequent visitors to the hotel, but according to Shona, there had been nothing unusual about his last visit.

Feeling annoyed that he had had a wasted journey, Paul's spirits were low as he entered the hotel's small dining room the following morning. He was carrying his overnight bag into the restaurant when he felt a light tap on the shoulder. It was Riley, one of the porters.

"Excuse me, sir," Riley said, "but guests are asked not to take bags into the restaurant. We have a side room off reception for luggage."

Paul frowned but handed his holdall to Riley.

"If you just ask at reception when you're ready to leave, someone will retrieve your property," Riley said.

The dining room was busy when he entered, and Paul was shown to a small table set for one at the back of the room. He ate a hearty breakfast, read the local paper and poured a second cup of coffee. He wasn't relishing telling Karl his journey had been a waste of time.

On entering the foyer, he was pleased to see it was Shona who was working on reception. She smiled timidly at him from beneath her long fringe. *Not so coy last night*, Paul smirked to himself, recalling the couple of hours they had spent in her room.

"Good morning, Shona," he said. "Can I settle my account and collect my bag, please?"

She smiled and took Paul's credit card from him. "Of course. I hope you enjoyed your stay with us."

He raised his eyebrows. "Yes, it was very enjoyable."

"I'll just get your bag," she said as she disappeared behind a door at the back of reception. "Is this it?" She handed Paul a dark-blue overnight bag.

"No, it's similar, but this isn't mine. My bag is black."

"Sorry," she said, "this is always happening when the hotel is busy. I won't be a minute."

Again, she went behind the door and returned with Paul's black holdall.

"That's the one." Paul smiled. "I…" He narrowed his eyes. "Shona, can I see the register for when Stefan Finch was last here?"

"What for?" Shona asked.

"I just want to check something." He reached over the desk and picked up the register.

Shona glanced left and right. "Paul, you really shouldn't be looking at that. It's private."

"Don't worry, I won't tell anyone if you don't. I just want to see who—" Paul scanned the register. "Shit! I don't believe this." He took out his phone and photographed the page.

"What is it? What have you found?"

Paul closed the register with a bang and leaning over, kissed Shona on the cheek then hurried out of the hotel.

30

Paul's train arrived at Leeds station at eleven o'clock that morning. He went straight to Thomas Walker's pawnbrokers in Briggate, a single storey red-brick building set back from the main road. The small windows were dirty with heavy mesh on the inside, giving the shop a gloomy and unwelcoming appearance.

Thomas Walker, the original proprietor, had died over ten years earlier. It was his son, Arthur, who now ran the business. Arthur was standing behind the wooden counter when Paul entered.

"Good morning," he muttered, not bothering to look up from his newspaper. "Feel free to look around, mate."

Without responding, Paul walked swiftly over to Arthur and, reaching over the bench, grabbed him roughly by his shoulders.

"What the fuck—" Arthur said.

Paul pulled Arthur closer, so his face was only inches away from his. "You and I need to talk," he said.

Arthur struggled, but Paul did not relinquish his hold. "Talk about what? I've done nothing."

"I want to know about the girl that pawned the Rolex the other day."

"I don't know what you're talking about."

"Who paid you to inform?"

"You've got this all wrong, mate. I never—"

"Arthur, I'm going to count to five," Paul said. "When I get to five if you haven't told me what I want to know, I'm going to hurt you. Really hurt you. Do you understand?"

Arthur whimpered like an injured animal. "Please, I don't—"

"One... two... three..." Paul began. He could feel Arthur trembling under his grasp.

"Four," Paul said, releasing one shoulder and bringing back his fist.

"Please," Arthur squealed. "There's no need for this. I've

done nothing wrong."

"Well?"

"A bloke phoned and said he'd had his watch stolen by an ex-girlfriend. He said he would pay me fifty quid to let him know if it was brought in."

Paul unclenched his hand. "What was this bloke's name?"

"Stefan. He said his name was Stefan Finch."

"And you let him know as soon as the girl came in to pawn the watch?"

"Yeah, that's all I did," Arthur nodded ferociously. "I told him her name and address and where she worked. She's the one that nicked the Rolex, not me."

"Did Stefan come here himself?"

Arthur shook his head. "No, two blokes came. They said Stefan was busy. I told them about the girl, and they paid me fifty quid."

"What did these men look like?"

Arthur shrugged. "I don't know, just blokes. One of them was a big bugger with a red beard."

"Where's the watch now?"

"I offered to sell it back, but they said I could keep it, so I polished out the engraving and—"

"Did the men say anything else about Stefan?"

"No, and I didn't ask."

Paul released his grip and Arthur scurried to the far corner of the shop. "What's this all about anyway?" Arthur said, straightening his crumpled shirt. "It was Stefan Finch's watch. He can do what he wants with it."

Walking towards the door, Paul stopped and turned to face Arthur. "When you spoke to Stefan Finch on the phone, he'd been dead a week."

31

When Charlotte entered the flat, Marion rushed towards her and hugged her tightly, kissing her cheek. "Oh, darling, I'm so glad to see you," she said. "It's been ages."

"Nearly a year." Charlotte grinned as she followed Marion into the kitchen.

"I'm sorry your bedroom's a bit on the small side, but I can't really manage anywhere bigger than this flat."

"It's fine, Marion, stop worrying." Charlotte smiled, taking off her coat. "It's you I've come to see, not the flat." She walked over to the window and looked out. "You have a lovely view of the park."

"Yes, I go for a walk there most days, now that I don't go into town as often."

Charlotte sighed and turned towards Marion. "I don't understand why you didn't want to stay with me and Patrick in Dublin. We've plenty of room in that big house, and you know we loved having you."

Marion poured two glasses of wine and handed one to her granddaughter. "It's always nice to visit, dear, but I need my own front door. Besides, you were newly married. You didn't want me hanging around."

"That's not true. I loved having you stay."

"Yes, but did Patrick? It's his home too, don't forget."

"Patrick didn't mind, besides he's rarely at home. He's always working somewhere."

"I can't fathom why he didn't join his father's law firm instead of working freelance and travelling all over the place."

Charlotte frowned. "Patrick likes the variety of the work," she said. "And he enjoys travelling. He gets bored, staying in one place all the time."

Marion tutted. "He's a married man now. He should be at home with you, not gallivanting around the globe."

Charlotte folded her arms. "Marion, that's not fair. Patrick is a good husband. He makes sure I have everything I need."

Marion shrugged. "Will he be joining you?"

"He should be here in a couple of days. He just wants to make sure Shamus is stable."

There was an uneasy silence. It was Marion who spoke first. "So how are you enjoying married life? It'll be your second anniversary soon, won't it?"

"Two years next month."

"No thoughts of starting a family?"

Charlotte giggled. "Not right now, Gran, but we do want children."

"Gran? That's the first time you've called me that." Marion smiled. "I like it."

"Sorry but, well, it's all been a bit strange, hasn't it? I didn't know you existed until Erica—"

"Yes, poor Erica. It was tragic what happened. I do miss her."

"So do I," Charlotte said quietly. "Cancer's very cruel."

"Her death left Joe devastated."

"Oh, are you still in contact with Joe? I haven't seen him since the wedding."

Marion nodded. "Yes. He was here the other day."

"What's he up to these days?"

Marion shrugged again as she poured more wine. "He said he was going into business with Matthew."

"Really? What sort of business?"

Marion grinned. "You're not going to believe this, but they've bought a casino in Manchester. They're going to call it The Lady Luck."

Charlotte gasped. "Why on earth would they want to buy a casino?"

"I suppose they're both at a loose end and looking for something to occupy them. I must say, a casino isn't a business I would want to get involved with."

"I'm meeting Matthew tomorrow," Charlotte said. "I'll ask him what's going on then."

Marion was silent for a moment. She fixed Charlotte with a stare. "Are you sure it's a good idea meeting Matthew again? After what his father did, I would have thought—"

"Matthew is my half-brother. It's unfair to hold him responsible for what his father... our father did."

Marion sighed. "I suppose so, but please promise me you'll be careful."

Charlotte chuckled. "You really are a fusspot, Gran. Shamus warned me to be careful too, just the other day."

"What? Be careful about Matthew?"

"No, he was concerned about Patrick. He thinks he controls me too much."

Marion sipped her wine. "And does he?"

"Of course he doesn't. He's just... protective. After what happened with Karl, I suppose it's understandable."

Marion reached out and gently took hold of Charlotte's arm. "You will keep out of Karl's way while you're over here, won't you?"

Charlotte smiled. "Stop worrying. I don't think there's much chance of our paths crossing, do you? Now, I really must give Patrick a ring and let him know I've arrived safely."

"Give him my love," Marion said as Charlotte turned and left the room.

32

The Emerald Club was bustling when Paul eventually arrived that night. Using the back stairs, he went straight to Karl's office.

Karl sneered. "Good of you to join us. I hope your trip was worth it," he said and indicated for Paul to get a drink.

He poured himself a whisky and one for Karl. "Actually," Paul said, handing Karl his drink. "I found something very useful." He sat across from Karl's desk and relayed details of his visit to the Five Pipers in Edinburgh. "It was when the receptionist handed me the wrong bag that the penny dropped," he said. "If my bag could be mistaken for someone else's, then so could Finch's briefcase."

Karl frowned. "Surely Finch would know it was the wrong one. You said it cost two thousand quid, and it had his initials on?"

"Yes, it was very distinctive. But what if someone else had the exact same briefcase with the same initials?"

Karl screwed up his nose. "It sounds a bit far-fetched, don't you think? Two identical briefcases with the same initials?"

Paul smiled. "I agree." He leant back in the chair and stretched his long legs out in front of him. "But look at this." Paul took out his phone and showed Karl the photo he had taken of the hotel's register. "These are the names and addresses of all the guests who checked out of the hotel the same day as Finch. Two have the initials SF and one PF."

Karl stared at the image for a few seconds. "So, you think one of these three has Finch's briefcase? Sorry, mate, but I don't buy it."

"Don't you think it's worth checking? After all, what have we got to lose?"

Karl was silent for a moment and sipped his drink. "All right," he said at last. "You track them down, but I'm not holding out much hope."

"I'll start first thing tomorrow," Paul said, and he emptied his glass. "It should only take a couple of days."

Karl steepled his fingers and leant forward. "Don't take any longer," he said. "When I find the bastards who've brought trouble to my daughter's door, I'll—"

Paul held his hands up. "Don't worry, we'll find them."

Karl leant further forward in his chair. "Oh, by the way, it turns out that Jacqui never went to the Belmont. She got her mate, Rachel, to do the booking for her."

"Who's Rachel? Have you spoken to her?"

"Not yet. She's working in Dubai, but she'll be back soon. She has a sister who works at Christina's salon."

"Do you want me to go to the airport?" Paul said.

"No. You concentrate on those names. I'll meet the thieving bitch personally."

33

"We're going to need some sort of grand opening," Joe said as he walked around the casino with Matthew. "It will be expected."

"Yeah. We'll sort that out later," Matthew said. "We'll need to make a list of everything we're going to need."

Joe shrugged. "There isn't much. Jonny left the place well stocked. We could probably do with some new bar stools, and maybe a couple dozen more wine glasses, but apart from that, everything seems in good nick."

"What about the staff? You don't want to make any changes?"

Joe shook his head. "No, I don't think so. The croupiers all have good references. They've worked here for some time."

"Okay," Matthew said. "If you're happy, I'm happy. I'm going to meet Charlotte for lunch."

Joe smiled. "Give her my best, and tell her we'll catch up soon."

Matthew was feeling a little nervous at meeting Charlotte again. It had been two years since they had last met and he had realised she was the daughter of his father's mistress. He'd arranged to meet her at twelve-thirty in the beer garden of the Riverside Inn, a traditional public house on the outskirts of Leeds. He arrived ten minutes early and was surprised to see she was already seated at a table.

Smiling, he approached her and lightly kissed her on the cheek. "How lovely to see you again," he said. "You're looking well."

"Hi, Matthew," she said. "So are you."

"Can I get you something to drink? Gin and tonic, isn't it?"

Charlotte shook her head. "It's a bit early for gin. A white wine, please."

Matthew turned towards the entrance but stopped when a

young woman wearing a pale-grey dress and white tabard walked up to the table.

"Can I get you anything?" she asked.

"A white wine and a pint of bitter," Matthew said. "Could you bring a menu as well, please?"

She pointed to a large chalkboard fixed to the wall. "Everything's on there," she said, and disappeared into the pub, returning a few minutes later with the two drinks. "Well?" she said. "Have you decided?"

"I'll have a ham salad," Charlotte said. "What about you, Matthew?"

"I'll have the same, and a bowl of chips, please."

The waitress scribbled their order onto her pad and went back inside the pub.

Matthew reached out and took Charlotte's hand. "Joe was telling me you've got married. A solicitor, isn't he?"

"Yes, his name's Patrick. We live in Dublin now."

"I'm glad you're settled. You deserve some happiness."

"What about you? You're not married?"

"No, I'm not really interested. Besides, I'm too busy with work at the moment."

"Marion told me you and Joe are about to run a casino. It sounds exciting."

Matthew shrugged. "I don't know about exciting. It's a crazy idea really, but we'll see how it pans out."

"I wouldn't have thought you were into gambling, or Joe either for that matter."

He laughed. "Sometimes life guides you down paths you never thought you would go. It's … oh here's the food."

The waitress deposited their order on the table. "Anything else?" she said.

"No, thank you," Matthew replied. "This is fine."

They both ate their food and chatted happily for a while.

"Another drink?" Matthew asked when they had finished eating.

"No thanks. I'm going shopping this afternoon."

He chuckled. "What is it with women and shopping?

You're all the same."

"I love shopping, especially for shoes. Patrick says he sometimes thinks he's married a centipede."

Matthew smiled. "I'm glad things have worked out for you. After everything that's happened, I—"

"Please don't. I can't dwell on what happened to my mother. Karl Maddox is an evil man, and one day he'll get what's coming to him, but I need to put all that behind me now, and so do you."

Matthew's posture stiffened. "That's easier said than done," he said. "My mother's in an institution because of him. You don't really think I can forget about that, do you?"

Charlotte sighed. "What can we do after all this time?"

"Did you know Karl's got a wife? A woman he married before he even met Erica?"

"Joe told me about it. It's hard to believe that he could have hidden a secret like that for all that time."

Matthew's eyes narrowed. "Karl's very good at hiding secrets. Did you know he has two children to her?"

"Yes, twins, aren't they?"

"That's right, Alex and Christina. I think you know Christina."

Charlotte shook her head. "I don't think so."

"She used to be a working girl. She called herself Bunny back then."

"Bunny? You're saying Bunny is Karl's daughter? She can't be. I don't believe it."

"Bunny," Matthew said, "or should I say, Christina, is living in Maddox's house, along with her mother. Karl bought her a beauty salon to get her off the streets."

"So, they're playing happy families and carrying on like nothing has happened?"

"That's right. But that's all about to change very soon."

Charlotte stared at Matthew. "What do you mean by that?"

"Let's just say that Joe and I have a plan."

"What are you going to do? Please tell me. Maybe I can help."

"It's best you keep out of it," Matthew said frowning. "It could be dangerous."

Charlotte leant into Matthew. "It was my mother he murdered," she said. "I have a right to be involved. Surely, you can see that?"

"Charlotte, I don't think—"

"Please, Matthew. I want to help. Speak to Joe."

"All right, I will, but no promises. Agreed?"

"Agreed. And, Matthew?"

"Yes?"

"Maybe I will have another drink after all."

34

Karl was in good spirits as he arrived at The Emerald Club the following evening. The private lounge on the first floor did not open until nine, but the club was in full swing. Karl watched intently as three girls whirled around poles in perfect unison, first turning upside down and then sliding to the bottom, landing in the splits. He grinned, remembering how, years earlier, he had attempted to twirl around a pole, only to land unceremoniously in a crumpled heap on the floor. Fortunately, his unwieldy attempt had only been witnessed by Joe.

He smiled to himself and made his way up the stairs to his office. He was surprised to see Peter standing at the top. "What's the matter?" Karl said. "You look like shit."

"Dad's waiting in your office," Peter said solemnly. "He needs to speak with you urgently."

Karl rushed into his office and looked across at Victor slumped on the couch. Victor Borowicz was big and beefy. His face, usually crumpled into smiles, was pale and strained. His eyes were red and swollen, and Karl could tell his friend had been crying.

"For fuck's sake, Victor, what is it?"

Victor had his head in his hands. His broad shoulders shook as he sobbed.

"Come on, mate. What's happened?"

Victor sniffed loudly as he took out a handkerchief from his pocket and blew his nose. "Sorry, Mr Karl," he said at last. "I... I... I didn't know who else to turn to."

Karl poured a large whisky and handed it to his friend. "Here," he said. "Drink this." Victor took the glass and downed the contents in one gulp.

"Well?" Karl said. "What's up?"

"It's Katya," Victor said at last. "She's... she's my sister's girl."

"What about her?"

"She's gone. She's been taken. I don't know what to do."

"You're not making sense, Victor. What do you mean, she's been taken?"

"Trafficked," Victor said. He clenched his jaw. "She's been taken away in the night like some animal to market."

"When was she taken?"

"About two weeks ago."

"Are you sure she was trafficked? She couldn't have gone off somewhere with a boyfriend or—"

"Katya wouldn't just go off without telling her mother. She's a good girl. No, she's been taken." Victor grabbed hold of Karl's arm. "Will you help me? Will you help me find my niece?" he said.

"I'll ask around," Karl said, "but I don't know anything about traffickers."

"You don't, but you know people who do. Please, Karl, I'm begging for your help. My sister is out of her mind with worry. We all are."

Karl replenished Victor's glass and poured himself a drink. "Do you have a photograph of your niece?"

"Why do you want a photograph? Do you know something? Do you know who these people are?"

Karl shrugged. "A girl turned up at my daughter's salon a few days ago claiming to have been trafficked. I just wondered if there was some connection, that's all."

Victor jumped to his feet. "Where is this girl? I want to speak to her."

"Calm down, mate. We're not going to get anywhere with you carrying on like that. Do you have a picture of your niece or not?"

Victor retrieved a small photograph of Katya from his jacket pocket. "This was taken last Christmas," he said. "You can see that she's very beautiful."

Karl studied the photograph of Katya, a beautiful young woman with shoulder-length black hair and sparkling blue eyes. "Does your sister have any idea how the abduction happened?"

Victor sighed heavily. "Katya worked as a receptionist at

the Hotel Superior in Budapest. She went to work one day and never came home." Victor glared at Karl. "What is it?" he said. "You know something, I can tell."

Karl rubbed his chin. "I don't know anything for sure. I've got to speak to some people."

Victor took hold of Karl's arm. "You know who has my niece, don't you? Please, Karl, if you know anything, you must tell me."

Karl shrugged him off. "Victor, there's nothing you can do here. Go home to your wife and try not to worry. I'll be in touch as soon as I hear anything."

Peter stood, holding the door open for his father. "Dad, if anyone can find out where Katya is, it's Karl," he said.

35

Once Victor had left the office, Karl telephoned Christina. "I need to speak with Nadia again," he said. "Bring her to the salon. I'm coming over."

"Is everything okay, Dad?" Christina asked.

"No, it isn't okay," Karl said. "It's anything but okay." He slammed down the receiver and walked out of his office and down the stairs.

Peter was standing in the foyer. "Anything I can do, boss?" he asked.

"You come with me. I think Nadia knows more than she told me."

Alex, who was standing in the doorway, stepped forward. "Can I do anything to help, Dad?"

"No, I want you to go over to Manchester. There's some furniture being delivered at ten o'clock tonight. Check it's okay, will you?"

"That's an odd time to deliver furniture. It's not a knock-off, is it?"

Karl held up his finger. "Alex, just do as you're told. I don't have time for this."

Alex shrugged. "Okay. I'll go now."

Less than half an hour later, Karl and Peter arrived at Christina's salon. Nadia and her sister, Sophia, were already waiting in the office.

Karl wasted no time on pleasantries. "Do you know this girl?" he asked, handing Nadia the photograph given to him by Victor. "Was she with you in the van?"

Nadia took the photograph and stared at it for a few seconds. She was trembling slightly, and her hand shook. "Katya," she said softly. "Her name is Katya. We worked together at the hotel."

"Was she taken too?"

Nadia nodded. "She managed to get out of the van and run towards the building, but Luke caught her and dragged her back. She almost made it."

Karl stepped forward and leant in close. "Nadia, I want you to think very carefully. Did either of the men say where they were taking the girls?"

She hesitated for a second. "When I was hiding in the bushes, I could hear them talking. Luke said they were going to Birmingham, but I don't know where."

"Are you sure he said Birmingham?"

Nadia nodded. "I heard Luke talking on his phone to someone about what had happened, and then he told George to hurry up to Birmingham. He said they were already late."

"Did you hear anything else?" Karl said. "Anything at all?"

"Luke did say something about another job they had to do when they had delivered the girls."

Karl clicked his fingers. "What sort of job? Think, girl, think."

"Leeds. He said the boss had a job for them in Leeds."

"Did he say what kind of job?"

"I don't know. He just said they had to go to Leeds. George didn't seem happy about it though. He said he hated Leeds."

"What do you want me to do with Nadia, Dad?" Christina asked. "Should I make her stay at home with her sister?"

"No, let her carry on as normal in the salon. I'll get one of the guys to keep an eye on her, so she'll be safe."

Karl headed towards the door, followed by Peter.

"Who do we know in Birmingham that's likely to be mixed up in this?" Peter asked as they walked towards Karl's car.

"Birmingham's a place I've never bothered with," Karl said frowning. "I know the bloke who runs most of the clubs over there, but I doubt he'd be mixed up in this type of shit."

"Do you want me to pay him a visit and see what I can find out?"

Karl shook his head. "No, this is something I need to deal with. You stay at the Emerald and keep things normal."

"Okay, boss, if you're sure. Let me know if you need any help over there. I've heard they don't take kindly to visitors."

36

No one had ever been able to diagnose what exactly was wrong with Isaac Croft, despite the numerous x-rays, scans and other tests he had undertaken over the years. What Isaac lacked in health, however, he more than made up for in intellect with one of the highest IQs ever recorded by MENSA.

Isaac was an albino. At forty-five, he weighed less than nine stone and was just under five-foot-tall with a slight curvature of his spine. His wispy-white hair hadn't been cut in over ten years, and he wore it pulled back from his thin, angular face with a rubber band. Because of his poor eyesight and problems with light, Isaac always wore dark glasses. These had the effect of giving him a menacing look. Despite his poor health and peculiar appearance, however, Isaac Croft was one of the most revered, as well as one of the most feared men in Birmingham.

Isaac was in his lavishly furnished private quarters at Temptations, one of his many strip clubs throughout the city. He was about to settle down to his dinner of chicken consommé and boiled fish with brown rice when there was a light tap on the door. It was Ben, his right-hand man.

"Yes, Ben?" Isaac said. "What is it? I'm eating."

"Sorry for the interruption, sir," Ben said, "but you have a visitor."

"At this hour?"

"It's Karl Maddox, sir. He says he needs to speak to you urgently."

"What does he want? Tell him to make an appointment."

The door of the sitting room burst open. "Stop pissing about, Isaac," Karl said, striding into the room. "We need to talk."

Isaac placed his spoon down. "Don't you bastards from Leeds have any manners? I'm trying to eat."

"You can eat when you hear what I have to say."

"What is it you want?" Isaac chuckled. "I thought you'd

been shot. You should be in the morgue, not harassing me in my own home."

"Lucky for me, the idiot who shot me couldn't hit a barn door."

"Ben, show Mr Maddox the way out," Isaac said, pointing a bony finger towards the door. He turned to Karl. "Next time, make an appointment."

Ben was tall, muscular, and had once been a renowned bare-knuckle fighter. He attempted to grab Karl by the arm, but Karl turned sharply and with one blow, sent him sprawling across the floor.

"I said stop pissing about and listen to me," Karl said and watched as Ben struggled to his feet. "Get out," Karl ordered. "My business is with your boss."

Ben looked towards Isaac for instruction. After a few seconds, Isaac nodded. "Wait outside," he said. "I'll call if I need you."

When Ben left the room, Isaac turned to his visitor. "I could have you torn apart for what you've just done," he said. "How dare you come here and—"

"For fuck's sake, Isaac," Karl said. "Shut up and listen."

Isaac sighed loudly. "Well? What is it that's so important?" Isaac said and wiped his mouth with a napkin. "You have five minutes."

Karl sat on the wooden chair across the table from Isaac. "Have you heard anything about sex traffickers?"

"Of course, I've heard about them. I was watching a documentary about it only last week."

"I'm serious. Have you been approached about placing girls in your clubs who've been trafficked?"

Isaac glared at Karl for a few seconds, two spots of colour forming in his otherwise chalk-white cheeks. "How dare you?" he said. "I haven't built up my business by using trafficked girls. You know that. Why do you ask?"

"Because, a few nights ago, a van full of young girls, from Romania, was trafficked to Birmingham. I need to find them and find out who brought them."

Isaac chuckled again. "Why? Do you want to put them in your own clubs?"

"Don't be stupid. I wouldn't touch them with a barge pole."

"Then, why the interest? These days girls get trafficked all the time."

"One of the girls is the niece of a good friend of mine," Karl said.

"And you think this girl's working for me?"

"No, but I think you might know the bastards behind it. We both know there isn't much that happens in this city that you don't know about."

"Flattery now, eh?" Isaac cackled. "Sorry, Karl, but this is the first I've heard about it. I'll put feelers out though and see what I can find."

"I'd appreciate it, Isaac."

"Noble as your cause sounds, Karl, I think there's another reason you need to find these people."

"Not much gets past you, does it?"

"Are you going to tell me what's going on?"

"No," Karl said.

Isaac shrugged. "Well, never mind, I'm sure it'll all come out in the wash, eh? Do you want a drink before you leave? Whisky isn't it?"

Karl nodded. "That would be good, thanks."

"I must say it takes balls to come here alone. You must be pretty desperate."

Karl remained silent.

A few minutes later, Ben entered the room with a bottle of whisky and one glass.

"Aren't you having one?"

Isaac sighed. "I don't drink. Well, it's more that I can't drink these days. I have terrible repercussions if I do, but you help yourself. By the way, I hear you're opening a club in Manchester."

"Yeah, that's right, the Amethyst. It should be open in a couple of weeks. Do you want a VIP ticket for the opening?"

"I haven't been out of this room for the best part of five years, as well you know," Isaac said. "But you're right, there isn't much that goes on in this city that I'm not aware of."

Karl remained silent as he poured himself a drink and then studied the label. "Nice whisky," he said.

"Yeah, it's better than that shite I serve the punters. Talking of punters, I hope you're not planning to open any clubs in my city. I'd hate for us to fall out."

"No, mate, Birmingham is all yours. You have my word on that."

"I heard your son Alex will be running the new club."

"Yeah, that's right. I thought I'd give him a chance to show me what he can do. He'll be taking them all on eventually."

"Keeping it in the family, eh?" Isaac said. "By the way, Karl, I suppose you've heard Jonny Dalton's sold the casino in Manchester?"

"The Lucky Ace? When did this happen?"

Isaac grinned. "A couple of weeks ago. I heard he got on the wrong side of some people and had to make a quick getaway."

"You seem to hear a lot of things considering you're housebound."

"I do, don't I?" Isaac smirked. "Do you want to know what else I heard?"

"No, but I'm sure you're going to tell me."

"I heard that your old buddy, Joe, has bought the casino off Jonny. What do you think about that?"

37

Paul parked his Peugeot twenty yards from the driveway to the red-brick detached house that was the address given for S. Ferguson in the register at the Five Pipers Hotel. He studied the house and its surroundings. An expensive property, he noted, with a double frontage and a large garage big enough to hold three vehicles. He walked up the gravel path to the blue-painted door and rang the bell.

It was opened almost immediately by a stout, middle-aged woman with a crop of bright ginger hair. "Yes?" she asked pleasantly, her pale-blue eyes glinting in the afternoon sunshine.

"Good afternoon," Paul said. "I'm doing a survey on behalf of the hotel industry, and I was wondering if you could spare me a few minutes to—"

"Of course," she said, her chubby face creasing into a broad smile. "Come in and have a cup of tea. I've just made it."

Paul followed the woman into a spacious living room with highly polished furniture and pretty floral curtains.

"Sit down, dear. I won't be a minute."

Paul sat on the chintz couch. He hadn't been sure what kind of reception he would receive, knocking on strangers' doors and asking them questions about hotels, but it certainly wasn't this.

"Milk and sugar?" she asked, putting her head and shoulders through the serving hatch.

"Just milk, please," Paul said.

The woman brought in a tray of drinks and a plate of chocolate biscuits. "Help yourself," she said, handing the plate to Paul.

He took a biscuit before picking up his clipboard. "Firstly," he began, "may I have your name please?"

"Mrs Ferguson," the woman said. "Mrs Susan Ferguson."

"Well, Mrs Ferguson," Paul said, "I—"

"Oh, call me Susan, dear. Everyone does."

"Susan," Paul continued, "I'm conducting a survey on behalf of some of the largest hotel chains in the country, to see how customers rate the service they have received."

She sighed. "It's been a long time since I stayed in a hotel. I don't get out much these days, what with my arthritis and—"

"Oh, I thought you stayed at a hotel in Scotland recently? They gave me your name."

"That wasn't me, dear. That would be my daughter Sally. She's travelling around Scotland."

"Is she still in Scotland?"

"As far as I know she is. She wanted to go backpacking with her friend, but her dad said she could only go if she stayed in a proper hotel every night. You can't be too careful with young girls these days. You hear such terrible things."

"The survey wants to know what sort of luggage was taken to the hotel. How many suitcases, for instance, or if you took a briefcase? I take it Sally wouldn't have had a briefcase with her?"

"No, of course she wouldn't. She had a rucksack, that's all. What would she want a briefcase for?"

"Well, thank you, Susan," Paul said and drained his cup. He stood and walked towards the door. "You've been very helpful."

"If you want to wait half an hour, my husband should be home," Susan said. "He stays in hotels sometimes when he goes to conferences. Maybe he can help with your survey."

"Your husband goes to conferences?"

"Yes, a couple of times a year. He's going next month actually to the Senior Police Officers' Conference in London."

"Your husband's a policeman?"

"Yes. He's Superintendent Arthur Ferguson."

38

It was just after ten o'clock the following morning when Paul arrived at the second address which had been in the register of The Five Pipers Hotel. This was a run-down mid-terrace cottage on the outskirts of Bradford. Paul gave a sharp rap on the door. He waited several seconds, but nothing happened. He knocked again, this time a little louder.

Paul could hear bolts being drawn back and several locks being turned before the door was partially opened, a heavy chain keeping it secure. A short, heavily tattooed man in his mid-twenties looked through the opening. "Yeah?" he said, "what do you want?"

Paul took a step back and smiled. "Good morning," he said. "I'm conducting a survey on—"

The man made to close the door. "Piss off," he said. "I'm busy."

Paul put his arm out, touching the door. "It will only take five minutes of your time," he said, "and there's twenty pounds for your trouble."

The man sniffed. "You're not one of those Jehovah people, are you? They were round here last week and—"

Paul shook his head. "No, I'm not a Jehovah's Witness," he said. "I want to talk to you about hotels, Mr...?"

"Fenton," the man said. "Philip Fenton."

Paul held up the clipboard he was carrying. "I understand you were stayed at The Five Pipers recently, in Scotland?"

The man frowned. "So what?"

"I'd like to ask you some questions about your stay at the hotel," Paul said.

Fenton sniffed loudly. "There's nothing much to tell. I was in Scotland on business, and the car broke down." He pointed to a battered Volkswagen parked at the side of the house. "I'm getting rid of it soon. The bloody thing's always breaking down."

"How was your stay, Mr Fenton?" Paul asked. "Was the hotel comfortable?"

Fenton shrugged. "It was all right, I suppose, apart from that bastard porter, Riley."

Paul frowned. "Oh, what did Riley do to upset you?"

"He stopped me taking a bird up to my room."

"You had a girlfriend with you?"

Fenton put his finger to his lips. "Shush," he whispered, "the wife's inside." He quickly unchained the door and joined Paul in the garden. "She wasn't a girlfriend exactly," he said, a broad grin spreading across his face. "She was a tart I met in a bar. Beverley, I think they called her. Nice bit of arse she had too. That bastard Riley wouldn't let me take her up to my room."

"It's hotel policy not to allow hookers into the hotel," Paul said. "Riley would have been in trouble if they found out."

Fenton shrugged but said nothing.

"Well, I'm sorry things didn't work out for you, mate," Paul said, "Now, getting back to my survey. Can I ask you about your luggage?"

"Luggage?"

"The survey wants to know what sort of luggage you had with you. Suitcase, rucksack, briefcase. That sort of thing."

"I just had a rucksack," he said. "I wasn't planning on an overnight stay."

"You didn't have a suitcase then, or a briefcase?"

Fenton began to chuckle. "What do I want with a briefcase? Do I look like a city gent?"

Paul smiled. "Well, thank you, Mr Fenton," he said. "You've been very helpful."

Fenton scowled. "You said there was twenty quid in it for me?"

Paul smiled as he took a twenty-pound note from his pocket. "There you are," he said, handing the money to Philip Fenton. "And thanks again."

Paul's phone rang as soon as he got into his car. "Karl, I was just going to ring you," he said. "I've checked out the first two names from the hotel register. I'm sure neither of them is involved. I'm going to visit the third person later this afternoon in—"

"Forget about that," Karl said. "I always thought it was a stupid idea. I need you back here now."

Paul sighed. "Okay, if you're sure, but I still think we should—"

"There've been developments."

"I'm in Bradford at the moment," Paul said. "I can be with you in less than an hour."

There was a click as Karl put down the receiver.

39

Karl slammed down the receiver after talking to Paul and turned sharply to his wife. "Did Christina come home last night? I didn't hear her come in."

"No, she stayed at a friend's house."

"What friend?"

"I don't know." Lisa shrugged. "It's none of my business, or yours, for that matter."

"Of course it's our business. She's our daughter."

"Stop worrying about her. I've told you before, Christina can take care of herself."

Karl tossed down his newspaper and thumped the table with his fist. "Lisa, I want to know who my daughter spends her time with, and I don't want her staying out all night either."

"Christina doesn't want us interfering in her life."

"While she's under my roof, she obeys my rules."

"You'll drive her away if you carry on like this," Lisa sighed. "She's a grown woman with a life of her own." There was an uneasy silence. It was Lisa who spoke first. "Have you decided what you're going to get her and Alex for their birthday this Saturday?"

"Shit, I'd forgotten! What do you suggest?"

"I thought we could buy Christina a new car. Hers is a bit battered."

Karl frowned. "I don't know about that."

"What about Alex?"

"What about him?"

"Have you given any thought about what to buy him for his birthday?"

Karl shrugged. "What does he want?"

"Why don't you give him the Amethyst?"

"Are you out of your mind?"

"Why not? You've bought Christina her own business. It seems unfair not to do the same for your son."

"I'm letting Alex manage the Amethyst when it opens, but

there's a big difference in managing a club and actually owning it. The responsibilities are enormous."

"You'll never know if you don't give him a chance. After all, you won't be around for ever. He'll be in charge of all the clubs sooner or later."

Karl frowned. "Thanks for that."

"In fact, I was thinking, why not give him a small percentage in all of the clubs, so he gets to know how they operate. He'll be able to take some of the workload off your shoulders."

Karl sat back in his chair. "I'll think about it, but no promises. By the way, they're not expecting a party are they?"

"No, of course they're not. Christina is going out for a meal with some of the staff from the salon, and I'm sure Sarah will have arranged something with Alex."

Karl snatched up his newspaper. "That's something, I suppose."

"Why are you being grumpy about having a party anyway? I thought you liked parties?"

"No, Lisa, I like making money, and unless I get over to the club, there'll be no money for cars or parties."

"Money's not getting tight, is it, Karl? I thought the businesses were doing well."

"They are, but there's always someone out there waiting to jump into your place the minute you turn your back."

Lisa sighed as she began to fill the dishwasher.

"What's the matter with you, anyway?" Karl asked. "You're looking miserable today."

"I'm just tired. I'm ready for a holiday."

"A holiday?"

"Yes, Karl, a holiday. When was the last time you left work and relaxed on a beach? A break would do you good too."

"In my business, you can't afford to relax and take holidays." He placed the newspaper back on the table and stood.

"You could if you let Alex help more."

Karl frowned and turned to put on his jacket. "You go on

holiday if you must, but there's too much happening here at the moment for me to leave."

"You mean this business with Victor's niece?"

"How did you know about that?"

"Alex told me. I think you're wasting your time trying to find her. From what I've heard about trafficked girls, you'll be lucky to see her again."

Karl shrugged. "We'll see."

"Have you found this damned briefcase yet? Christina's terrified those men will come back to the salon. She said her friend Rachel—"

"Christina has a big mouth," Karl said. "I'll speak with Rachel when she's back in the country. Now, if you don't mind, I have work to do."

40

Karl brought his fist down hard on the table. "Did you know about this?" he yelled, "or do I have to rely on that freak, Isaac Croft, to let me know what's going on?"

"I hadn't heard a thing about it," Paul said quietly, "but then why would I? A casino isn't part of our business, is it?"

"I don't give a fuck about the casino," Karl said. "It's that bastard Joe back on the scene that worries me."

"Forget about him. Joe's nobody."

"Never underestimate him, Paul. Joe's dangerous. You've no idea how dangerous."

"I'm sorry, but I don't see how he poses any sort of threat to the business. If he's bought the casino then——"

Karl threw his hands out. "Why has he bought it, that's what I want to know? What does he want with a casino a few hundred yards from the Amethyst?"

Paul shrugged. "I'll poke around and see what I can find out."

"You do that. I want to know who's backing him. Someone must be. Casinos don't come cheap. I want you to go and have a good snoop around at the grand opening on Saturday. See what you can find out."

"Okay, if that's what you want," Paul said. "I don't suppose your mate, Isaac Croft, knew anything about the traffickers? Dad's out of his mind with worry."

"He's doing some digging. If anybody can find out what's going on, Isaac can."

"He's an odd sort of bloke though, isn't he? Peter says he's an albino."

Karl smirked. "He might be odd, but he's got his finger on the pulse. Nothing much gets past him. He's a vicious little bastard too, not the sort of bloke you want to cross."

"How come a freaky twat like him came to be so powerful?"

"Isaac's body might be knackered, but his brain works like a computer." Karl grinned. "He was the only child of wealthy parents. When he was growing up, he had the best of everything, but he yearned for excitement in his life. That's why he turned to crime, I suppose."

Paul frowned. "So, his power is just down to cash?"

"His money helped buy him the best muscle out there, but Isaac is clever. He's a brilliant planner. He's behind most of the serious crime in Birmingham." Karl began to chuckle. "Don't be fooled by his appearance. If you cross him, Isaac has no compassion, no mercy. He'll have you killed in the blink of an eye."

"He can't be that savvy if he didn't know about the trafficking."

"Well, he knows now, so wait and see."

Paul shrugged, again. "What do you want me to do about the last name in the hotel's register?"

"Leave it. This business with Joe is more important. I want you to find out everything that's going on at that casino."

"Okay, if you say so, but I still think—"

Karl put both hands flat on the desk and took a deep breath. "Paul, just do what I say. There's something not right with the whole setup, I know there is."

There was a light tap on the door, and Alex entered the office. "I checked that furniture over at the club," he said, and walked over to the cabinet to help himself to a whisky. "It all looks great."

"Good," Karl said. "We should be ready to open in a fortnight. Have you got the VIP guest list prepared?"

Alex frowned. "Guest list?"

"We always invite VIPs to the opening of our clubs. Local people of influence. I thought you knew that."

"I'll get it sorted," Alex said.

"Get Marco to help. He knows everybody in Manchester."

Alex scoffed. "I don't need Marco's help. I'll deal with it."

"You'd better not balls it up," Karl warned. "This is your chance to show me what you're made of."

"I said I'll deal with it. I know what I'm doing."

"You're sure you have enough hostesses and dancers?

Alex rolled his eyes. "Of course I have. Stop worrying. Every girl has been picked by me personally."

"What about Sarah? Is she okay about moving back to Manchester?"

Alex took a long sip of his drink. "Sarah will do as she's told."

Karl scowled. "Is everything all right between you two? Sarah doesn't come round to the house anymore. Lisa was wondering if she'd done anything to upset her."

"Sarah's a moody cow, that's all. She's not very sociable."

"If you're going to make a go of running the Amethyst, you are going to need her on board. You do know that?"

Alex drained his glass and slammed it down on the table. "Don't worry about Sarah and me. Everything is fine."

Karl sat back in his chair and eyed his son. "All right, if you say so," Karl said. "By the way, what are you doing on Saturday to celebrate your birthday?"

"I wasn't planning on doing anything."

"I thought Sarah would be arranging something," Karl said.

"I don't think she even knows it's my birthday."

"Have you been shagging another woman? Is that what's upset her?"

Alex folded his arms. "When the hell do I get time to shag anybody?"

Paul got up and walked towards the door. "I'm off, Karl. I'll get on with what we discussed."

"Thanks, Paul."

When Paul left the room, Alex turned to Karl. "What's that all about? What's he up to?"

"Nothing for you to worry about," Karl said. He grimaced and rubbed his leg. "Now, pass me those pain killers, will you? My leg is killing me today."

41

The room was cold and damp. A shaft of light came from a small window high on the wall, a window that was covered in heavy mesh. Paint peeled from the walls, and the only door was solid wood with two heavy bolts on the outside. On the floor were half a dozen thin mattresses and a bundle of blankets. One corner of the room had a plywood partition, behind which was a toilet and a small washbasin. In the centre, a large table and six wooden chairs. This had been home to the girls brought from Romania a few days earlier.

It was midday. All five girls were seated at the table, eating sandwiches, when the bolts were pulled back from the other side of the door, and two men came into the room.

"Take that one to the house in Park Row," the younger of the two men said and pointed to a pretty brunette. "And those two over to Brooke Street."

"What about the other two?" his companion, a thick-set man in his forties, asked. "What do you want me to do with them?"

He grinned. "Don't worry about them. They're going to work in a club in Manchester."

"Manchester? Why the fuck have they been brought to Birmingham?"

He smirked. "A special request. All I know is the boss wants those two taken to Manchester."

The older man walked over to one of the girls and putting his hand in her hair, roughly pulled her head backwards. "Maybe I'll come and visit you in the club," he said, leaning over and putting his face close to hers. "Would you like that?"

The girl struggled to free herself from his grip, but his hold remained firm. "Well, would you like that?" he whispered as he leant in and tried to kiss her on the lips.

"Get away from me," she screamed. "Leave me alone."

The man laughed, and pulled the girl towards him. "Maybe I should take you upstairs now. What do you say?"

"No," she shrieked, desperately trying to push him away.

"Please don't."

He laughed again. "No chance. You're coming with me." He grabbed the girl's arm and dragged her towards the door.

"For Christ's sake, haven't you had enough?" his companion said. "You've been at it with them since they got here."

"It's a perk, mate. Every job has to have perks, right?"

"Well, you haven't got time to do her now. The boss wants these three moved. They're being put to work tonight."

He grinned and loosened his hold on the girl. "Okay. Keep your hair on. I'll be back later, and we can finish off what we started."

"I'll give you a hand," the younger man said, as he grabbed two of the girls and pushed them towards the open door. The other man took hold of the third girl and followed. The only noise was the sound of the bolts sliding back into position, and then there was silence.

"We have to get out of here," one of the remaining girls said. "I can't bear that animal to touch me again. I'd rather die than…"

"Stay strong, Katya," Anna whispered. "You heard what they said. We're going to be taken to work in a club. It should be easier to escape from there."

"I don't see how, they'll be watching us all the time."

"Don't give up hope. Remember Nadia? She managed to get away."

"I don't think she got away. They probably caught her and killed her, just like they'll kill us when they've finished with us." Katya lowered her head into her hands and, not for the first time since her capture, began to sob uncontrollably.

42

"What time did she say she'd be here?" Joe asked as he straightened the optics behind the bar.

Matthew took a drag of his cigarette. "Don't worry, she's just a few minutes late. She'll be here."

"I don't understand why you told Charlotte about this place. You know if things kick off, it can be dangerous?"

Matthew stubbed out his cigarette and drank the remnants of his whisky. "Charlotte's a big girl. She has a right to know what we're planning. I owe it to her. We both do."

The outer door opened casting a beam of strong sunlight into the dimly lit casino, and Charlotte walked into the room. She was dressed in jeans and a pale pink sweater, her long blonde hair lying loose on her slender shoulders.

"Hi, guys," she said and kissed first Matthew, and then Joe on the cheek. "So, this is your casino? I must say it's very impressive."

Matthew beamed. "Good to see you," he said and gave Charlotte a hug. "Glad you like it."

"It's not meant as a commercial venture," Joe said. "We bought this place for one reason only, don't forget. To bring down Karl Maddox."

Matthew grinned. "Of course I haven't forgotten, but that doesn't mean we can't have fun, does it?"

Charlotte turned to Joe and reached for his hand. "We're going to do this for Erica." She smiled. "Now, I want you to tell me what I can do to help."

"Charlotte, Joe and I have been talking. We think it's too dangerous for you to get involved."

"But Matthew, I—"

"I'm sorry, Sis, but we both think you should stay away."

Charlotte spun round to face Joe. "Is that what you both think?"

"It's for the best," he said. "When things start to kick off, it will get rough. We don't want you put at risk."

Charlotte sighed. "All right, but please, let me spend just

one evening here. I've never been inside a casino before."

"If we agree," Joe said, "do you promise to do as we tell you?"

"I promise."

Joe turned to face Matthew. "What do you think?"

Matthew sighed. "It can't do any harm, I suppose. What about lunch? What do you fancy?"

Charlotte grinned. "Italian every time, and then you can both explain to me exactly what it is you're planning to do to Karl Maddox."

Matthew wagged a finger. "All in good time."

"You will let me know if there's anything I can do to help, won't you?"

"Yes, of course we will," Matthew said. "Now let's hurry, or Mario's will be full."

43

It was Saturday night. The stretch limo pulled up outside the salon and Christina, and half a dozen of her staff climbed into the vehicle, chatting excitedly. Champagne flutes were laid out and two bottles of champagne chilled in the ice buckets.

Christina smiled as she began to pour the liquid into each glass. "Dad's been so generous. He's provided the car and the drinks, as well as paying for the meal."

"Lucky you," Victoria said. "I wish he was my dad."

Christina shook her head. "No you don't." She handed each girl a flute. "Believe me, you don't."

"Happy birthday, Christina," they all chorused and sipped their drinks.

"How far is it to the restaurant?" Maria asked.

"About fifteen minutes but I've arranged for the driver to take us the scenic route through Leeds. That'll give us time to finish our drinks." The girls began to giggle.

"Do you know, I've never eaten Italian food before," Nadia said.

Sophia frowned. "Not even a pizza?"

"No, not even a pizza. I'm so looking forward to it."

Three-quarters of an hour later, the limousine pulled up outside 'The Italian Experience', a new restaurant in the north of the city.

"Here we are," Victoria said. "I know you'll all love it. I come here all the time. The food's great."

Christina rolled her eyes. "Let's hope so. You've been on about this place all week."

The group were shown to a circular table in the large bay window looking out onto the street. The table had a white linen cloth and gleaming silver cutlery. The napkins were alternate colours of the Italian flag, white, red and green. A small arrangement of flowers sat in the centre of the table.

"Oh, Chris, this is lovely," April said. "It's a pity Rachel couldn't be here too."

Christina smiled. "Well, if she will go partying around Dubai, it serves her right."

A smartly dressed waiter approached the table and handed everyone a red leather-bound menu. "Can I get drinks for you, ladies?" he asked in a strong Italian accent.

"Alfie?" April gasped. "Alfie, what are you doing here?"

He turned to April with his mouth open. "April, I—"

"Why, Alfie?" April snatched up a napkin. "Why did you leave without a word? I thought you loved me and—"

An older waiter came over to the table. "Alfredo, you're needed in the kitchen," he said. "I'll deal with the ladies." Alfie turned and hurried away.

"Is that your boyfriend who disappeared?" Christina asked, putting her arm around April's shoulders.

April nodded as tears trickled down her cheeks. "I thought Alfie had gone back to Italy. I can't believe he was here all the time."

"You know Alfredo?" the waiter asked April.

"I used to," she said softly. "We were… we were very close once."

"Alfredo is the nephew of the owner," the waiter said quietly. "He is… how do you say in English… he is a bit of a ladies' man. If you don't mind me saying, young lady, you are better off without him."

April smiled weakly. "Yes, I think you're probably right."

Christina clapped her hands together. "Let's forget about men for tonight. In my experience, they're nothing but trouble." The group burst into laughter.

Three bottles of white wine were ordered, and everyone studied the menu and made their choice. Twenty minutes later, the food was delivered to their table.

"This looks fab," Maria said, as she set about a large plate of carbonara.

"What did you say they call this?" Nadia asked.

"That's lasagne," Sophia said. "Are you enjoying it?"

"Mm, it's delicious."

The group ate and chatted happily, even April began to

relax and enjoy the evening.

"I'm just going out for a cigarette." Christina wiped the tomato sauce from the corner of her mouth. "I won't be long."

She left the table and walked through into the deserted foyer heading for the door. She stopped as she heard a familiar voice behind her. A voice she had hoped never to hear again.

"Good evening, Christina," he said. "It's good to see you."

Christina shuddered. "Hello, Guido."

"Hello? Is that all you have to say to me after all this time?"

Christina slowly turned. She was shocked to see how much he had aged in the two years since she had last seen him.

"I think you and I need to talk, don't you?" he said, grabbing her by the wrists.

She tried to pull away from him, but Guido's hold remained firm. "We have nothing to talk about," she said. "Get away from me."

Guido forced her into a small storage room off the foyer and closed the door.

"What are you doing in Leeds, anyway?" she asked. "Your restaurants are in London."

"I decided to branch out. Leeds seemed as good a place as any."

She attempted to get past him, but he barred her way. "Please, I have to get back to my friends, they—"

"You heard what happened to me, I suppose?"

"No, what do you mean?"

Guido held up his hands, both of which were covered in white cotton gloves. "This happened," he said. "Some bastard crept into my restaurant one night and attacked me. He thrust both my hands in hot fat."

Christina gasped and moved towards him. "Why would anyone do such a terrible thing?"

"The coward didn't give a reason."

"I didn't know anything about this. I give you my word."

He sneered. "Your word means nothing."

"And yours does?"

"What do you mean by that?"

"You persuaded me to be your mistress, remember?" Christina said, a slight tremor in her voice. "You promised we would get married. I gave up everything to be with you."

"You didn't need much persuasion as I remember."

"Do you have any idea how much you hurt me, Guido," she said as tears began to run down her cheeks. "Finding you in bed, our bed, with another woman?"

Guido reached out and grabbed Christina's arms, pulling her closer towards him. "You forget that I told you I had a wife already," he whispered. "You could never be anything more to me than a distraction."

Christina struggled to free his grip. "You said you'd leave her and marry me."

"That was pillow talk, you silly girl. I could never divorce Bella."

"You bastard. I hate you," she yelled, finally managing to free herself from his hold.

He scoffed. "Is that why you stole the money?"

"I had a right to that money," she said and pushed him in the chest. "After all your broken promises, you owed me that much."

"I owe you nothing," he said. "Nothing."

The door opened slightly, and one of the waiters leant timidly into the room. "Guido," he said quietly, "you can hear the shouting in the restaurant."

"Okay, okay," Guido said, closing the door on the waiter.

He turned to Christina. "I want my money," he said. "All twenty thousand pounds."

"I… I don't have it."

"Then maybe you should resurrect Bunny." A faint smile danced across his lips. "Bunny could earn the money easily enough."

"How did you—?"

"I know everything about you, Christina. You didn't think you could rob me and just walk away, did you? I know where you live and where you work."

"Do you have any idea who my father is? What he's capable of?"

"Of course I know. Karl Maddox was once the most feared gangster in Leeds. His grubby little fingers were in every dirty business going. But Daddy's not in the best of health since he got shot, is he? He doesn't have the clout he once had."

"You don't know what you're talking about. If I told him that you—"

Guido smiled and pushed his face closer to hers. "Told him what? That I once cared for you and trusted you? Will you tell him how you stole from me and disappeared into the night like a thief? Maybe you should tell him why you chose to become a common whore?"

Christina backed away slightly. "I was an escort, and he knows all about that."

"Does he know you became a whore because of your drug habit?" Guido sneered. "I don't think he does. Karl only knows what you've told him, and we both know what a liar you are."

"I'm clean now. I haven't touched the stuff in ages," Christina said. "Please, you can't tell Dad."

"What do you think Karl would do if he knew his little girl had been a junkie?" Guido smirked. "We both know what he thinks about drugs. I bet he wouldn't have given you that salon if he knew about that, would he?"

"Please, Guido, you can't tell him. Please, I'm begging you."

He walked towards the door and turned to face her. "I don't care what you have to do," he said, "but you get me my money. Otherwise, I will make your perfect little life not so perfect. Do you understand me?"

Christina nodded weakly.

"You have seven days." The door slammed behind him. Christina closed her eyes and fought back the tears.

A waiter came over to the table and discreetly handed

Victoria a white envelope. "Guido asked me to give you this," he whispered.

Victoria took the envelope and smiling, placed it in her bag. *'One hundred pounds just for persuading Christina to have her party at Guido's restaurant,'* she thought *'The easiest money I'll ever make.'*

44

Lady Luck Casino opened its doors at seven o'clock and was soon bustling, everyone anxious to see what, if any, changes the new owners had made. Apart from the walls being freshly painted pale-grey, little refurbishment had taken place. The roulette tables were still where they had always been, so were the blackjack tables. Half a dozen extra slot machines had been added, and comfortable high stools had been placed along the front of the bar. Hostesses walked around the gaming floor, taking orders for free food and soft drinks. Most of them had worked for Jonny Dalton previously.

Joe circled the casino, welcoming punters. Matthew was upstairs in the office with Charlotte, monitoring events on screens through the various CCTV cameras around the building.

It was nine o'clock when Joe approached a man sitting alone at the bar. "Good evening, Paul," he said. "I'm surprised to see you in the casino. I didn't think you were a gambler."

Paul shrugged. "I heard you'd bought this place," he said. "I must say I was surprised as well. I didn't think gambling was your thing either."

"Well, it just goes to show, we're both full of surprises."

There was an uneasy silence between the two men as they sized each other up.

It was Joe who spoke first. "I take it you're still working for Karl?"

Paul nodded. "That's right."

"How is the old bastard these days?"

Paul shrugged. "Karl's Karl," he said.

"Well, make sure you tell him I said hello. I hear he's got his new family around him these days."

"That's his business," Paul said, making direct eye contact with Joe. "It's not mine, and it's certainly not yours."

Joe shrugged. "Okay, fair enough. Can I buy you a drink, for old time's sake? After all, the night is still young."

"Another time maybe," Paul said, as he got up from the

bar and walked towards the exit.

"Well, goodnight," Joe said. "I'll see you around."

"Oh, you will," Paul said quietly, "I can promise you that."

When Paul left, Charlotte joined Joe at the bar. He grinned. "Well at least we know Karl's aware we're here," he said, handing her a glass of white wine. "He's sent one of his goons to spy."

Charlotte frowned. "You know him?"

"Yeah, that was Paul Borowicz. He worked for Karl at the Emerald when I was running the Sapphire in Sheffield."

"He's probably on his way now to tell Karl."

Joe smiled. "Of course he is. Stop worrying, Charlotte. Everything's going to plan."

"Joe, I think it's time I was leaving," Charlotte said. "It's after midnight, and I have an early start tomorrow."

Joe lowered his lips to her ear. "You can't go yet," he whispered. "The fun's just about to start."

Charlotte looked at Joe and raised her eyebrows.

Joe nodded towards the door. "Over there. The guy who's just walked in."

"What about him?"

"That's Alex Maddox."

Charlotte turned to see a tall, immaculately dressed man with dark hair stood by the roulette table. His arm wrapped around the shoulders of a young black woman in a tight-fitting green silk gown.

Charlotte smiled. "They make a nice couple. Who is she?"

Joe chuckled. "That, my dear, is Katie."

"Katie?"

"Katie works for me."

45

Charlotte watched as Alex removed a large wad of notes from his inside pocket and exchanged them for gambling chips. He placed a quantity of the chips on the roulette table, and the wheel was spun.

"Thirty-one," announced the croupier as the wheel came to a halt.

Katie flung her arms around Alex's neck. "Darling, you've won." She giggled. "Your luck's definitely in tonight, Alex."

He placed more chips on the table, larger amounts this time.

"Number eleven," said the croupier. Again, Alex collected winnings.

"Joe, I thought the idea was for Alex to lose money," Charlotte whispered. "He seems to be doubling his stake."

Joe smirked. "Give it time. He's been lucky so far, but that won't last."

Charlotte picked up her coat from the rack and kissed Joe lightly on the cheek. "I'm sorry, but I really do have to leave," she sighed. "I have a taxi waiting outside to take me to the hotel."

"I thought you were staying at Marion's?"

"I am, but it's too late to go over to Leeds tonight. Patrick is coming over tomorrow so I must be there to meet him."

"All right. Go if you must," Joe said, as he walked Charlotte to the door. "But you'll miss all the fun."

Charlotte smiled. "Let me know how tonight ends and say goodbye to Matthew for me."

After Charlotte left, Joe made his way to the roulette table and stood directly behind Alex. He watched as Katie nibbled on Alex's ear, encouraging him to make more bets. Gradually, the pile of betting chips in front of him began to dwindle.

"I think I'll try Blackjack," Alex said, getting up from the roulette table. "Maybe I'll have more luck there."

Katie linked her arm in his. "All right, darling," she said. "How about another drink? I could murder a vodka."

Alex signalled to one of the hostesses to bring over two drinks as he took his place at the Blackjack table, Katie by his side.

Two hours later, Alex and Katie left the casino arm in arm. Joe made his way up to the office. Matthew sat behind his desk, surrounded by a bank of monitors, each one recording the activities around the casino.

Joe poured himself a whisky from the decanter. "Do you have any idea how much Alex lost tonight?" he said.

Matthew grinned. "I saw. I just hope he comes back."

"Of course he'll come back. Katie will make sure of that."

"What about the bloke at the bar? He's one of Karl's goons, isn't he? Do you think he'll be making trouble?"

Joe shook his head. "No, Karl wouldn't dare try anything, not while he thinks I still have the knife he used to kill Charlotte's mother."

"Well, let's hope you're right," Matthew said. "Do you know something, Joe? I think I'm going to enjoy running a casino."

46

Sarah stood with her hands on her hips. "What time did you get in last night, or should I say this morning?" I was hoping we could have gone out for dinner last night to celebrate."

Alex rolled his eyes. "Celebrate what?" he said as he poured himself a coffee. "Getting another year older? There's nothing to celebrate about that."

"I take it you're still going ahead with this club in Manchester?"

"Of course I am. Why wouldn't I?"

"I meant what I said, Alex. I'm not going with you. If you go to Manchester, you go alone."

Alex spun around to face Sarah and grabbed her by the shoulders. "As long as you're my wife, you'll do exactly as I tell you." He shook her. "Understand?"

"You're hurting me," she said. "Let go."

Alex released his grip, pushed her against the wall and glared at her. "You're coming with me to Manchester," he said, "so you'd better get used to the idea."

Before Sarah could reply, Alex's mobile rang. He glanced at Karl's name on the screen then back to Sarah. "We'll talk about this later," he said as he walked through into the lounge.

"Morning, Karl," Alex said. "How are you today?"

Karl grunted. "Never mind that. I want you over at the Emerald now."

"Why? What's up?"

"Just get your arse over here now."

"Okay, Karl. I'm on my way." Alex pushed the phone into his pocket and turned to Sarah. "I'm going over to the Emerald. You'd better have started the packing when I get back."

Karl and Paul were already in the office when Alex arrived. He was surprised to see a tray of coffee mugs, instead of the usual whisky glasses on the table.

Alex smiled. "Is everything all right?"

Karl stared at him. "Isaac was right about Joe buying the casino," Karl said. "Paul went there last night and spoke to him."

Alex's eyes darted towards Paul. "You were at the casino?"

"Yeah. I went to have a look around."

"What time?"

Paul frowned at Alex. "Early," he replied. "Why do you ask?"

Alex shrugged. "Oh, I was wondering if you had placed any bets. Beginner's luck and all that."

"I don't gamble," Paul said. "Gambling's a mug's game. Everyone knows that."

Karl sneered. "Not everyone. Eh, Alex?"

Alex puffed out his cheeks. "Do you have to keep bringing that up? Haven't you ever made mistakes?"

"Wind your neck in, Son, I'm only joking. In fact—" The desk telephone rang, and Karl leant over to answer it.

"Hello?... Isaac?... Yes, mate, I can be there right away." He replaced the receiver and retrieved his jacket from the stand. "That was Isaac Croft," he said as he headed towards the door. "He wants to see me urgently."

"Do you want me to come along?" Paul asked.

"No, you stay here. Isaac was never one for company. I won't be long."

47

When Charlotte arrived at Marion's late the following morning, Patrick was already there. She smiled. "Darling," she said, rushing towards him, arms outstretched. Patrick kissed her gently on the lips.

"Where have you been? Marion and I were getting worried."

"I went to see Matthew and it got late, so I stayed the night in a hotel. I wasn't expecting you until this evening."

Patrick huffed. "I caught an earlier flight. How is Matthew?"

"He's well. He owns a casino in Manchester."

"A what?" Patrick said.

"I know, I couldn't believe it at first, but he's bought the Lady Luck Casino with Joe. I was there last night and—"

"You were at a casino?"

"Don't worry, Patrick, it was all perfectly respectable. Joe says—"

"I don't care what Joe says," Patrick said. "I don't want you going there again, ever."

"But, Patrick—"

Patrick glared at her. "I'm not arguing, Charlotte. I mean what I say. Now come upstairs and help me unpack."

Patrick ascended the stairs, closely followed by Charlotte.

Marion walked into the kitchen and busied herself finishing the lamb casserole. She could hear raised voices coming from the bedroom, and she sighed. When the couple came back into the kitchen, Charlotte slumped onto a seat and lowered her head.

"Are you all right, love?" Marion said.

Charlotte nodded but did not reply as she continued to stare down.

Marion placed a plate of food on the table. "How's your father doing? Charlotte was saying he's in hospital."

Patrick sat and picked up a fork. "It's his heart. The doctors don't think he has long."

"That's a shame. Erica said Shamus was a real gentleman."

Patrick shrugged as Marion handed a plate of food to Charlotte.

"Where are you planning to visit while you're in Yorkshire?" Marion said. "Have you decided?"

"I'm afraid I have to work for the next couple of days," Patrick said. "A client wants me to deal with an urgent situation."

"Oh, Patrick, you promised we could spend some time together," Charlotte said, turning to her husband.

He reached over the table, taking her hand in his. "And we will, once I've finished this assignment. We'll do whatever you want, darling, I promise."

Charlotte sighed heavily. "How long will the job take?" she asked quietly.

Patrick shrugged. "Two days. Three at the most." He turned to Marion. "This really is delicious, Marion. You must give the recipe to Charlotte."

48

Isaac sat in an armchair with a thick woollen blanket wrapped around his frail body, waiting for Karl to arrive.

Karl burst into the room. "You said you had information?"

"Hello to you too," Isaac said.

"I don't have time to piss about. What have you found out?"

Isaac grinned. "First things first," he said, lacing his fingers together. "Would you like a drink?"

"No, I don't want a drink. I want to know what you've found out."

Ben entered the room with a tray containing a bottle of whisky and one glass.

"Have a drink," Isaac said. "You're going to need it."

Karl poured himself a whisky, swallowing it in one gulp. "Well?" he said. "Let's hear it."

"It would seem you're right about there being a trafficking gang," Isaac said, "but you were wrong about it being a Birmingham operation. Birmingham is just one of many drop-off points."

"Go on," Karl said.

Isaac pulled the blanket up to his neck and gave a wry smile. Karl narrowed his eyes at him and ground his teeth as Isaac continued. "The gang take requests for girls to be brought from Eastern Europe. Last week girls were delivered to Birmingham. Next week it could be Glasgow or Sheffield."

"Who's running this gang? Did you find that out?"

"I don't know the ringleaders yet, but I'm working on it. What I do know is who's transporting them into the UK."

"Who?"

"If I tell you that, Karl, what's in it for me?"

"What do you want?" Karl said scowling.

"Well, quid pro quo, mate, that's what they say isn't it? You scratch my back…"

"Isaac, I don't have time for playing games."

"I want to know everything that's been happening," Isaac

said. "I know there's a lot more to it than you've told me, and until I know everything, I'm keeping schtum."

Karl was silent for a moment, trying to work out what was the least he could get away with telling Isaac. In the end, he realised everything was linked – Stefan Finch and the missing briefcase, Nadia's escape from George and Luke, Jacqui's death. He took a deep breath, poured himself another drink and proceeded to tell Isaac all that had happened.

Isaac remained silent throughout. Occasionally he would nod or shake his head slightly, but Karl's rendition was not interrupted. When Karl eventually finished, Isaac took an envelope from a drawer and handed it to him. "This is the name of the haulage company that bring in the girls," he said. "Their lorry is due into Dover the day after tomorrow at about midnight."

"Thanks," Karl said as he reached over and took the envelope.

"Well, I think that concludes our business," Isaac said as Karl walked towards the door. "Oh, Karl, there is one more thing."

Karl turned sharply. "What?"

"If I see or hear of you being in Birmingham again, there will be consequences. Understand?"

Karl put up his hand. "Understood," he said, turned and hurried out of the club towards his car.

Isaac chuckled and picked up the telephone. "Hello? Is that the Dover Port Authority? I have some information about a sex trafficking operation going on in your port. Interested?"

49

"It's for you," Lisa said, handing the telephone to Karl. "It's April."

"Yes, April, what is it?" Karl said. "Have you heard from Rachel yet?"

"Just now. She'll be arriving at Manchester Airport about two o'clock this afternoon."

"Two o'clock, eh?" Karl glanced at the kitchen wall clock and saw it was nine-thirty. "I should be able to make it."

"I was going to the airport to meet her myself."

"No, you stay at the flat. I'll collect her."

"But, Karl, I—"

"Do as I say," Karl said. "You stay at the flat, and I'll bring her there. I need to speak to her urgently."

April sighed. "All right, I'll wait here."

Karl put down the receiver and turned to Lisa. "I'm going to the airport," he said. "I'll get this bloody briefcase business sorted out once and for all."

"Don't you think you should take Peter with you? It could be dangerous."

Karl scoffed and rubbed his leg. "The day I can't handle some stupid tart is the day I pack in. I'd better take a couple of pills before I go. My leg is aching this morning."

"I'll get them for you," Lisa said, going to the kitchen cupboard and retrieving the bottle. "You seem to be taking a lot more of these lately. Do you think you should see the doctor and change your prescription?"

"I might do that. The pills make me feel dizzy and sick every time I have a drink."

"That's because you're not supposed to drink alcohol while taking them," Lisa said. "Anyway, laying off the booze for a while won't do you any harm."

Karl glared at Lisa but did not respond as he headed to the door. "Give Peter a ring and tell him where I've gone. Let Paul know as well. I should be back at the club later."

"All right," Lisa said, "but do be careful, Karl."

50

Karl was halfway to Manchester Airport when he heard the siren. Looking in his rear-view mirror, he could see the police patrol car, its blue light rotating, signalling for him to pull over.

"Shit," he muttered and steered the car into a layby. "What the hell do they want?"

"Do you know whose car that is?" the ruddy-faced police sergeant asked, addressing the probationary constable sat next to him.

"No, sarge," the younger man replied.

"That's Karl Maddox's car. You've heard of Karl Maddox?"

"Didn't he get shot by Inspector Glendenning a couple of years back?"

"Yes, that's him," the sergeant said as he opened the car door and paused. "David Glendenning was a mate of mine. We went through training together."

"What happened, sarge? Nobody seems to know why he shot him."

The sergeant stared towards the car in front. "Karl Maddox knows," he said. "The lying bastard tried to say David was off his head." The officers got out and marched towards the car.

Karl had already removed his driving licence from his wallet when the two policemen approached. "What's the problem, officers?" he asked with just a hint of a smile. "I wasn't speeding."

"Is this your vehicle, sir?" the sergeant said.

"You know it is. Why have you stopped me? I've done nothing wrong."

"That's to be established," the sergeant said. "Have you been drinking, sir?"

"What?"

"I said, have you been drinking? I believe I can smell alcohol on your breath."

Karl rolled his eyes. "No, I haven't been drinking."

"I require you to take a breath test, sir," the sergeant said. "Failure to do so will result in you being arrested. Do you understand?"

Karl shrugged. "All right. Play your silly games if you must, but hurry up. I have an appointment."

"Fetch the breathalyser, constable."

The constable hurried towards the police car and retrieved the kit.

The sergeant grinned. "You can do this one, lad. It will be good practice. Take your time. There's no rush." He smiled at Karl.

The constable looked nervous as he instructed Karl on the procedure. No stranger to taking the test, Karl promptly blew into the device and handed it to the young man. All three watched as the breathalyser gave its reading. It was green. No trace of alcohol.

"Well?" Karl said. "Sorry to disappoint you, but as you see, I have not been drinking. Now, I have to be somewhere urgently." Karl turned on his car ignition.

"Not so fast," the sergeant said. "Turn off your engine, Mr Maddox. We're not done yet."

"What now? I wasn't speeding, I've not been drinking, so what the hell are you pratting about at? This is starting to look like harassment to me."

"Police harassment? No sir. Just routine. I think your brake light may be defective. I'm requesting my colleagues from the traffic division inspect the vehicle immediately. I want to make sure it's roadworthy."

"The car's only twelve months old. It's maintained regularly and—"

"Can I remind you, Mr Maddox, that refusal to allow this examination to be carried out will result in you being arrested? Now, step out of the vehicle, please, sir, and sit in the patrol car."

Karl groaned, got out of his vehicle and accompanied the officers to their car.

Half an hour later, a police van arrived at the roadside.

"I want tyres checked," the sergeant said to his colleague. "Brakes, lights, the lot."

The officer looked at the new Mercedes and back to the sergeant. He shrugged, but began his work as instructed. Karl checked his watch and stared out of the window as the examination was carried out. He knew there was nothing wrong with the car, but he also knew that the sergeant was determined to cause him trouble.

It was then a small, red Mondeo pulled up in the layby and a short, grey-haired man with a neat goatee beard climbed out. He was immaculately dressed in a dark suit. The man spoke to the sergeant for a few minutes and then headed towards the police car where Karl was sat.

"Do you mind if I join you?" he asked. He smiled as he opened the rear car door and sat next to Karl.

"What's going on?" Karl said. "Who are you, and what do you want?"

"Good afternoon, Mr Maddox," the newcomer said. "My name is Jeremiah Beauchamp, senior partner in Beauchamp, Bonneville and Clements. I'm a solicitor."

"Well, good for you."

"Mr Maddox, I have been asked to represent you by a mutual friend who witnessed you were being... how shall I put this tactfully... harassed by the police."

"What friend?"

"Mr Paul Borowicz. I believe he is an employee?"

"How did he know?"

"Mr Borowicz received a phone call from a friend of his who witnessed your... your predicament. He rang me and asked me to intervene."

"And has your intervention worked?"

"Oh, yes. The police say you are free to go."

Karl looked up and saw the officers gathered together around their van.

"Bastards," he said and stepped out of the car.

"Perhaps it would be best not to exacerbate the situation, Mr Maddox," the solicitor said. "Just drive away and say nothing."

"Say nothing? They—"

"Mr Maddox, you will be paying a good deal of money for my advice. Please don't waste it. I'll be in touch."

Karl clenched his fists tightly as he walked towards his car. He checked his watch again. It was one-thirty. He realised that he could not get to the airport by two o'clock. He could only hope that the plane was late or that getting through customs would be slow.

51

Rachel left the airport and headed towards the taxi rank. She rummaged inside her handbag as her mobile rang. "April. I was just about to ring you."

"Hi, Rachel! How was Dubai?" April asked.

"Beautiful. I'll tell you all about it when I get home. I'm just about to get a taxi."

"There's no need to do that. Karl's on his way to pick you up."

"Karl? Christina's dad?"

"Yes. He wants to ask you about a briefcase."

"Briefcase? Oh that. I'd almost forgotten about it."

"You mean, you have it?"

"Yes, but what's it got to do with Karl Maddox?"

"It's a long story. I'll tell you about it when you get to the flat. Where is it?"

"I put it in the floor safe," Rachel said.

"I didn't know you had a floor safe."

"It's under the rug. I'll… Oh, there's a guy holding up a card with my name on it. He's too young to be Christina's dad, though."

"Karl must have changed his mind and sent one of the men to pick you up."

Rachel shrugged. "I don't care who gives me a lift. I can't wait to get home. I'll see you in a couple of hours." She walked over to the man and smiled. "Hi, I'm Rachel. Did Karl send you?"

"Yes," replied the man as he reached down and picked up Rachel's luggage. "My vehicle's over here."

He walked briskly through the car park towards a white van, with Rachel following in close pursuit. Sliding open the side door, he put the suitcase inside. Before she had time to realise what was happening, Rachel was lifted up from behind and pushed into the van, the side door sliding firmly shut behind her.

52

Christina parked outside Rachel's apartment and glanced at her watch. It was just after two. She knew her friend was the best chance she had of borrowing the twenty thousand pounds Guido was demanding. She pressed the doorbell, and the door was opened by April.

April smiled. "Hi, Chris. Rachel's not arrived yet I'm afraid."

"I'll wait," Christina said, making her way into the apartment.

"I've just spoken to Rachel on the phone. She was getting a lift from the airport with one of Karl's men."

"Oh, I thought Dad was collecting her himself?"

April shrugged. "He must have changed his mind. But guess what? Rachel did have the briefcase after all."

"Are you sure? Where is it?"

"She said it was in her floor safe. I was just about to look when you arrived."

"I didn't know Rachel had a floor safe," Christina said. "Where is it?"

"She said it's beneath one of the rugs."

Christina looked around the room. There were several rugs on the shiny granite floor. She lifted the one in front of the couch and scowled. "There's nothing here." She examined the tiles. "Let's try the rug over there."

Both women lifted the heavy rug at the back of the room, revealing more granite tiles.

"No, there's nothing here either." April sighed.

Christina leant forward and began to examine the tiles more closely. "Look at this one," she said, running her fingers gently over the surface. "There's a small dimple in the tile. Perhaps it…" As she spoke, she pressed the slight indentation, and the tile slid silently to one side.

"How clever," April said, leaning over Christina's shoulder. "I'd never have found that in a million years."

Christina reached into the aperture. "So, this is what all the fuss has been about?" she said and triumphantly removed a brown leather briefcase. "I wonder what's inside that's so special?" Christina examined the bag closely. "It has a combination lock. It will be impossible to get it open without damaging the case."

April frowned. "Perhaps Rachel knows the combination? She won't be long. Let's wait until she gets here."

Christina stood, holding the briefcase closely to her. "All Rachel did was steal it from a dead man. She'll have no more idea of the combination than we do."

"I still think we should wait for her," April said.

"This can't wait," Christina said and, tucking the briefcase under her arm, headed for the door. "Tell Rachel I'll give her a call later."

53

Peter was working at the desk in Karl's office when Christina arrived at the Emerald Club. "Is Dad about?" she asked. "I have something to show him."

"No," he murmured, not bothering to raise his head from the paperwork. "He's gone to the airport to pick up Rachel."

"Dad didn't go to the airport. Someone else picked her up. I thought he'd sent you or Paul."

Peter sat bolt upright. "What do you mean, he didn't go? I saw him leave myself at half-past twelve. He should be on his way back by now."

"I've just been to Rachel's flat. April spoke to her when her plane landed, and she said a man was waiting for her."

Peter tapped the desk with his pen. "What man? That's news to me."

"Could Karl have sent Alex?"

"No, Alex is busy at the Amethyst. He won't have time to go picking anyone up from the airport."

Christina frowned. "We'd better ring Dad and find out what's going on."

The telephone on the desk rang. "It's Karl," Peter said, picking up the receiver. "Hi, boss, we were just talking about you."

"I see," Karl said. "I want you to go round to Rachel's flat and see if she's there yet."

"What happened? I thought you were picking her up."

"I was, but the bastard police pulled me over. By the time I got to the airport she'd left."

"Give me the phone," Christina said, reaching over and snatching it from Peter. "Dad, guess what? I've found the briefcase."

"Where was it?"

"It was in Rachel's flat all the time."

"Do you have it with you now?"

"Yes," she said, "but it has a combination lock, so I can't get it open."

"Don't worry about that, I'll open it when I get there."

"By the way, Dad, April said Rachel was picked up at the airport by a man. Do you know who that was?"

"I've no idea," Karl said. "Put Peter back on, will you?"

"Sure, Dad," she said, handing the receiver back to Peter. "Yes, Karl?"

"I want you to put the briefcase in the office safe," Karl said. "I have a feeling we might have visitors. I'll deal with it when I get there."

"Okay, boss, I'll do it now."

"Is Paul there?" Karl said.

"He went over to Manchester to give Alex a hand."

"Oh shit! I'd forgotten about that. I'll give him a ring."

54

Paul was in the Amethyst Club when Karl rang. "Hi, boss," he said, "did everything work out okay with you and the cops?"

"Yes, eventually, but if it hadn't been for Beauchamp, I'd still be there. He said your mate had witnessed it?"

"Yeah, his name's Freddie Smith. He used to be a minder at the Sapphire Club a couple of years back. Freddie rang me as soon as he realised the police were hassling you."

"Well, tell him thanks from me when you see him."

"Sure thing," Paul said. "Did you manage to get to the airport in time to meet Rachel?"

Karl tutted. "No. She'd gone when I got there, but that little tart had the briefcase all along."

"So, where is it now?"

"It's in the safe at the Emerald. I'm on my way there."

"Do you need me to come over?"

"No," Karl said. "I need you to make sure everything's in order for Saturday."

"Okay, boss, if you're sure. By the way, do you realise how much cash Alex has spent on refurbishing this place?"

"You think he's overdone it?"

"That's not for me to say, but he's not spared any expense."

Karl sighed deeply. "If that little shit's gone over the budget, I'll…" There was a short silence. "There's not much I can do about it at the moment. I need to sort this bloody briefcase business out first."

"Okay," Paul said. "I'll meet you at the club as soon as I can."

"Was that Karl?" Alex asked from the doorway. "What did he want?"

"Just business," Paul said. "Now, turn on the sound system. Let's see what sort of job the electricians have made of it."

Alex pressed the switch, and the room was filled with loud dance music, with strobe lights flashing tantalizingly around the walls. The five podiums with the silver poles glistened under the lights.

Alex gazed around the room. "Doesn't it look great? The Amethyst is going to be the best club in Manchester."

"It will be the most expensive," Paul said. "You've certainly gone to town on the furnishings."

Alex folded his arms. "Karl wants the club to look good," Alex said defensively, "there's a lot of competition out there. The Amethyst has to be the absolute dog's bollocks if it is to get the punters in."

Paul shrugged but did not respond.

Alex walked over to the door, leading to the foyer. "Have you seen the VIP lounge upstairs now that it's been finished?"

"Not yet," Paul answered.

Alex grinned. "Let's do it together. You'll love it."

Paul followed Alex past the small reception desk in the foyer to the door marked 'Private'. Beyond the door was a staircase leading to the VIP lounge. On entering, Paul stared open-mouthed at the opulence of his surroundings. The walls were covered in a pale-lilac silk paper, and a thick, mauve carpet covered the floor. A dozen or so purple velvet couches were scattered around the room, along with several smoked glass tables. A well-stocked bar was on one wall.

Alex held out his arms and grinned. "Well, what do you think?"

"Great," Paul said. "It looks great."

"The punters will love it up here. Those that can afford it, that is."

Paul narrowed his eyes at Alex. "Let me give you a word of advice. Members who pay to come into this lounge are referred to as guests, not punters. That's one of your father's rules."

Alex shrugged. "Guests? Punters? Who gives a fuck? They're all pervs as far as I'm concerned." He walked across to the bar. "Fancy a drink?"

"No thanks," Paul said. "I have to get back to Leeds."

"Tell Karl I'm staying in Manchester tonight. I've got a load of stuff to finish off."

"Do you need a hand?"

"No," Alex said, "that's all right. I can manage thanks."

"Well, if you're sure. By the way, have you found somewhere to live over here yet?"

"I'm renting a flat about a mile away," Alex said. "I move in a couple of days."

"Is Sarah happy with it?"

Alex took a swig from his glass. "I don't give a shit. She'll do as she's told."

"If there's a problem, Alex, you should tell your dad."

Alex turned and glared at Paul. "It's nothing to do with Karl. Sarah's my wife, and she'll do what I say."

Before Paul could respond, Alex's mobile rang. "Hi, Katie," he said. "Hold on a sec, babe." He turned to Paul. "Well, thanks for your help today."

"Sure," Paul said as he headed for the door. "See you later."

55

Christina watched as Peter carefully placed the briefcase inside the office safe. "Ask him to ring me," she said, walking towards the door. "I have to get back to the salon."

"Okay, Chris. Karl shouldn't be long now, and stop worrying about Rachel. She probably got some punter to pick her up, and she'll be out on the town somewhere."

"I hope you're right." Christina frowned as she left the office and headed outside towards her vehicle.

It took Christina fifteen minutes to get to the salon. Victoria hurried over to her as soon as she arrived. "Oh, thank goodness you're here. I've never seen the salon this busy."

"What's happened? Are we double-booked?"

"No, just short-staffed. April hasn't come in today, she's meeting her sister, and Nadia is sick."

"You should have rung me. I'd have come earlier."

Victoria put her hands on her hips and sighed heavily. "That's the problem, Chris. I couldn't ring. That bloody junior you set on dropped the salon's phone. It's smashed to bits. I haven't had time to get it replaced, and I forgot my mobile this morning and—"

"Oh, never mind, I'm here now. Give me a minute to collect a smock. It's been ages since I did a shampoo and blow." She grinned. "I just hope I can still remember how."

Victoria smiled. "Don't worry, it's like riding a bike. Oh, by the way, some bloke rang for you earlier."

"What bloke?"

"He wouldn't give a name, but said to tell you the clock was ticking."

"He said what?"

"The clock was ticking. Do you know what he meant?"

Christina frowned and shook her head. "I have no idea."

56

Rachel's heart pounded in her chest. Her body ached from the unnatural position she was lying in. She tried to move, but her wrists and ankles were tightly bound. The man with the ginger beard had seen to that. A cotton cloth of some kind had been thrust into her mouth and then fastened securely by her own silk scarf. Rachel wasn't sure how long she had been in the van, at least an hour she reasoned, maybe two. The vehicle was stationary now, but no one had come. Her head throbbed as she tried to make sense of what was happening. Outside the van, she could hear muffled noises. She strained to hear what was being said, but without success.

Luke parked the van in a secluded alleyway and lit a cigarette. "I'm going to ring the boss," he said to his companion. "See what he wants us to do with her."

"Can't we just find where she's put it and then—?"

"And then what?"

"Well, let her go?" George said meekly.

"No, we can't let her go, you moron. She's seen both of us. I don't fancy spending the next few years inside for kidnapping."

"We can't kill her," George said, dragging his hands through his hair. "I'm not doing that. I won't."

"Who said anything about killing her?" Luke smirked. "Once she's told me what I want to know, I'll scare the shit out of her. She won't dare open her mouth."

Beads of sweat ran down George's face. "You will let her go?" he asked quietly.

"Of course I will, now stop worrying."

There was an uneasy silence.

"I fancy a coffee," George said at last. "There's a snack van up the road. Do you want one?"

"Sure. I'll ring the boss while you're gone."

"You do that," George said pointing a finger at Luke. "But make sure he knows there's no way I'm getting involved in murder."

"Oh, I will. I'll make sure he knows that," Luke said quietly. "By the way, mate, get me a sausage roll to go with the coffee, will you?"

George nodded. "I'm feeling a bit peckish myself."

Luke watched as George walked up the road in the direction of the snack van. Once he was out of sight, he walked to the side of the van and slid open the doors.

Ten minutes later, George was back at the van with two coffee cups and a couple of paper bags containing the food. "They didn't have any sausage rolls left, so I got you a pork pie instead." He grinned, handing one of the bags to Luke. "I hope that's okay?"

"Yeah, that's fine. Now hurry up and get in the van. We have to be somewhere."

"Where are we going?"

"You'll see," Luke said as he started the engine.

"What about the girl? Has she said anything about where she put the briefcase?"

"Yeah, she told me where she hid it."

"Good. Are we going to fetch it?"

Luke smirked. "Sure we are, but I have something to take care of first."

George gave a sideways glance but said nothing as he bit into his pork pie and slurped his coffee. Ten minutes later, the van bounced its way down a rough dirt track into a small clearing.

George frowned. "What are we doing here?" He peered around at the isolated location. "I don't understand."

"Give me a hand to get her out of the van," Luke said. He jumped from the cab and walked towards the side door. "Hurry up, George. We don't have all day."

George rushed to Luke's side and reached inside to grab Rachel. He had pulled her halfway out of the van before he saw the blood. "Fuck!" he said and allowed her limp body to fall to the ground. "She's dead. You've killed her, you bastard.

What the fuck did you do that for? She's only a kid."

Luke scoffed. "She's a whore. A whore and a thief who's caused the boss a load of trouble."

George groaned. "No! No! This isn't right. You shouldn't have done that. I don't want any part in this. I'm—" George saw the glint of the knife, just for a second, as Luke lunged towards him. He felt a sharp pain as the blade was driven into his chest. Then he felt nothing.

"It's done," Luke said. "Both of them."

"Good," replied the voice at the other end of the phone. "George was a liability. He made too many mistakes."

"Well, don't worry about him, boss, he won't be making any more. Do you want me to go and pick up the briefcase now?"

"Yes, but be careful. Another girl is living in the flat, remember."

"Well," Luke said, "let's hope for her sake that she's not at home when I get there, or she'll be joining big sister."

The voice chuckled. "You're a callous bastard. I'm just glad we're on the same side."

"We are as long as you keep paying."

"Don't worry, Luke, you'll get your money. All you have to do is bring the briefcase to the usual place at eight o'clock."

"I'll be there."

George groaned as he slowly struggled to his feet. He tried to focus, his vision blurred, but he could make out the crumpled body of Rachel in the undergrowth. He staggered the couple of hundred yards to the main road. Frantically, he felt around his jacket pocket for his mobile, as slowly he dialled the emergency number before passing out once more.

57

It was a twenty-minute drive from the clearing in the wood to Rachel's flat. Luke made the journey in twelve. He stopped at the roadside, glanced in his mirror, and spotted April hurrying from the flat. Luke pulled up alongside the preoccupied girl, jumped from the cab and grabbed her from behind, forcing her into the back of the van.

She tried to scream but Luke held a knife to her throat. "We're going back to the flat," he said. "There's something there that doesn't belong to you."

Tears trickled down April's cheeks. "Please, please don't hurt me."

Luke pressed the knife closer. A small dribble of blood ran down the blade. "Pack that in, now."

"If this is about the briefcase, it's… it's not in the flat," April said through her sobs.

"What do you mean it's not there? Rachel said—"

"You've seen Rachel?"

Luke grabbed April's arm and squeezed. "Never mind about Rachel," he said, pushing his face nearer. "What have you done with the briefcase?"

She winced. "Christina has it."

"Who the fuck's she?"

"She's Rachel's friend."

"And you're sure she has it?"

April nodded. "Rachel told me where she had hidden it, and Christina took it."

"You'd better not be lying," Luke said and released his grip. "Where is Christina now?"

"She's probably at the salon," April said, rubbing her arm. "Please, where's my sister? What have you done with her?"

"If you want to see your sister again, you'll keep quiet," he said. "You're coming with me until I get that briefcase."

"Where is she?" April yelled, banging frantically on the side of the van. "Help," she screamed. "Help me, somebody."

Reaching over, Luke punched the girl hard in the face,

causing her to fall back onto the floor of the van. "Shut the fuck up, you stupid bitch," he said. He climbed down from the back of the vehicle and fastened the sliding door securely. He jumped into the cab, and turning on the engine, drove in the direction of the salon.

58

Peter was in the office when Karl arrived back at the Emerald.

"Where is it?" Karl said. "Where's the briefcase?"

"It's in the safe. Christina found it at Rachel's flat."

Karl pushed past Peter and went over to the safe. In seconds he retrieved the briefcase, placing it on his desk. "It feels like there's something heavy inside," he said gently shaking it. "It's probably a laptop."

"That's what I was thinking," Peter said. "There's a combination lock on the case. It's not going to be easy to get it open."

Karl removed a knife from his desk. "If you can figure out the combination, be my guest," he said. "Hold it still while I cut."

Peter frowned. "That's an expensive briefcase. It's a shame to ruin it. Shouldn't we—?"

"I don't give a fuck about the case," Karl said. "My daughter's been threatened. One of my girls has been killed and... we don't have time to piss about. We have to find out what's inside." Karl ran the sharp knife along the bottom seam of the case, causing a wide incision. He placed his hand inside. "Yes, it's definitely a laptop," he said. "Hold the bag steady while I finish cutting."

Soon the briefcase was split wide open, and Karl put his hand inside and pulled out a laptop. "Got it," he said, throwing the case onto the floor and placing the computer on his desk.

"We're going to need the password," Peter said. "We can't get in without that."

"Password? How the hell do we find that?"

"It's not easy. Do you know anybody good with computers?"

"Nobody I can trust, but I'm sure Paul will know someone who understands this shit."

Karl's mobile rang. It was Paul. "How long are you going to be?" Karl said. "I need you to—"

"I'll be there in about half an hour," Paul said breathlessly, "but Karl, there's a problem."

"What kind of problem? I've got more than enough problems to be getting on with."

"You'd better turn on the news," Paul said. "I've just heard it on the car radio."

59

Karl turned on the news channel on the small television in the office. A reporter was shown at Dover docks describing how a lorry belonging to Delaney Logistics had been stopped for a routine check. Inside the vehicle had been eight young women from Romania. The driver of the lorry, a man named Albi Kolkovsky, had been detained at the scene and police were anxious to trace the owner of the haulage firm, Harry Delaney.

"I don't believe this," Karl said. "Isaac told me the lorry was due into Dover tomorrow night. I was going down there myself to—"

"It's a good thing you didn't," Paul said. "You could have got caught up in it."

Karl shrugged. "I suppose so, but this isn't helping me find what's happened to Katya."

"Maybe the police can get information from the driver they've arrested?"

"The police? Don't make me laugh. They couldn't find their thumb if it was stuck up their arse. No, if Katya's to be found, we're going to have to find her ourselves."

"How are we going to do that? That haulage firm was our only proper lead."

"We still have the laptop," Karl said. "Once we figure out the password."

"Paul's bound to know somebody who can get into the computer and—"

The office door burst open, and Lisa rushed into the room. "Have you seen the news?" she asked. "Those young girls being trafficked?"

"What do you want, Lisa?" Karl said. "I'm busy."

Lisa slumped onto the couch and turned to Peter. "Get me a stiff drink, Peter. I need it."

Peter poured Lisa a whisky and handed it to her. Lisa carefully raised her shaking hand, holding the glass, to her lips.

"Why are you so upset about it anyway?" Karl asked. "It's not as if you know any of the girls."

"No, I don't, but I do know the owner of the haulage company. I know him very well."

Karl grabbed Lisa by the shoulders. "Delaney?" he said. "You know him?"

"Yes, I know Harry Delaney. I worked for him for almost ten years. We were... we were close once." Lisa swallowed the remaining whisky in one gulp before continuing. "I'm sure Harry's not responsible for this, though. He can't be."

"Where is he?" Karl said.

"I don't know. I haven't seen him in over three years."

"How close were you? Were you lovers?"

Lisa's eyes widened. "What?"

"I asked you if you were fucking him. It's a simple enough question."

"I've told you it was a long time ago. I haven't seen him in ages."

"What sort of bloke is this Harry Delaney?"

"Harry was always kind to me, but—"

Karl scoffed. "But what?"

"There were rumours that Harry was being forced into doing stuff."

"What sort of stuff?"

"He started bringing booze and cigarettes across the Channel. He'd never done anything like that before."

"Who was forcing him?" Karl said.

"I've no idea. He never confided in me about that side of the business, but I knew he was scared of someone."

"You must have met some of his contacts. Think, woman."

"Harry was a very private man. I can't believe he'd be involved in trafficking girls. He wouldn't do that."

"Where can I find him?"

"I've no idea. I might still have his private phone number at home, but it's over three years old. He's probably changed it."

Karl briefly looked upwards. "Go and find it. I need to meet Harry Delaney before the police find him."

Lisa hurried out of the room.

"Do you want me to go with her, boss?" Peter asked.

"No, I need you here to open up the club."

60

Paul arrived at the Emerald Club just before six. As he entered the car park, he almost collided with a young woman, staggering towards the entrance, crying hysterically.

"Is everything all right?" he asked as he got out of his car and approached her. "Is there anything I can do?"

"I... I... I need to see Karl," she blurted through her sobs.

"I'll take you to his office," Paul said, guiding her through reception and up the stairs to the office.

"I found this young lady outside," he said as he entered the room.

Karl sat behind his desk, cradling a large whisky and soda. He recognised Victoria immediately. He had seen her several times in the salon.

"What's up?" he asked, rushing to her side. "Is it Christina? Has something happened to my daughter?"

"He... he took her," Victoria said. "He came into the salon and took her."

"What do you mean, he took her? Come on, girl, pull yourself together. Where's Christina?"

Paul handed her a glass of whisky, and she shakily accepted it. She took a sip, grimaced and gave the drink to Karl. "No, thanks," she said softly. "I don't like whisky."

Karl slammed the glass on the table. "My daughter. What's happened to my daughter?"

"It was Luke. He came into the salon half an hour ago and... and he grabbed Christina and put her in a van."

Karl blew out hard. "Was the red-haired bloke with him?"

"No, just Luke."

"Why the fuck didn't you ring me straight away?"

She put her hands to her face. "The salon phone's broken and I'd forgotten my mobile, and everyone else had left for the day and—"

The telephone on the desk rang. Karl picked it up immediately. "Yeah?" he answered.

"If you want to see your daughter again, you know what I

want," a voice said.

"If you touch one hair on her head, I'll—"

"You're in no position to threaten anybody," the voice goaded. "She's not been harmed... yet."

Karl was silent for a moment. His heart was pounding and his breathing became erratic. "All right, you win," he said at last. "Where do you want to meet?"

"I'll ring you tomorrow."

The telephone clicked into silence.

Karl thumped the desk with his fist. "Bastard. The fucking cowardly bastard." He turned sharply to face Victoria. "Tell me exactly what happened."

The girl, trembling, wiped her eyes with a tissue. "We were locking up," she began. "Everyone else had left. There was only Chris and me in the salon."

Karl huffed. "Come on, I haven't got all day. What happened?"

Victoria glanced at Karl as he loomed over her. "Well?" he said.

"Luke burst in and pushed Chris up against the wall. He shouted something about a briefcase. Chris said she didn't have it and he slapped her hard across the face." Tears rolled down Victoria's cheeks.

"Stop that wailing," Karl said. "That's not helping."

Victoria put her hand on her chest and took a deep breath. "He... he had a knife. He held it up to her face and threatened to—"

"Did he cut her?" The veins in Karl's neck pulsated. "Did he?"

"No. Chris told him she had left the briefcase with you at the Emerald. He got really angry. That's when he grabbed her by the hair and forced her outside and into his van."

"But Christina was all right when she got into the van? You're sure she wasn't hurt?"

"She was crying, and her lip was bleeding, but she was okay."

Karl briefly looked upwards. "Well, that's something I

suppose."

"There's… there's something else."

"What?"

"When Luke slid the side door of the van open, I got a glimpse inside. I was looking out of the window and—"

"What did you see?"

"Another girl was on the floor of the van. She looked unconscious."

Karl frowned. "That would be Rachel."

"No, it wasn't Rachel. I'm almost certain the girl was her sister, April."

61

About the same time Karl was speaking to the kidnapper of his daughter, Alex was entering Lady Luck Casino in the company of Katie.

Alex grinned. "I'm feeling lucky tonight, babe." He handed over two thousand pounds for casino chips. "I'm sure lady luck is well and truly in the building."

Katie smiled and kissed Alex lightly on the cheek. "Of course, she is, darling," she murmured softly. "I'll be back in a few minutes. I just need to—"

"As long as it's not to powder your nose," Alex said. "It looks perfect the way it is."

"I won't be long," she said and made her way towards the ladies' toilets. Joe was waiting for her in the corridor. Katie rushed to him and frowned. "How much longer do I have to spend with Alex? He's driving me mad."

Joe stepped back and held up his hands. "We have to be careful, Katie," he said. "Alex has already lost over twenty thousand. He can't go on much longer without asking for credit."

She sniffed. "Make sure he does. He's talking about leaving his wife, and he wants me to move in with him. I can't keep putting him off much longer without him—"

Joe gently spun Katie around in the direction of the door leading to the gaming floor. "Trust me," he said. "Alex will soon have more to think about than seducing you. All you have to do is keep encouraging him to gamble."

"He doesn't need much encouragement, believe me," Katie said. "Once he gets in front of the roulette wheel, he just can't resist." Katie gave Joe a peck on the cheek. "Well, I suppose I'd better get back." She sighed. "A fool and his money…"

"Good luck," Joe said as he watched Katie walk over to the roulette table and sit beside Alex, who was already engrossed.

"He's lost the two grand," Matthew said as Joe entered the

office a couple of hours later. "I've been watching him all night. He's written another cheque for three thousand."

Joe went to the drinks cabinet and poured two whiskies. "A few more days and his cheques will be worthless." He grinned, and handed a glass to Matthew. "That's when we go into action."

Matthew leant back in his chair, smiling. "I don't know about you, but I'm rather enjoying running a casino. It's a lot more fun than I thought it would be."

"Don't get too comfortable," Joe said. "We're not here to have fun. We're here to bring Karl Maddox's grotty little empire to its knees."

"Of course we are, but that doesn't mean we can't have a little fun on the way, does it?"

Joe slammed his glass down on the desk. "Matthew, don't lose sight of what we're doing here," he said. "Karl Maddox destroyed your family and mine, and we're going to destroy his. All of them."

Matthew shrugged, and lit a cigarette. "You can't hold them all responsible," he reasoned. "Christina hasn't done anything wrong."

Joe raised an eyebrow. "You know Christina?"

"Yes, I've met her, and to be honest, I rather like her."

Joe leant over and grabbed Matthew's shoulders, putting his face close to his. "You like Karl Maddox's daughter? Are you completely insane? You do know she used to be an escort. She called herself Bunny back then."

Matthew drew on his cigarette. "Of course I know. Actually, I met Bunny a couple of times."

"I don't believe I'm hearing this. You actually bunked up with her?"

"I didn't know she was Karl's daughter, not at first," he said. "She was just a beautiful young woman, and I… I was lonely."

Joe slumped onto the couch. "She's supposed to have given up whoring. Don't tell me she's still at it?"

"No, of course she isn't. We meet up occasionally for

dinner or the theatre. She really is a nice girl."

Joe gritted his teeth. "She's not a nice girl. She's bad blood, just like her father and her brother." He got up from the couch and walked over to Matthew. "Does she know who you are? Does she know that your father tried to kill hers?"

Matthew shook his head. "No, of course she doesn't. She thinks my name is Matthew Warwick and that I'm an IT consultant."

Joe walked over to the window and gazed out onto the street. "Please, Matthew," he said at last, "promise me you won't see Christina Maddox again. I think you're playing a very dangerous game."

"I think we both are, Joe."

62

It was a loud bang, somewhere outside the room above, that caused April to open her eyes with a start. It took several seconds for her to make sense of her surroundings. She was lying on a wooden floor, both hands fastened securely behind her back with a tie-wrap. The only source of light was a street lamp shining through the small barred window high up on the wall. She struggled to sit and realised that she was in some kind of storeroom. Tins of food were neatly arranged on wooden shelving along all four walls, and a large table stood in the centre of the room with cardboard boxes stacked on top. The pleasant aroma of freshly baked bread and garlic wafted into the room.

"Help," she shouted. "Please help me." Her voice sounded tinny as it echoed around the room. "Please, someone, help me." She sobbed as tears rolled down her cheeks.

"April, is that you? It's Christina. I'm over here by the window."

April's heart pounded in her chest, and tears stung her eyes. "Christina?" she said. "What's happened? Why are we here?"

Christina shuffled along the floor to be closer to April. "It's all right," she whispered. "Don't be frightened."

"But what are we doing here? What do these people want?"

"They're after the briefcase that Rachel stole."

April huffed. "Then give it to them."

"I don't have it. I gave it to Dad."

"Why? What's so special about that damned briefcase anyway?"

Christina shrugged. "I've no idea," she said, "but Dad will sort it out. You'll see."

"What if he doesn't? I'm scared, Chris. I want to go home."

"Don't worry. Dad won't let anything happen to us."

"What about Rachel? What have they done with her?"

Christina frowned. "What do you mean?"

"She never arrived home from the airport. When Luke came to the apartment, he knew that the briefcase had been in the floor safe. Only Rachel could have told him that."

"He probably let her go once she told him where to find it."

April slowly shook her head. "I don't think he'd do that, do you?"

Christina bit on her bottom lip. "April, we've got to—"

The door to the storeroom opened, and two men wearing balaclavas came in. One of the men stood by the doorway while the other walked over to April and checked her hands were secure. Then he did the same to Christina. "Thirsty?" he asked. Both girls nodded. "I'll bring you some water." He walked towards the door and returned a few minutes later with a bottle of water. Carefully, he helped them take turns to drink.

April sighed. "Well, at least they're human," she said once the men had left. "If they were going to kill us, they would have done it by now."

Christina remained silent.

"Are you okay, Chris? You're very quiet."

Christina did not reply.

April stared at her friend. "Chris, what's wrong? You're scaring me."

Christina took a deep breath. "I'm… I'm okay," she said. "I was just thinking what Dad will do when he gets his hands on these bastards."

63

Karl drummed his fingers on his office desk. Peter and Paul Borowicz stood by the window.

"When you meet this bloke tomorrow," Peter said, "I could get some of the lads together and—"

"And risk getting my daughter killed?"

"But you can't let them get away with it. I think—"

"I don't give a fuck what you think. Christina's safety comes first. Nobody does anything unless I say so. Understand?"

Peter shrugged. "Whatever you say."

Karl sat in silence for a few minutes, his eyes closed. "Paul," he said at last, "what was the name of that guy who repaired the leather couch in the club when it got ripped the other week? Jimmy something?"

"Jimmy Cohen," Paul said. "He has an upholsterer's shop up on the Headrow."

"Tell him I have an urgent job for him. I'll be round at his place first thing tomorrow."

"Yeah. I've still got his number on my phone."

"After that, I want you to find me a laptop, exactly the same as the one in the safe."

"I'll see Russ," Paul said, a faint smile on his face. "He has dozens of computers in his shop. He's bound to have this model."

Peter frowned. "I don't understand," he said. "What are you going to do?"

Paul grinned and turned to his brother. "We're going to give the bastard his property back," he said and winked at Karl. "Isn't that right, boss?"

Karl slapped his hand on the desk. "That's exactly what we're going to do, providing Jimmy Cohen can repair the briefcase to look as good as new."

"That shouldn't be a problem," Paul said. "You cut it open along the bottom seam so—"

"I still don't get it," Peter said.

Paul grinned. "The combination lock on the briefcase hasn't been touched. He'll open it up and see that the laptop is still in the bag."

Peter scratched his head. "But won't he know it's a different computer?"

Paul rolled his eyes. "He will when he turns it on, but I'm banking on him sending one of his lackeys to collect. He'll probably be given the combination of the briefcase so he can check the laptop is inside, but I doubt he'll have the password."

"By which time we'll have Christina back," Karl said.

Paul grinned and dialled Jimmy Cohen's number.

64

It was the early hours when Alex and Katie finally left the casino.

"It's been a shitty night," Alex mumbled as he climbed into the taxi. "Anyone would think I'd broken a mirror and walked under a ladder with the rotten luck I've had."

"You can't win every time, darling," Katie said. "I'm sure next time will be better."

"I've got the club to open in a couple of days," Alex slurred. "The Amethyst opens its doors to the great British perverts. Remember?"

"Are you excited?"

Alex shrugged and lit a cigarette. "I couldn't give a shit anymore. It's supposed to be my club, but Karl's put Marco in charge of security. He's a nosy bastard. I'm sure he's checking up on me."

"Darling, you're starting to sound paranoid. Marco's there in case there's any trouble, that's all."

Alex snorted. "Marco was in the club tonight on the pretence of last-minute training of the minders. I think he was there to see what I was up to."

Katie put her hand on Alex's arm. "You don't think he knows you've been visiting the casino?"

"The shit would really hit the fan if he did," Alex said. "He'd be straight round to Karl. You can bet your last pound on that."

Katie leant into Alex and gently ran her tongue along his ear. "Darling," she whispered, "you're not going to let some hired help dictate to you how you spend your money, are you?"

Alex grinned. "Too right I'm not. I'm just going to have to be smarter than him. That's not going to be difficult, the man's a moron."

"Karl doesn't seem to think so."

"Karl? What does he know? He's washed up, a has-been." Alex stubbed out his cigarette and put his arm around Katie's shoulders. "Anyway," he said, "I don't want to talk about Marco. I thought that tonight you and I—"

Katie shrugged Alex's arm away and gently kissed him on the cheek. "I'm sorry, darling," she said, "but I can't see you tonight. I have an early start in the morning and—"

"What do you mean? I thought we were spending the night together at yours?"

"Not tonight, Alex. Like I said, I—"

Alex slapped Katie hard across the face. "You fucking bitch. I need you, Katie, don't you understand that? I thought we were—"

Katie moved further away from Alex and rubbed her cheek. "You have a wife waiting at home, don't forget."

"Get out, you fucking whore." He leant over her and attempted to open the taxi door.

"Alex, please. You can't just—"

"I said, get out!"

The driver brought the taxi to a halt at the side of the road. "Is everything all right back there?" he asked. "Are you okay, miss?"

"Mind your own fucking business," Alex said. "She's getting out of the car. Isn't that right, Katie?"

Katie undid her seatbelt and opened the door. She was halfway out of the vehicle when Alex grabbed her arm and forced her back inside. "Not so fast," he said. "I've changed my mind. You're coming with me."

Katie tried to prise his fingers from her arm. "Let go, you're hurting me."

Alex's hold remained firm as he dragged her back into the car and closed the taxi door.

The driver leant over the seat. "That's enough," he said. "Let the lady go, or I'm calling the police."

Alex glared at him. "Don't be fucking stupid. Do you know who I am?"

"No, mate, I don't, but I want you out of my cab."

Alex sprung forward and attempted to head-butt the driver. The driver dodged to the side and then, leaning forward, landed his clenched fist hard on Alex's jaw.

"Bastard," Alex yelled as blood trickled from his mouth. "I'll kill you."

The driver jumped out of the vehicle and pulled open the rear door. "Get out," he said. Grabbing Alex by the hair, he dragged him from the car. "Think yourself lucky you're pissed, or I'd really kick the shit out of you."

Alex landed hard on the ground. His vision was blurred, but he could make out Katie in the back of the taxi speaking into her mobile as the vehicle sped away into the night.

A red Mondeo pulled up a few yards away. The driver watched as Alex clambered to his feet, and precariously made his way along the road, meandering from one side to the other. Once Alex had reached his flat, the car drove off into the darkness. It was late. Too late to let Karl know what his son was up to, Marco reasoned. That would have to wait until tomorrow.

65

Karl and Paul were at Jimmy Cohen's shop just after six the following morning. Jimmy smiled broadly as he unlocked the door. "Good morning, gentlemen. What is it you want me to do that is so urgent?"

Karl placed the damaged briefcase on the bench. "I want you to fix this," he said.

He examined the case, noting the tear along the seam. "It's an expensive make, Karl," he said at last. "One of the best on the market."

"Can you fix it? Can you make it good as new?"

Jimmy nodded. "Yes, I can do that. It shouldn't be a problem. I can have it ready for you this afternoon."

Karl shook his head. "No, mate, that's no good. I want it done now."

Jimmy gave Karl a sideways glance and sighed. "Okay. I can have it fixed in about an hour."

"Oh, there's one more thing," Karl said.

"What's that?"

"I want you to repair the briefcase with this computer inside." He handed the laptop to Jimmy. "Do you think you can manage that?"

Jimmy frowned as he studied Karl. "I can try," he said, "but it will be more awkward to repair. It could take a little longer."

"I'll wait," Karl said.

Jimmy went into the back of the shop, leaving Karl and Paul in the front area.

"Will you be okay to wait on your own?" Paul asked. "Only I want to track down Martin Morris."

"The computer whiz-kid? Yeah, you do that. Get him to meet me at the Emerald. We'll see if he's as good as they say he is."

An hour and a half later, Jimmy Cohen handed the repaired briefcase to Karl. "Good as new." He beamed. "Although I say so myself."

Karl smiled as he examined the bag. "Very nice," he said and handed Jimmy an envelope of cash. "You've done a great job. Thank you." He walked towards the door and then turned slowly to face Jimmy and ambled back across to him. "Make sure you keep your mouth shut about this," he said and leant over the counter. "This is between you and me."

"Sure thing," Jimmy said and edged away. He watched as Karl left the shop and rubbed the small beads of sweat from his forehead with the back of his hand. "This never happened," he said to himself.

66

The phone rang in Karl's office just before ten o'clock. "Yeah," he said.

"Karl, it's me, Marco."

"Marco, get off the line, mate," Karl said. "I'm expecting an important call any minute."

"But Karl, I—"

"I said, not now. I'll call you later." Karl slammed down the receiver.

It was almost midday before the phone rang again. This time, it was the call he had been waiting for.

"Do you have it?" said the same voice Karl had heard the previous night.

"Yes, I have it. Let me speak with my daughter."

"Sorry, but Christina can't get to the phone right now. Don't worry, she's perfectly safe... for now."

"If you dare to hurt her, I'll—"

"Calm down, Karl," the voice said. "Nobody's going to hurt her if you do exactly as I say."

"Where do you want to meet?"

"Be at the back of the Corn Exchange in half an hour. And, Karl, make sure you're alone."

"All right, I'll be there, but let me speak to Christina first. I—"

The receiver clicked, and the caller was gone.

Peter moved closer to Karl. "Was that them?"

Karl nodded. "He wants me to meet at the back of the Corn Exchange."

Peter raised his eyebrows, a faint smile across his lips. "Do you want company?"

Karl shook his head. "No, he said to go alone."

"Fuck that," Peter said. "We can be discreet, eh, boys?" He looked towards the two minders stood near the door. "There are plenty of places to park up around the Corn Exchange building." The two men nodded in agreement.

Karl stood. "No. I can't risk it. If anything happens to Christina I—"

"Boss, you can't go on your own."

"Nothing will happen to me as long as they think I have the laptop," Karl said. "Once Christina's safe, we'll find the bastard responsible, you can count on that."

It was just after twelve-thirty. As instructed, Karl parked behind the Corn Exchange. He climbed from his car when he saw Christina and April walking towards him, their hands fastened behind their backs. Directly behind them was a man Karl knew, from the description given by Nadia, must be Luke. The group stopped about ten feet from Karl.

"Dad," Christina said as she saw her father. "I knew you'd come."

Karl didn't move. "Are you okay? Have they hurt you?"

"I'm all right, Dad," Christina said quietly, tears trickling down her cheeks. "Please be careful. He has a gun in his pocket and—"

Luke grabbed both women by the hair. "Do you have it?" Luke said.

Karl walked towards him, carrying the briefcase. "Don't worry, it's here," he said and gently placed the bag on the ground. "Now let them go."

Scowling, Luke reached into his pocket and took out a knife. He leant forward and cut the tie wrap on April's wrists and pushed her forward. "Fetch."

April crept towards Karl rubbing her wrists. She bent down and picked up the case.

"Bring it over here," Luke said. "Hurry up."

April hurried back towards Luke.

"Let Christina go," Karl said. "You have what you want."

"I need to make sure you haven't—"

"Haven't what? I couldn't get the fucking thing open. You can see that. Now let my daughter go."

Luke snatched the case from April and pressed the buttons on the combination lock. The case sprung open, revealing the laptop.

There was a screeching of brakes, and a dark-green Audi raced into the street stopping alongside Luke. He got into the back seat, and the car sped away towards the town centre.

Christina ran towards her father. "Dad, I thought they were going to kill me," she said sobbing.

Karl took his daughter in his arms and hugged her tightly. "It's all right," he said and kissed her on the head. "He's gone now." He took a penknife from his pocket and cut the tie-wrap binding her wrists. "Are you sure they didn't... didn't hurt you?"

Christina shook her head. "No, Dad, they just kept us locked in a room."

"Do you know where? Could you find it again?"

"We were blindfolded when we were put into a van," April said as she joined Karl and Christina. "We have no idea where we were held."

"Dad, please take me home." Christina buried her head into Karl's chest. "I'll answer your questions later, but right now, I need to go home."

Karl opened the car's rear door. "Okay, get in the car, both of you."

67

It was early the next morning before Lisa found the phone number she had for Harry Delaney. Karl rang the number but got no reply.

"Harry was never an early riser," Lisa said. "I'll ring him about ten. He should be awake by then."

Karl snorted but made no comment. "How's Christina this morning?"

"She was sleeping when I looked in, so was April. I didn't want to disturb them. They were both in a bad state when you brought them home."

"Christina will be all right. She's made of tough stuff," Karl said. "When I get hold of that bastard that took her, I'll—" His mobile rang. He grunted. "Yeah?"

"Good morning, Karl," Paul said. "It's good news about Chris, eh? Your plan went like a dream."

"Never mind that," Karl said. "Have you found this computer wizard? We need to get into that damned laptop."

"That's why I'm ringing. There's a bit of a hitch I'm afraid."

"What sort of hitch?"

Paul sighed. "Martin Morris is banged up in Wakefield nick."

"He's what?"

"The dick-head got three years for housebreaking. He's not due for release for another eighteen months."

Karl huffed. "What are we going to do now? Do you know anybody else who can work out the password?"

"Nobody that's half as good as Martin. But, Karl, I have an idea."

"I hope it's a good one?" Karl said.

"If Martin can't come to us, maybe we can go to him."

"What? Have you lost the plot? You think I can just go into the nick and ask him to retrieve the password on a stolen computer?"

Paul laughed. "No, of course you can't go, but Jeremiah

Beauchamp can."

"Beauchamp? I don't understand."

"He's now Martin's newly appointed solicitor. He can visit the prison anytime to confer with his client, along with his junior, of course. Yours truly."

"I don't know, Paul," he said. "It sounds risky."

"Of course it's risky, but we don't have much choice. We have to act quickly."

"But how will——?"

Paul chuckled down the phone. "Solicitor-client confidentiality. We'll be in a private room away from the screws. They won't have a clue what we're doing."

Karl was silent for a moment. "Do you think Beauchamp will agree?"

"If the money's right, I know he will. In fact, I've already been to see him."

"You've done what?" Karl said. "When?"

"Last night. He's spoken to the prison this morning and made an appointment to visit first thing Monday."

"It's taking a big chance, Paul. If things go wrong——"

"Karl, those bastards have my cousin. God knows what they're doing to the poor kid. I need to find her fast. There's no time to be cautious."

"Okay, mate, you're right. Actually, the more I think about it——"

"I'll meet you at the club later," Paul said. "By the way, what's happening with Christina? She can't go back to work while those maniacs are loose. Who knows what they'll do?"

"She'll be staying here at the house. I'll leave a couple of the guys to watch her. The salon will have to manage without her for a few days and… Oh fuck, there's somebody on the landline. I'll speak to you later." Karl picked up the receiver. "Yeah?"

There was only silence. "Who's there?" It was several seconds before the caller spoke.

"I suppose you think you're smart, eh, pulling that stunt with the laptop?"

Karl sat upright in his chair. "You made a big mistake threatening my family," he said. "I will find you and when I do…"

Again, there was a silence. "Look, Karl, maybe we got off on the wrong foot. We don't have any argument with you or your family. We just want what's ours."

Karl sneered. "The laptop must be pretty important to go to the lengths you have."

"It just has information for our business, that's all."

"You mean your sex trafficking business?"

"How the hell did—?"

"I know a lot about you, you fucking scumbag," Karl said. "Are you the animal that killed one of my girls at the hotel?"

"That was an accident. The silly bitch fell."

The phone went silent again, and Karl was about to put down the receiver.

"Tell me what you want?" the voice said. "How much will it cost to get the laptop back?"

"I want the girl," Karl said.

"Karl, mate, you can have as many girls as you want. You just have to ask."

"Her name is Katya."

"I don't know any Katya. She—"

"Katya was one of the girls you brought to Birmingham from Romania."

"Karl, I don't know who's been feeding you this horseshit but believe me, I—"

"I have Nadia, the girl that got away from Luke and George," Karl said. "Nadia has told me you took Katya."

"Karl, there must be some mistake. I don't know anyone called Nadia or Katya."

"If you want your laptop returned, you'll stop this bullshit and give me Katya."

Again, the phone went silent. "All right, I'll see what I can do, but it might take a couple of days. I'm not sure where Katya is at the moment."

"Find out. I want the girl returned unharmed.

Understand?"

"Yes, Karl. I'll be in touch."

The telephone clicked into silence.

Karl smiled and turned to face Lisa. "Well, it looks like things are moving. Give Delaney another ring. He's the key to all this shit."

"All right," she said and dialled Harry Delaney's number for the tenth time that morning.

68

Joe was in the Arndale Centre buying new shirts from his favourite shop. He didn't notice the attractive auburn-haired woman until he collided with her, causing her to drop her shopping bags. "Oh, I'm so sorry," he said. "I didn't see you there and... are you all right? I haven't hurt you, have I?" Joe smiled at the woman with a flawless complexion and pale-amber eyes.

She forced a smile. "I'm fine. I wasn't paying attention either."

"Well, at least there's nothing broken," Joe said. He bent down and picked up a lampshade and two cushions. "Moving house?"

The woman sighed heavily and nodded as she put the items back in her bag.

"Please, let me buy you a coffee by way of apology. It's the least I can do."

"Thank you, but—"

"I'd make it something stronger only it's a bit early." Joe grinned. "Please say you'll join me. It'll make me feel better about colliding with you like that."

"Well... if you're sure?"

"We can get a drink over there," Joe said, steering her in the direction of a bistro café. "It looks quite nice."

Joe and the woman sat at a table next to the window, sipping excellent coffee and looking out onto the shopping mall. "I'm Joe by the way," he said. "And you are?"

The woman smiled. "Sarah," she said.

"Well, it's very nice to meet you, Sarah. I hate shopping, don't you?" He pointed at his carrier bags on the seat next to him. "I'm used to my wife doing the shopping."

"Why hasn't she come with you if you hate it so much?"

"She died," Joe said quietly. "She had cancer."

"I'm so sorry. That's terrible. She must have been very young."

"How long have you lived in Manchester?" Joe asked.

She sighed. "Not long. My husband moved here for work," she said. "I lived here a couple of years ago when he worked at the… when he was working here."

Joe studied her as she fidgeted with her wedding ring. "Is everything all right?" he asked. "Only you look upset." She lifted her head to face Joe, her eyes were brimming with tears. "Is there anything I can do?" he asked.

She shook her head. "I'm fine," she said quietly. "It's just… well everything really. A new home, a new city… It all gets a little overwhelming."

"My advice is to take it one step at a time," Joe said. "Don't try and do everything all at once."

She gave a faint smile. "Yes, I suppose you're right."

"Furnishing your new home must be exciting," he said.

She shrugged but made no reply.

"What line of business is your husband in?" Joe asked.

"He's a… he works with his father."

"Working in the family business, eh? That's good, isn't it?"

Sarah shook her head. "You don't know his father." She turned to face Joe. "What is it you do?"

Joe shrugged. "Oh, nothing very exciting."

"That's not an answer," she said. "Tell me."

"Well, if you must know, I'm part owner of The Lady Luck Casino here in Manchester. It's been open a couple of weeks now." Joe gazed at her as she scowled. "I take it you don't approve of gambling?"

"Actually, no I don't. It can take over your life. Destroy your life if you're not careful."

"Only if you let it," Joe said.

She sniffed. "I suppose so." She swallowed the last of her drink. "Well, I must be going, Thanks for the coffee."

Joe smiled. "It was my pleasure." He held out his hand. "Sarah…?"

She shook his hand and picked up her shopping bags. "Sarah Maddox."

Joe raised his eyebrows. "Well, Sarah Maddox, perhaps we can do this again soon?"

"I'd like that," she smiled as she walked towards the door. Joe watched her until she was swallowed up into the crowds of shoppers in the mall.

69

"Harry? Harry, it's me, Lisa."

"Lisa? What the… Are you all right? Where are you?"

"I'm fine, Harry. I have someone here who wants to speak to you. He—"

Karl snatched the phone from Lisa's hand. "Delaney," he said, "we need to meet. Where are you?"

"Who are you? What do you want with me?" Harry said. "Are you with the police?"

"Don't be stupid. You do know they're looking for you?"

"I had nothing to do with those girls," Harry said. "I just provided the vehicles. I didn't know what those bastards were using them for."

"I believe you," Karl said. "Lisa's told me you were being forced to—"

"Lisa told you? I don't understand. I thought nobody knew about it."

"She told me you were being forced into smuggling. What I want to know is who's been using your trucks?"

"I… I can't help you," Harry said. "They'll kill me if I tell."

Karl sneered. I'll kill you if you don't. Now, if you want to save your miserable skin, you'll tell me what I want to know."

"Put Lisa back on."

"It's not Lisa you need to talk to, mate, it's me. Now, for the last time, who are these people?"

"I can't tell you. I daren't tell you. You've no idea how dangerous they are."

"And you don't know how dangerous I am. I'm your only chance of coming away from this shit in one piece."

"How do I know I can trust you?"

"You trust Lisa, don't you?"

"Yes, but—"

"Stop pissing about, Delaney. The police won't believe you're not involved."

"But I didn't know," Harry said. "It was just supposed to be a few fags and booze. They never said they were moving girls."

"Can you prove it? If the police pick them up first, they'll put all the blame at your door, you do know that?"

"No, that's not right. I wasn't involved. I swear to God. I wasn't involved."

"Then let me help you. Tell me who they are."

"I... I have to think about it," Delaney said. "Work out what's best."

"You don't have time. We have to move now."

"No, I have to think about this. Tell Lisa... tell Lisa, I'm sorry."

The phone clicked, and then there was silence.

70

When Christina eventually managed to fall asleep, it was a restless, troubled sleep which left her exhausted when she woke. Had she imagined Guido had been her captor, she wondered? She closed her eyes, but the image would not go away. That of a man standing in the shadows, his hands covered in white cotton gloves.

It was mid-morning before she came downstairs. Still in her dressing gown, Christina trudged into the kitchen and picked up the coffee pot.

"I'll make some fresh," Lisa said, rushing into the room. "You sit down, love, and I'll get you some breakfast."

Christina shook her head. "No thanks, Mum," she said slowly. "I couldn't eat a thing."

Lisa placed her arm around her daughter's shoulders. "Are you sure those men didn't hurt you?"

Christina scowled and pushed her mother away. "Mum, stop fussing. I've told you I'm all right." She sat down at the table. "Where's Dad?"

"He's at the Emerald. I can get him back if you want?"

"No. I'm fine."

"Have you seen your friend this morning? Is she all right?"

Christina shrugged. "April's still sleeping. Stop worrying, I've told you they didn't hurt us."

Lisa sat across from her daughter at the table and gently held her hands. "Your dad and I have been talking," she said quietly. "We think it's best if you stay at home for the next few days, just until your dad sorts out this mess."

She pulled away from her mother's hold. "I can't do that," she said. "I have a business to run."

"Victoria can take charge for a while, I'm sure she's capable. Your dad thinks it's safer for you to stay in the house."

"But, Mum, I can't—"

"Christina, it's been decided. You and April are to stay here until Karl says otherwise."

"I'm going back upstairs," Christina sighed heavily. "April should be awake by now."

"All right, dear, let me know if you want anything, won't you?"

Christina smiled weakly and nodded. "Are we still going to the Amethyst tonight?"

Lisa frowned. "We'll have to see what Karl says, but I wouldn't think so."

"But we have to go. Alex will be so disappointed if his family aren't there to support him on the opening night. He's worked so hard."

"Those men are still out there, Christina, don't forget that. You need to be careful. We all do."

"They're not interested in me. They just want that damned briefcase. I don't know why Dad doesn't give it to them and have done with it."

"It's not that simple, you know that."

"But why can't—"

The kitchen door opened, and April entered the room. She was already washed and dressed. "Good morning," she said.

Lisa smiled. "Good morning. Did you manage to sleep well?"

April nodded and turned to her friend. "Have you heard anything from Rachel yet?"

Christina shook her head.

"I'm going to call the police," April said, taking out her mobile. "Something's happened to her. I know it has."

"No, you mustn't do that." Christina grabbed the phone from April. "If the police get involved, Rachel will be in serious trouble. She stole from a dead man, remember? She could go to jail."

"But I can't just stand by and do nothing. She could be hurt or… or worse."

"Leave it to my dad, he'll find her."

She sighed and put her phone away. "All right, but if I haven't heard from her by tomorrow, I'm definitely calling the police."

71

Karl arrived at the Amethyst just after nine o'clock, accompanied by Lisa, Christina and April. The music was loud, and strobe lighting bounced around the room. Scantily clad young women danced on the podiums, expertly winding their bodies around the glistening, silver poles.

Christina rushed over to her brother, who was standing by the bar and hugged him. "Congratulations." She smiled. "The club looks fantastic."

Karl walked over to Alex, held out his hand and smiled. "Well done, Son," he beamed. "You've done a great job"

Alex smiled. "I'm glad you like it." He kissed his mother and sister lightly on the cheek.

"Where's Sarah?" Karl asked. "I thought she'd be here for support."

Alex frowned and shrugged. "She might call in later," he said. "She had a headache or something, but I don't think clubs are her thing." He glanced at Karl. "I've reserved a table," he said, leading the party upstairs to the lounge. "You can see everything that's going on, but it's not so noisy."

Their table was by a glass screen with full views of the podiums below. "I hope this is all right," he said, smiling. "I've ordered champagne. It should be here in… oh here it is now. Thanks, Anna."

Anna was tall and slim with sleek-black hair falling over her slender shoulders. She carried a tray with an ice bucket containing a bottle of champagne and four crystal flutes. "Good evening." She smiled – a smile which did not extend to her dark-brown eyes.

"Oh, lovely," Christina giggled. "Isn't this exciting? Hasn't Alex done a wonderful job with the club?"

Lisa smiled. "He certainly has." She poured champagne into the glasses. "The club looks absolutely wonderful. Don't you think so, Karl?"

But Karl was not listening. He was transfixed with the girl who had brought the drinks. Not by her beautiful face, or her slim, sexy figure. It was the green tattoo on the back of her wrist – a tattoo in the shape of a three-leaf clover. He watched Anna intently as she moved around the room handing out drinks.

Lisa tapped his arm. "Is everything all right, Karl? You look miles away."

"Of course it is," Karl said. "You enjoy your champagne. I'll be back in a minute." Karl left the table and wandered over to Anna, stood by the bar. "Have you worked in many clubs?" he asked.

She shook her head. "No," she said softly. "Not many."

"I didn't think so. I thought you looked a little… how can I put this, I thought you looked a little uncomfortable."

She took a deep breath and swallowed hard. "I don't know what you mean," she said and looked away.

Karl narrowed his eyes. "Where are you from? You're clearly not English."

She turned sharply to face him. "Why do you ask that?"

"Were you brought here from Romania?"

Anna's eyes widened, but she remained silent.

"Is someone forcing you to work here?"

Anna said nothing.

"Tell me who. Maybe I can help."

"I don't know what you mean. I—"

Karl grabbed her wrist. "I've seen this mark before. Who did this to you?"

She turned away and busied herself pouring more drinks. "I have to work. Please leave me alone."

"I'm looking for a girl. Her name is Katya."

Anna turned around to face Karl. "You know Katya?"

Karl nodded. "I have to find her. Do you know where she is?"

"No, but—"

Alex walked over to Karl and Anna. "Is everything all right?"

"Yes, I was just asking this young lady if she was enjoying working at the club. It seems that she does."

Alex flashed a smile at Anna. "The table over there need more drinks," he said. "Take care of it. Then I want you downstairs. It's starting to get busy."

She nodded and rushed to the table at the far side of the room, carrying a tray of champagne.

"Let's go and find your mother, shall we?" Karl said. "She'll be wondering where I've gone."

Alex nodded but said nothing. When they got to the table, all three women were drinking and giggling.

"Steady on, Lisa," Karl said. "If you're not careful you'll need carrying home."

"Oh, stop fussing, darling," she said. "I'm enjoying myself. After the last three days I think I deserve to, don't you?"

Karl frowned, and sat back down at the table.

"I have to be downstairs," Alex said after a few minutes. "Meet and greet and all that. Will you be all right?"

"Yes, of course, darling," Lisa said. "You carry on, Alex. We're fine. Hasn't he done a wonderful job?" Lisa slurred, as she downed her fourth glass of bubbly. "I told you he would make a good job of running a club, didn't I?"

Karl remained silent, his eyes following the girl Anna as she disappeared downstairs. He knew she must have been one of the girls brought over from Romania. What he couldn't work out was what was she doing in the Amethyst? Surely Alex couldn't be involved in trafficking? He was about to go downstairs and speak with her again when one of the doormen came rushing over to his table.

"Mr Maddox?" he said breathlessly.

Karl scowled. "Yes, what do you want?"

"There's a telephone call for you, sir, down in reception. The caller says it's urgent."

"Did they give a name?"

"No, sir, just that it was urgent."

Karl huffed and made his way to reception and picked up the receiver. "Yeah?" he said.

"Karl? It's Paul."

"This better be good, I think I've—"

"George, the guy with the beard. He's here at the club."

Karl frowned. "What's he doing at the Emerald?"

"He's been stabbed."

"Stabbed? Then why isn't he at Jimmy's getting seen to?"

"He's been to the hospital and discharged himself. He says he needs to speak to you urgently."

"What about?"

"I don't know."

"Have you asked him?"

"Of course, I've asked him, but he won't speak to me. He says he'll only talk to you. I think you need to come over, Karl. He's not looking too good."

"All right, I'll be there in an hour, but if that arsehole's wasting my time…" Karl went into the main club and approached Alex. "I have to get back to Leeds straightaway. Get a taxi for the girls when they're ready to leave and keep an eye on your mother. I don't want her getting more hammered than she already is."

"Okay, but why the rush? I thought this was your night off."

"Business," Karl said and headed for the door, followed by Alex. He paused. "By the way, I'll be through to see you tomorrow at about ten. Make sure you have all the financials ready."

"Don't tell me you're checking up on me?"

"I just need to know where my money's going, that's all."

"You can see where it's gone. Just look around."

"Don't you raise your voice to me," Karl said. "I want to see the accounts and copies of contracts for all the dancers working here."

Alex frowned. "Why do you need those?"

"Just checking everything's legal," Karl said. "My clubs are clean, and I want to make sure they stay that way." Karl walked through the exit and out into the car park. "Ten o'clock, Alex. Don't be late," he said over his shoulder as he approached his car.

"Karl, have you got a minute?"

Karl turned and saw Marco walking towards him. "Sorry, mate," he said. "I'm in a hurry." He climbed into his car and started the engine. "I'm back here tomorrow morning. We can speak then."

72

It was nine o'clock that evening when Sarah walked into the casino. Joe hurried over to her, smiling. "Hello," he said. "I wasn't expecting to see you in here."

Sarah walked over to a small booth and sat down. "I wasn't expecting to be here either," she said.

"I'm glad you came, but what made you change your mind?"

Sarah shrugged. "Curiosity, I suppose. I've never been inside a casino before."

"Well, what do you think of the Lady Luck?"

"It looks very nice… for a casino."

Joe smiled. "Nice? Is that the best you can do?" he said. "Can I get you a drink?"

"A white wine, please."

"Coming right up," Joe said signalling to one of the waitresses with his order. He grinned. "Don't tell me you've changed your mind about having a flutter?"

She scowled. "Of course not."

"No? Then why did you come?"

Sarah blushed. "I just came to… to see you, I suppose."

He reached out and took her hand. "I'm flattered," he said. "I was going to call you and—" The waitress came over and placed two glasses on the table. "Anything else, Joe?" she asked.

"No thanks," he said, not taking his eyes off Sarah.

She picked up the glass and sipped at the contents. "Mm," she murmured, "I was ready for that."

"Hard day?"

She sighed. "Every day's a hard day at the moment. You have no idea."

"Tell me. Maybe I can help."

Sarah lifted her head sharply, her eyes brimming with tears. "Nobody can help," she said softly. "Nobody."

"Is it your husband? Alex isn't it?"

Sarah nodded.

"What has he done to upset you so much?"

She stifled a sob and sipped the wine. "I'm sorry, Joe. I shouldn't have come. Alex is expecting me. He's opening the club tonight, and I should be there."

"The Amethyst? You're going to the Amethyst?"

"You know about that? How——?"

Joe shrugged. "I've heard of it, but you don't have to go if you don't want to. You could always stay here."

"No, I can't. His whole damned family will be there."

"You don't like his family?"

"Lisa's okay and Christina, I suppose," she said, "but I hate his father. He frightens me."

"Why's that?"

"It's hard to explain. He's never hurt me or anything, but there's just something about him that makes me uncomfortable."

Joe reached out and gently took Sarah's hand in his. "Have you spoken to Alex about it?"

"Alex won't hear a thing said against him."

"Your father-in-law's Karl Maddox, isn't he?"

She frowned. "Yes, he is, but how——? Do you know Karl?"

Joe shrugged. "I used to a few years back. He was married to a friend of mine."

"You knew Erica?"

"Yes, I knew her," Joe said softly. "She was a beautiful woman."

"I don't know what went off between them. It all happened before Alex met up with his father, but Karl won't have Erica's name mentioned in the house."

"How is Karl these days? I heard he got shot a couple of years back."

"Alex says he was shot by a deranged policeman, but Karl never talks about that either."

"He doesn't seem to talk much about his past, does he? Back in the day, Karl used to be up to all sorts of shady deals. I suppose he hasn't changed much?"

Sarah ran her finger around the rim of her glass. "You

mean the business with the briefcase?"

"What briefcase?"

"One of his escorts nicked a briefcase from a client. Karl has it now, but somebody's trying to get it back. Alex says it's the same people who're involved in trafficking girls."

Joe frowned. "I didn't know anything about this. Tell me more."

"I don't know all the details, only what Alex has told me, but I know Karl's up to his neck in something."

"You say girls are being trafficked?"

She nodded. "Yes, it was on the news the other night. Girls from Romania had been found in the back of a lorry."

"And Karl's involved in that?"

"No, I don't think so. He's helping his friend Victor. His niece has been taken, and Karl is trying to get her back."

"Victor?" Joe said quietly. "I haven't seen him in years."

"Victor's two sons both work for Karl at the Emerald."

"Yes, I heard that," Joe said thoughtfully. "Sarah, let me get you another drink. You and I need to talk."

73

Karl drove to the Emerald Club in record time and went straight up to his office. Paul sat in one of the armchairs, and George was slumped on the couch.

"You look like shit," Karl said. "What's happened to you?"

"They tried to kill me," George said almost in a whisper. "The bastards tried to kill me."

"Well, you never were a good judge of character, were you? From what I've heard, that lot you're working with now are worse than the Kennedy's ever were."

George nodded. "Yeah, they're evil, and they're dangerous."

"What do you expect me to do? You're either very brave or very stupid coming here. I told you what would happen if you ever came back to Leeds again, remember?"

George grimaced in pain as he attempted to stand. "I was hoping we could put all that shit behind us." He breathed heavily. "I've had enough. I'm going to go back to Scotland, as far away from those crazy bastards as I can."

"Well before you piss off up north, I hear you've got something important to tell me. Do you know who took my daughter?"

George shook his head. "I don't know anything about that. That must have happened after Luke stabbed me."

"Why did he stab you? I thought you two were best buddies."

George lowered his head but remained silent.

"Well," Karl said. "What is it you have to tell me? I don't have all night."

"It's about the girls."

"What about them?"

"I know where they're kept."

Karl walked over to George and grabbed his arm. "Tell me," he yelled. "Tell me where they are, or I'll kill you myself."

George winced as he tried to release Karl's grip. "I will," he said, "but you have to help me get away from them.

They've tried to kill me once, and they'll try again."

"What have you done to piss them off anyway? You're only the lackey."

"I might be their lackey," George said quietly, "but I'm a lackey who knows stuff, lots of stuff."

Karl released his grip on George. "Who's running the operation?"

George shrugged. "I don't know. I've never met the top man."

"Then what do you know?"

George's breathing became erratic. "Water," he gasped, clutching his chest. "I need some water."

Karl indicated for Paul to fetch him some. Karl looked on as George lifted his trembling hands, holding the glass to his lips. He slumped back in his seat and wiped away the beads of sweat running down his ashen face.

"Steady on." Karl took the glass from George's grasp. "You're in a bad state. You need to get to the hospital."

George shook his head. "I'm not going back to the hospital," he whispered. "I just need to rest for a bit."

Karl went over to the drink's cabinet and poured himself a whisky. "Want one?" he asked. Not waiting for a reply, he poured a second glass and handed it to George.

"Now then, let's get down to business. Tell me everything you know about what's been going on."

George took the whisky and greedily gulped down the contents.

"I'm waiting," Karl said.

"Like I said, it was that mad bastard Luke that stabbed me," George said at last. "He killed a girl too."

"What girl?"

"The girl he picked up at the airport. Her name's Jacqui or Rachel, I'm not sure which. She's the whore who took the boss's briefcase."

"Where is Rachel now?"

"We left her in the woods, just off the pathway."

"Why did Luke try to kill you?"

George shrugged. "He said I was making too many mistakes. He blamed me for one of the girls that Albi delivered escaping. Albi's—"

"I know who Albi is," Karl said. "Go on."

"The girl got away, and I got the blame, but it wasn't my fault. I only—"

"Why did you let Nadia escape?"

"She was just a kid, she looked terrified. But how did you know about her?"

"Never mind how I know," Karl said. "What about the girl who fell from the balcony. Was that you or Luke?"

"It was an accident," George said quietly. "Luke thought she had the briefcase, and she got scared. She ran onto the balcony and... Nobody pushed her. She just fell."

"You'd better be telling me the truth about that," Karl said. "If I find out you're lying—"

George shook his head. "I'm not," he said. "I swear that's what happened."

"You said you know where the girls are being kept?"

"I know where Luke took them once we'd picked them up at Dover. I kept the addresses of all the drop-offs in my notebook."

Karl huffed. "Where is your notebook?"

"I've left it with a friend. They're taking care of it for me."

"What friend? Where do I find him?"

"It's not a him. Her name is Stella."

Karl banged his empty glass down on the table. "Stop fucking about, man. Where do I find Stella?"

"You get me fixed up and safely on my way to Glasgow, and I'll tell you."

"Come on, George," Karl said, "we don't have much time. Tell me what I want to know, and you'll be on your way."

"No chance," George said. "From now on, I don't trust anybody."

"All right, you win," Karl said as he picked up the telephone. "Alex? Alex, I need you over at the Emerald right away. Bring your medical bag with you."

74

It was the early hours of Sunday morning when the telephone rang. "Hello?" Charlotte said sleepily. She listened to the caller before putting down the receiver. She gently shook her husband, who was sleeping next to her. "Patrick," she whispered. "Patrick, darling, wake up."

Charlotte was in the kitchen when Marion came down that morning. She smiled. "You're up early. It's not eight o'clock yet."

"It's Shamus," Charlotte said softly. "There was a phone call early this morning from the hospital to say he had died in his sleep."

"Oh, darling, I'm so sorry," Marion said, putting her arms around Charlotte. "I know you were very fond of the old man."

"Patrick has gone over to Dublin to make the arrangements. He should be back tonight."

"If there's anything I can do, please let me know."

Charlotte smiled weakly. "Thanks, Gran," she said. "I'll get dressed, and then I'm going to go out for a walk. I need some fresh air."

"Do you want me to come with you?"

Charlotte shook her head. "No, I think I'd prefer to be by myself."

"All right, darling, if that's what you want. I'll make us some breakfast first, though. You've got to eat."

"I can't face food right now. I'll just have a glass of juice."

It was ten o'clock when Charlotte approached Maddox Mansion on the edge of the park. She stared at the house. It looked the same as she remembered when she had visited Erica and Karl a few years earlier. The door opened, and a young woman stepped outside and lit a cigarette. Although her once long, red hair was now an attractive bob and a subtle shade of auburn, there was no mistaking her. The woman standing on the doorstep was definitely Bunny.

Charlotte walked tentatively up the herringbone drive towards the house. "Bunny?" she said and smiled. "Is it really you?"

Christina stared at the young woman. There was something about her which was vaguely familiar.

"It's me, Charlotte. I never thought I'd see you again. How are you?"

"Charlotte, of course." Christina smiled as she recognised the young woman she had met in the hotel years ago. "How lovely to see you." She walked towards her and hugged her gently. "It's been ages. What are you doing here?"

"I'm visiting family in Leeds." Charlotte grinned. "Bunny, I can't believe I would bump into you of all people."

"It's lovely to see you again," Christina said, "but I don't use the name Bunny anymore. My name is Christina now."

"Christina? That's nice. But what are you doing here? This is Karl Maddox's house, isn't it?"

Christina nodded.

"Then how come—?"

"It's a long story," Christina said. "Perhaps we could meet for a drink later, and have a proper catch-up?"

"I'd like that."

Charlotte reached into her bag and took out a pen and a piece of paper. She quickly scribbled down her telephone number and handed it to Christina. "Ring me when you get the chance," she said. "I'd love to hear what you've been up to."

"Christina," called a female voice from inside the house. "Christina, come inside."

Christina shrugged and put out her cigarette. "Coming, Mother," she called. She turned to Charlotte. "I'll ring you in a couple of days, okay?"

Charlotte nodded and watched as Christina turned and walked back into the house, closing the door behind her.

Marion was in the kitchen when Charlotte got back to the

flat. "Oh, there you are," she said. "I was beginning to think you'd got lost. You've been gone ages."

"I went for a walk in the park," Charlotte said. "I needed to clear my head."

"Patrick rang about an hour ago wanting to speak to you. He said he won't be coming back tonight after all. He should be here tomorrow, or Tuesday at the latest."

"Oh, that's a shame."

"Yes, dear, but don't worry, I'm sure we can find lots to do. They've opened a new shopping mall down by the river. We could go there tomorrow if you like."

"Perhaps, Gran, but I was hoping to visit Joe and Matthew again before I have to go back to Ireland. You don't mind, do you?"

Marion walked to the fridge. "Of course I don't mind," she said. "But this evening I'm going to have you all to myself. I'm taking you out to a restaurant for a slap-up meal, and I won't take no for an answer."

Charlotte smiled. "That'll be lovely. I haven't eaten anything at all today. I'm starving."

"I'll make us both a sandwich to put us on," Marion said as she opened the fridge door. "Which do you prefer, ham or cheese?"

75

George opened his eyes slowly and struggled to take in his surroundings.

"Feeling better?" asked a voice somewhere in the room.

"Where am I?" he whispered. "What time is it?"

"You're still at my club," Karl said, walking into view. "You're in the night watchman's room."

"How long have I been out?"

"Just a few hours. The doc says you'll be fine in a couple of days."

"Yeah, I feel a lot better," George said through shallow breaths. "I don't suppose there's a coffee on offer?"

"Yeah, but first, we have unfinished business."

"Oh, you mean Stella?"

"Yes, Stella. Ring her and get her to fetch the notebook to the club."

"I don't want to get her involved. She's… she's a good girl."

Karl moved closer. "Does she know what's in it?"

"She doesn't know anything. She's just looking after it for me, that's all."

"Ring her and tell her to meet you here with the notebook."

"But, Karl, I—"

Karl looked upwards. "It's not up for discussion, George," he said as he handed the telephone to him. "Get her to bring it here this afternoon."

Hesitantly, George took the receiver from Karl and dialled a number. When he had finished the call, Karl walked over to the door.

"Well?"

"She'll be here at three," he said.

"Good. I'll get you that coffee. I have to go out for a while, but Peter will take care of you until I get back."

76

Karl drove to the Amethyst. The club was locked, and there was no one around when he arrived. He quickly dialled his son's number. His call was eventually answered by Sarah.

"Good morning, Karl," she said sleepily.

"I need to speak to Alex. Put him on, will you?"

"Alex is still asleep, he's exhausted. He didn't get home until the early hours."

"I told him to meet me here at ten," Karl said. "Get the lazy sod out of bed and down to the club now."

"Is everything all right?"

"That's what I'm here to find out. By the way, where were you last night? I was expecting you at the club."

"I wasn't feeling well. I had a headache, so I stayed home."

"You should have been there at the Amethyst. Your place is beside your husband not nursing a bloody headache."

"I have to go," Sarah said. "I'll let Alex know you're waiting for him at the club." Before Karl could respond, the phone went dead.

Cursing, he sat in his car, drumming his fingers on the steering wheel. It was twenty minutes before a red Mondeo pulled up in front of the club and Marco, head of the club's security, got out.

"Good morning, Karl," he said. "You're an early bird."

Karl scowled. "That's more than can be said for my idle son. I told him to meet me here this morning."

Marco busied himself opening the front door of the Amethyst and then dealt with the alarm. "Fancy a coffee while you wait?" he asked. "I was going to make one for myself."

"Yeah, why not?" Karl said as he followed Marco into the club. "How did it go last night? I had to leave early."

"It went... great. The club was at full capacity, and there was no trouble from punters."

Karl fixed Marco with a stare. "What is it you're not saying, Marco? There is something I can tell."

Marco turned to face Karl "You asked me to keep an eye

on young Alex," he said.

"That's right, I did. Why, what's he been up to?"

Marco sighed heavily and turned away again, busying himself with making the drinks.

"Come on, man, spit it out," Karl said. "Don't tell me he's been chasing after the girls working here."

"No, no, it's nothing like that."

"Then what?"

The outer door opened, and both men turned to see Alex standing in the doorway.

"I thought we weren't meeting until ten?" he said to Karl. "It's only just after nine."

Marco puffed out his cheeks. "Do you want a coffee, Alex?" he asked.

"No, I don't want coffee. This place looks a disgrace. What time are the cleaners due?"

"They'll be here at ten."

"How are we for champagne? The VIP lounge seemed to get through most of it last night, the greedy bastards."

"We've still got a couple of dozen bottles. I'll do a stock check in the cellar later."

"Do it now," Alex said. "Karl and I have some business to discuss. When you've finished there, I want you to go to the wholesalers. There's a list in the office."

Marco shrugged. "Okay," he said. "Give me a shout if you need anything else."

Karl watched as Marco went behind the bar and descended the cellar steps. He turned to his son. "Marco's supposed to be head of security, not a bar manager." Karl frowned. "I thought you had somebody in place to take care of stock?"

"You mean Andy? I caught him helping himself to booze last night, so I sacked him."

"Have you got a replacement in mind? Marco can't do both jobs."

"Marco will do whatever I tell him. Now, what is it you want to talk about? I'm busy this morning."

Karl smiled. "My, my, who's got out of the wrong side of

bed this morning? By the way, thanks for coming over last night to take care of George."

"He's a lucky man. If the knife had gone in a couple of centimetres higher—"

"Well it didn't. What did you give him by the way? He went out like a light."

Alex grinned. "Oh, just a little something I've put by for emergencies."

"I could have done with him awake last night."

"The pain that man was suffering must have been excruciating. I had to knock him out. He had twelve stitches in the wound. Who is he anyway, and who stabbed him?"

"Nobody important," Karl said. "Do you have the paperwork I asked for? The accounts need to be checked at my office and—"

Alex turned sharply to face his father. "That's not what we agreed. You said the Amethyst was mine to run as I see fit. That means I deal with all the financials myself."

"That's not how I operate. All of the clubs submit their financials through my office at the Emerald. That's how it's always been done."

"For God's sake, I'm your son, not the hired help," Alex said. "Don't you trust me or something? Do you think I'm not capable of running a poxy club? You do know I'm a qualified doctor, don't you? Not some lowlife off the street."

"Steady on, Alex, there's no need for the hostility. Nobody's accusing you of incompetence."

"Then why do you insist on going through everything with a fine-tooth comb? You don't go through Christina's accounts at the salon, do you? Or maybe Christina's your favourite, the girl who can do no wrong."

Karl held up his hands. "Alex, calm down. Let's discuss this rationally."

"I'm through with being rational. You either trust me, or you don't."

"Of course I trust you, you're my son."

"Then let me run the club as I see fit. I don't want you

breathing down my neck, Karl. It's not fair."

Karl rubbed his chin. "All right, I suppose you have a point. Actually, I was planning on signing the Amethyst over to you eventually. I suppose now would be as good a time as any."

"Do you mean that? You'll give me the Amethyst?"

"Your mother thinks you're ready for the responsibility."

"What about you, Karl? Do you think I'm ready?"

"Well, I guess we'll soon find out, eh, son?"

Alex threw his arms around Karl and hugged him tightly. "Thank you, Karl. Thank you."

"Steady on, Son," Karl grinned. "I can see you've worked hard. You deserve it."

"You won't regret it, Dad, I promise."

"Dad is it now? Things are moving on."

"I'll give Sarah a ring," Alex said excitedly. "She'll be over the moon."

"Let's hope so," Karl said. "By the way, what time are you expecting Anna? I was hoping to have a word with her."

Alex chuckled. "What do you want to speak to Anna about? You don't fancy her do you, you dirty dog?"

Karl shrugged. "She's a pretty girl. Where did you find her?"

"I can't remember. You know what these girls are like. They come and go all the time. Why do you want to know about her?"

"No reason. Like I said, she's a pretty girl. Will she be working tonight?"

"I suppose so."

"Tell me, Alex, have you been approached by anyone wanting to place girls into the Amethyst?"

"Pimps you mean?"

"Well, sort of, I suppose. There are rumours that girls are being trafficked into the area and placed into clubs."

Alex folded his arms. "I can assure you there are no trafficked girls working in the Amethyst."

"Including Anna?"

"Including Anna."

"In that case, there's nothing more to be said. I'll have the paperwork drawn up today, and the Amethyst will be all yours."

Alex smiled and shook Karl's hand. "Thanks. You won't regret it, I promise."

"I'd better not," Karl said.

77

Stella arrived promptly at the Emerald at three o'clock. She was in her thirties, tall and slim with short blonde hair and blue eyes. She would have been pretty had it not been for the scar down the left side of her face – a scar stretching from the corner of her eye, across her cheek to her top lip. Stella had a pronounced limp and steadied herself with a wooden cane.

"I've come to see George," she said to Karl. "He rang me this morning and asked me to come here."

"Did you bring the notebook?"

"I have it," she said. "I'll give it to George, not to you."

"He's through here," Karl said as he led the way through the corridor to the room where George was resting. As Stella entered the room, George smiled broadly.

"Stella, you came," he said, holding out his arms to her.

She made her way unsteadily to the couch and bending, kissed him lightly on the cheek. "George, darling," she whispered. "Are you all right? Who did this to you?" She turned her gaze towards Karl.

"I'm fine," George said softly. "Karl helped me. He got me a doctor and—"

"You are going to be all right, aren't you?" she said gently stroking his hair. "I couldn't bear it if… if anything happened to you."

"Nothing's going to happen to me, I promise. We're going to leave here and go to live in Glasgow."

"Glasgow?" she shrieked with delight. "Do you mean it, George? I've never been to Scotland before."

"Touching as this reunion is," Karl interrupted, "I think you have something for me, Stella?"

"You did bring the notebook like I asked?" George said. Stella nodded. "Then give it to Karl." She opened her handbag and handed Karl a blue leather A5 notebook.

"Thank you," Karl said, taking the journal.

He opened it and scanned through the dozen or so pages. Each entry showed the dates of the pick-ups, the destination and the number of girls involved. "There are no names in here." He frowned, turning to George. "Don't you have any more details?"

George shrugged. "I just have the addresses where the girls were taken. It was Luke who dealt with everything else."

Karl huffed and tossed down the book. "Where can I find Luke?"

George shook his head. "I don't know where he lives. He always picked me up at my flat when there was a job."

"Can we go now, George?" Stella said. "Are you well enough to travel?"

George grimaced as he attempted to stand.

"Maybe you should give it a couple of hours," Karl said. "The doctor did say you should rest."

"I don't have time to rest," George said weakly. "I have to get as far away from here as I can. If they find out I'm still around—"

"At least wait until it gets dark," Karl said. "You can stay here until then."

"I think he's right, George," Stella said softly. "You don't look well."

George lay back on the couch, and Stella sat beside him, stroking his hand.

"How did you two meet?" Karl asked.

"George bought me from the traffickers."

"He did what?"

"I was brought to England about five years ago from Bulgaria. I was made to work in clubs at first, then in brothels. Eventually, I was put onto the street."

"Is that when you met George?"

"Yes, George was a regular client. He's a big man with a big appetite." She grinned affectionately as she gently stroked his hair. "One night, I was attacked by one of the punters. I was no good for work anymore. Nobody wants a scarred cripple, eh?"

"You're still beautiful to me," George whispered. "You always will be."

"They would have killed me, but George offered them money." She kissed George gently on the cheek. She turned sharply to face Karl. "Is there anything else you want to know? George needs to rest."

Karl shrugged. "I'll get Peter to bring you something to eat. You must be hungry."

"Thanks," George said and gently touched his wound. "I'm starving."

"I'll go to the flat and get our things together," Stella said. "I'll be back at six."

"There are some interesting addresses here," Paul mused as he studied the notebook. "They've certainly got quite a business going delivering girls all around the country. Do you think Katya is one of them? Maybe we should—"

"Paul, we're not the mafia," Karl said. "We don't have the manpower to go barging into all of the premises. There's over a dozen in Leeds alone."

"I just feel so helpless. We should be doing something."

"We are doing something. What time are you meeting Beauchamp at the prison tomorrow?"

"Nine o'clock," Paul said.

"Well, let's hope we can crack the password. We have to know what's so damned important on that laptop that those bastards are prepared to kill for."

"Don't worry. Martin Morris won't let you down. I don't suppose you've heard any more from Delaney?"

"No, not yet. He sounded scared shitless on the phone."

"Maybe he has good reason to be."

Karl frowned. "Maybe he has."

78

Martin Morris was forty-two years old. Each one of those years was deeply etched on his pale, thin face. His hair, once dark and curly, was now grey and wispy, forming a halo of straggly curls around his head. Martin had had an undistinguished career as a thief, spending fifteen years of his life in prisons. His one and only talent was his amazing ability with technology. Had he chosen to, Martin could have had a brilliant career in IT. However, working with computers did not compare to the thrill he felt when breaking into a building and taking whatever he wanted.

It was nine o'clock on Monday morning when Martin was escorted from his cell and taken to the small, windowless room on the ground floor reserved for meetings between inmates and their legal representatives. Martin was perplexed. He didn't understand what a solicitor could possibly want with him. The guard indicated for him to sit on a chair in front of a metal table. He didn't have long to wait before two men entered the room.

"Thank you, officer," the older of the two men said. "That will be all. You can wait outside while I speak to my client." The prison guard dutifully left the room, closing the door behind him. Martin studied the man closely. He was short, no more than five foot six, and had white hair with a neatly trimmed beard. Shrewd grey eyes looked out from behind his steel-rimmed glasses.

"Good morning, Mr Morris," he said. "My name is Jeremiah Beauchamp. I'm a solicitor, and this gentleman," he nodded in the direction of Paul, "is my associate."

Martin looked at the second man. He was a lot younger than Jeremiah Beauchamp and much taller. His appearance, however, was equally as smart, but his large, muscular frame and broad shoulders strained at the seams on his jacket.

"Good morning, Mr Morris," Beauchamp said. "I trust you are well?"

Martin scowled. "What is it you want? Have you come to

get me off?"

"Your guilt has been proven in a court of law," the solicitor said, looking at Martin over the top of his glasses. "There's nothing anyone can do about your conviction now, I'm afraid."

Martin glanced between the two men. "If you can't get me off, what is it you want?"

Paul, who had been silent up to this point, placed the laptop he held onto the table. "We want you to get us into this," he said. "Do you think you can you do that?"

Whatever Martin had been expecting Paul to say, it certainly wasn't that. He looked closely at the computer and smiled. "Of course I can do it," he said, narrowing his eyes. "But why should I? What's in it for me?"

"Money," Paul said. "You find the password, and there'll be one thousand pounds waiting for you when you get out."

Martin scowled. "A grand? You must be joking. I want more than that."

"How much do you want?"

"Two grand. If I get you into the computer, I want two thousand quid."

"Two grand just for working out the password?" Paul said. "That seems excessive."

"If you think it's that easy, you do it." Martin pushed the laptop across the desk towards Paul. "Go on, mate, be my guest."

Paul frowned. "All right. Two thousand it is. How long will it take you?"

Martin shrugged. "Five minutes, maybe ten. I'm a bit out of practice since I've been stuck in here."

"You'd better hurry up and get on with it then," Paul said. "The screws will be back soon."

Martin took the laptop and deftly ran his fingers over the keyboard. After a few minutes, the screen sprang into life. "There you go." He grinned. "That was easy. By the way, I've taken off the old password and replaced it with one of my own."

"You've done what?" Paul snatched hold of the laptop.

"I'll tell you what it is when I get my money."

"You stupid bastard," Paul said, grabbing him by the shoulder. "Do you have any idea who this belongs to?"

"No, but I don't think it belongs to you, mate."

"You're right, it doesn't," Paul said. "It belongs to Karl Maddox. Perhaps you've heard of him?"

The colour drained from Martin's cheeks. "Karl Maddox?" he whispered.

"That's right. Do you know what will happen to you when I tell him what you've done? Karl has a lot of contacts inside the prison and—"

"Look, mate, I... I... it was only a joke. My password is *alcapone47*."

"Al Capone?"

"Yeah, he's my hero," Martin said. "He died in 1947."

Paul typed the password into the laptop and satisfied it was correct, he closed the lid.

"What was the original password?"

"Eh? What does it matter? You're in now."

"What was it?"

"*worldwide*" Martin answered. "*worldwide69*".

"Thanks," Paul said as he entered it on his phone. "Well, I think that concludes our business."

"I will still get my two grand like you said, right?"

"Unlike you, I keep my word," Paul said, walking towards the door, closely followed by Jeremiah Beauchamp.

"By the way, if I might make a suggestion, Mr Morris," the solicitor said smiling. "Perhaps you might consider a change of career. You don't seem to be very successful as a thief."

Martin grinned. "It's funny you should say that. I was thinking that I might give up burglary and turn my hand to hacking people's bank accounts. What do you think?"

"That's not quite what I had in mind." The solicitor frowned as he hurried out of the room.

"That went well," Jeremiah Beauchamp said as he

approached his vehicle. "It's a pity you had to pay more than you intended, though."

"More?" Paul grinned. "I think we got the password pretty cheap. Karl authorised me to go to five grand."

79

Karl sat anxiously behind his desk at the Emerald club when Paul arrived just after ten. "Well, how did it go? Did you get the password sorted?"

Paul grinned. "I did. The new password is *alcapone47*.

Karl grimaced. "Al Capone? Who thought that one up?"

"It's that tosser Martin's idea of a joke."

Karl took the laptop from Paul and placed it on his desk. "Well, let's see what's on the bloody thing. *alcapone47* you said?" He nimbly tapped out the password, and the screen burst into life. "Great, we're in."

Paul joined Karl at the screen. "These must be the contacts abroad," Paul said. "There are phone numbers with international codes. I recognise +40 as Romania and +359 is Bulgaria."

"So, these are the people supplying the girls abroad, eh?" Karl said quietly. "And thanks to George's notebook, we know where they are held when they arrive in the UK. But we still don't know who is organising it."

"Hey, look at this, Karl," Paul said and tapped the screen. "The last entry was made the day Rachel nicked the laptop. It must refer to the girls brought in from Romania and delivered to Birmingham."

Karl studied the screen. "There's a London telephone number. Let's give it a ring." He dialled, and it rang three times before being answered.

"Hello," a well-spoken male voice said.

"Hi," Karl said. "Is John there?"

"John? I'm sorry, sir, there's no John at this number."

"Are you sure? I'm positive this is the number he gave me."

"You must be mistaken," the voice said. "This is the residence of Sir Anthony Howard-Cleeve."

"Who?"

"Sir Anthony Howard-Cleeve, MP."

"Oh, I must have taken the number down wrong. Sorry to

have bothered you." Karl replaced the receiver and turned to Paul. "You'll never guess who that was." He grinned and relayed the details of the call to Paul.

Paul smirked. "An MP mixed up with sex trafficking? Whatever next?"

"I want you to find out everything you can about him," Karl said. "It looks like he's involved in this somehow."

"Okay, I'll do that," Paul said, "but I've been thinking. There is something else we could try."

"What's that?"

"Remember the three names in the hotel register in Edinburgh?"

Karl rolled his eyes. "That was a complete waste of time."

"Two of the names were, but there was a third name, remember? I never followed that through."

Karl shrugged. "Okay, I suppose it's worth a try. What's the bloke's name?"

Paul took out his mobile and checked the photograph he had taken of the register. "Flynn," he said at last. "S. P. Flynn."

80

Marco sat back in his seat and sipped contentedly at the whisky brought to him by the flight attendant. In just two hours he would be in Benidorm, his favourite Spanish resort. Then it would be sun, sea, and if he got lucky, sex too.

It had come as a surprise when Alex had suggested he take a holiday. It came as an even bigger surprise when he handed him his complimentary plane ticket and hotel reservation. 'A little thank you for your hard work,' he had said. More like a bribe to keep his mouth shut. Marco grinned. If Karl knew the amount of time his son was spending at the casino… Still, it wasn't his place to say anything. After all, he was just the hired help.

Marco frowned. It was a pity Anna had to be moved on, but he had seen Karl sniffing around her, and he knew it wouldn't be long before he started asking questions. His cousin, Luke, hadn't been too pleased when he returned Anna, but at least Alex hadn't suspected anything. He was far too busy visiting the casino.

The stewardess came down the aisle.

He smiled. "A whisky," he said. "Make it a large one."

81

Charlotte arrived at the Lady Luck Casino just before lunch. "Charlotte." Joe beamed hurrying towards her. "What a lovely surprise. I thought you'd be back in Ireland by now."

She kissed him lightly on the cheek. "I'm going back later this week," she said solemnly. "Patrick's father died at the weekend."

"I'm sorry to hear that," Joe said as he gently steered her by the elbow into the club. "If there's anything I can do?"

"Thanks, Joe, but everything's being taken care of. Patrick's in Ireland right now arranging the funeral."

Joe sighed. "Matthew will be sorry he's missed you. He won't be back until this evening. He's gone to see his mother in the nursing home."

"That's a shame. I was looking forward to seeing him again before I leave. How is his mother? Is she getting better?"

"She's about the same, I think. Matthew doesn't talk about her much."

Charlotte frowned. "It must be terrible for him. Losing his dad like that was bad enough, but then having to cope with his mother's breakdown as well."

Joe shrugged. "All part of life's rich tapestry, I suppose. Anyway, Matthew's not here so you'll have to make do with me. How about lunch?"

"That would be lovely," Charlotte said, smiling. "I can't wait to hear what's been happening in the casino."

"Could you manage a dessert?" Joe grinned as he watched Charlotte eat the last of her lasagne. "I'm going to have a Tiramisu."

"Mm, sounds wonderful. I think I'll have the same."

"Should I get us another bottle of wine?" he said, smiling. "This one seems to have evaporated."

"Very funny," Charlotte said. "Yes, another bottle of wine would be perfect."

Joe ordered desserts, along with a second bottle of

Chardonnay.

"Tell me about Alex," Charlotte said. "Is he up to his eyes in debt yet?"

Joe shrugged. "He's started a credit line. He's ten thousand down at present."

"So, your plan's working?"

"It seems to be. He visits the casino most nights."

"And Karl has no idea?" she said. "That surprises me."

"From what I've heard, Karl's got enough problems on his plate at the moment."

The waitress came to the table with the wine. "I'm sorry," she said, "but we've run out of Tiramisu. We have lemon cheesecake, or there's apple pie or—"

"No, I don't think I'll bother," Charlotte said. "What about you, Joe?"

Joe shook his head. "No thanks, we'll leave it."

Charlotte turned sharply to Joe. "You said Karl has problems. What did you mean?"

Joe frowned. "I don't know all the details, but it seems he's got mixed up with sex traffickers."

Charlotte gasped. "Sex traffickers? Karl? I don't believe it. I know he's an evil bastard, but I can't believe he would get involved with that sort of thing."

Joe shook his head. "He's not involved exactly," he said. "It's… it's complicated. Anyway, I don't want to discuss the Maddox's murky little world. Tell me what you've been up to."

"Nothing much," Charlotte said. "Living with Gran isn't exactly living life in the fast lane. But tell me about you. Have you found anyone yet?"

Joe shook his head. "There'll be time for that when I've brought Maddox down."

"It's been six months since Erica died. You can't be expected to be on your own forever. Erica wouldn't have wanted that." Charlotte reached over the table and held his hand. "Time's precious, Joe, don't waste it. Live your life in the present, not the past."

"Is everything all right, Charlotte?" Joe stared into her tear-filled eyes. "You seem a little... tense."

She quickly pulled away from Joe. "I don't know what you mean," she said and drank the remnants of her wine.

"Charlotte, it's me you're talking to, remember? If anything is bothering you, you can tell me. You know that." He leant forward and gently held her hand. "Now, what is it?"

Tears ran down her cheeks. "Oh, Joe, I... I'm so unhappy," she sobbed. "I don't know where to begin."

"Is it Patrick?"

Charlotte nodded as she fumbled in her bag to retrieve a tissue.

"What is it? Please tell me."

"I... I think Patrick's seeing another woman," she dabbed her eyes. "He's hardly ever at home, and half the time he won't tell me where he's been."

"Have you spoken to him?"

"I've tried, but he just makes excuses."

"You say he's in Ireland at the moment?"

"He's supposed to be, but I tried ringing him last night and got no reply." She dabbed her eyes again. "This morning I rang the Dublin office and spoke to Deidre, his father's secretary. She said Patrick had been into the office yesterday and given instructions about the funeral, but she didn't know where he had gone after that."

"When are you expecting him back?"

"He rang Marion yesterday to say he won't be back in England for a couple of days."

Joe frowned. "So, you think he's seeing someone else?"

"It's the only explanation that makes any sense."

"You don't think it could just be work? You said he travels around the world with his job."

"Yes, all the time. It's impossible to get hold of him." Charlotte screwed up the tissue. "He doesn't have a base, a proper office."

"I thought he worked from his father's offices in Dublin?"

She shook her head. "He helped out when Shamus was ill a couple of times, but he rarely goes there."

"Perhaps now the old man is dead, Patrick might take on the practice?"

She poured herself another glass of wine, swallowing half the contents in one gulp. "He said not." She sighed. "I've begged him to join the firm, but he says he doesn't want to be tied to a desk."

Joe reached over the table and gently stroked her hand. "Charlotte," he said, "I don't think drinking is going to solve anything, Do you?"

Charlotte pulled away from him. "Are you suggesting I drink too much? How dare you?"

"What I'm saying is that I think you've had enough to drink for one day. Why don't you come back to mine and I'll make us some coffee?"

She glared at him, anger flashing in her eyes. She was about to speak when her mobile rang. "Yes?... Christina? How lovely to hear from you... Six o'clock? Yes, I can make it. I'll see you then."

Joe raised his eyebrows. "Christina? Don't tell me that was Karl's daughter?" he asked. "You're not in contact with her, are you?"

"Yes," Charlotte said. "As a matter of fact, I am. I bumped into her yesterday."

"But why would you want to meet up with Christina Maddox? Do you think it's a good idea?"

"Why wouldn't it be? Bunny, I mean Christina, has never done anything to hurt me."

"You do realise her father is Karl Maddox?"

She folded her arms tightly. "She can't be held responsible for that pig."

"You're being ridiculous. You must keep away from that family, do you hear me? They're bad blood, the whole lot of them."

Charlotte scoffed. "You're beginning to sound like Patrick. He's always trying to tell me what to do, who to see, where to go. I've had enough of it, do you hear?" She banged her fists down on the table. "From now on I'm going to do what the hell I like, and nobody's going to stop me. Not even you."

82

"Hello...? Hello...? Who's there?" There was silence. "Who is this?" Guido demanded.

"I know it was you," the voice said.

"You know what was me? Who is this?"

"It was you that held me prisoner in that room."

"Christina? Is that you?"

"I saw your hands, Guido. Hands that wore white cotton gloves."

"I don't know what you're talking about."

"You're involved with the sex traffickers."

"That's rubbish."

"Is it? Do you have any idea what Karl would do if he knew it was you who held me captive?"

"Christina, I... I think we need to talk. Let's meet and discuss this like two sensible adults. What do you say?"

"No, Guido. I don't think so." The phone went quiet again. It was a few seconds before Christina spoke. "Why?" she said at last. "Tell me why you would get involved with those people?"

"Money," he said. "I got involved because of the money. But I give you my word, you were never in danger. They weren't going to hurt you. They just wanted Karl to hand over the briefcase."

"They're killers. They killed Jacqui, and they've probably killed Rachel."

"I don't know anything about that. All I did was let them use my storeroom for a few hours."

"You know what would happen if Dad found out you were involved? It would be your head in the fryer next time, not your hands."

"What the hell are you saying?" Guido said. "That it was Karl who attacked me?"

"What I'm saying is, if you don't want my dad to come after you, you'll write off the twenty thousand pounds you say I owe you."

"That's a lot of money, Christina."

"It's a lot of pain, Guido."

"Do you promise to keep your mouth shut?"

"You have my word."

"You're certainly your father's daughter."

"Do we have a deal?"

"Yes," he said. "Yes, we have a deal."

83

Karl was at the Emerald Club when Paul rang. "How are you getting on, Sherlock?" Karl said. "Have you managed to track down the mysterious Mr Flynn?"

"Not exactly," Paul said. "According to his secretary, Mr Flynn died on Saturday night."

Karl scowled. "So that's that then. Yet another dead end, if you'll excuse the pun."

"I'm not so sure. The address in the hotel's register was that of a solicitor's office in Dublin. Shamus Phelan Flynn was the senior partner."

"And you say he died on Saturday night?"

"That's right," Paul said. "But the secretary told me that Shamus Flynn had been in hospital for the past month."

Karl frowned deeply. "Then how come he was in Scotland just a few days ago?"

"That's where it gets interesting," Paul said. "Shamus has a son, Shamus Patrick Flynn, and he is very much alive."

"Where do we find this prodigal son?"

"Nobody seems to know. Patrick travels the world doing freelance legal work. He lives in Dublin. I called around, but the house was empty. A neighbour I spoke to seemed to think he's in England visiting his wife's family."

"You think this Patrick Flynn could be the bloke we're looking for, the ringleader?"

Paul sighed. "I think it's the best lead so far."

"How are we going to find him? I can't spare you to camp out in Dublin indefinitely."

"I don't have to," Paul said. "The old man's funeral is next Friday. The obliging Deidre even told me which church. Patrick's bound to be there. Don't you think?"

"Find out all you can about him, and then I need you back here. Luke rang me earlier. He says he'll hand Katya over tomorrow night."

"Have you let Dad know?"

"No, not yet. I think it's best we make sure first before

building his hopes up, don't you?"

"I suppose so," Paul said. "Where are you meeting?"

"I'll tell you all about it when you get back."

"Okay. The next flight isn't for a couple of hours. I'll have another snoop around here before I leave."

"All right, but be careful."

"I will," Paul said. "By the way, don't forget to change the password back. We don't want them knowing we've copied their files."

"Don't worry, I've already taken care of that."

"Good. See you tonight."

Deidre peeped through the blinds and watched intently as Paul entered the street and drove away. She picked up the receiver and dialled a number. "Patrick? Patrick, it's me, Deidre," she said breathlessly. "I appreciate you told me not to ring you on this number unless it was urgent, but there's something you should know right away." She hurriedly relayed to Patrick the details of Paul's visit. "I didn't like the look of him, far too friendly to be genuine, so I'm afraid I told a little white lie."

84

It was just after six when Charlotte arrived at the Smoking Grill, a new and vibrant bistro in the centre of Leeds. The music was loud, and the restaurant was already filling up with office workers ready for a cold drink and a quick meal.

"Over here," Christina shouted from her table by the window.

Charlotte walked over to her and held out her arms. "It's lovely to see you after all this time." She smiled and hugged her friend affectionately. "I often wondered what had happened to you."

Christina grinned. "There's a lot to tell, but tell me about you first. I see you're wearing a wedding ring."

"Yes. I married a solicitor. His name is Patrick Flynn, and we live in Dublin."

"Do you have any children?"

Charlotte shook her head. "No. Patrick's far too busy with work to think about starting a family, but I'm sure we will soon."

"Where's Patrick now?"

"He's in Dublin. His father died at the weekend. Patrick's arranging the funeral."

"Oh, Charlotte, I'm sorry to hear that."

"Shamus was very old, and he'd been unwell for a long time."

"Will you be going back to Ireland?"

"The funeral's on Thursday so I'll be going back the day before," Charlotte said, "but enough about me, I want to hear all about you. What's been happening in your life?"

Christina giggled. "Well, for a start I gave up my... my job after I met a father I didn't even know existed."

"You mean Karl Maddox?"

She nodded. "Yes. I know he has a bad reputation, but he's been very good to me. He bought me a beauty salon in the city centre, and he's looked after Alex too."

"Alex?"

"My brother, well, actually, he's my twin brother. Dad's put Alex in charge of one of his clubs in Manchester. It's called the Amethyst."

"It sounds exciting. You're living in Karl's house now, aren't you?"

"That's right. It's a lovely house, but of course you'll know that already, won't you?"

"I stayed there a couple of days with Aunt Erica, but that was a long time ago."

"I heard Erica died."

Charlotte nodded. "Yes, a few months ago. She had cancer."

"What about the bloke she ran off with? Do you know where he is?"

"Joe? No, I haven't seen him since Erica's funeral. Why do you ask?"

Christina shrugged. "No reason. Dad is still mad as hell about what happened between them. He never talks about it much, but I think if he ever met Joe again he'd kill him."

Charlotte frowned. "Well, let's hope they never get to meet. Now, who do we have to sleep with to get a drink around here?"

Christina grinned. "Don't worry, I've ordered a couple of bottles of wine. Ah, here they come now."

"Two bottles?"

"I've invited some of my staff from the salon for a drink. I hope you don't mind."

"Of course not, the more the merrier."

Both women had almost finished their first glass of wine when Victoria, Sophia and Nadia arrived. Christina made the introductions.

"Where's April?" Christina asked. "I thought she was coming out tonight."

"She went off in a police car," Victoria said. "The police have found the body of a woman. They think it could be Rachel."

Christina brought her hands up to her face and gasped.

"Oh no, that's terrible. Let's hope they're wrong."

"Who's Rachel?" Charlotte asked. "Does she work with you at the salon?"

"No, Rachel's… Rachel's a friend," Christina said. "She's April's sister. She's been missing for a few days."

"Who would want to kill her?" Nadia murmured as she nervously wound her hair around her fingers. "April said one of Rachel's friends died a few days ago. She fell from a hotel balcony. Do you think she was murdered too?"

"Don't be ridiculous," Christina snapped. "That was an accident. The girl must have been drunk when she fell."

"April said—"

"Nadia, I don't care what April said. Now can we change the subject for goodness sake? It's starting to sound morbid."

Nadia shrugged but remained silent as Christina ordered another bottle of wine.

"Do you work at the salon too, Nadia?" Charlotte asked. "You look very young to be a stylist."

"I do nails," she said. "And I make tea and sweep floors."

"Nadia is a trainee nail technician." Christina smiled. "She's been with me a couple of weeks now, isn't that right?"

Nadia nodded.

Sophia put her arm around Nadia's shoulders protectively. "My sister is very lucky to be here," she said in almost a whisper. "She was kidnapped and brought to England by evil men who—"

"Sophia, that's enough," Christina said. "I've told you before not to speak of what happened."

"Are you saying Nadia was trafficked?" Charlotte gulped. "Were you, Nadia?"

Nadia's eyes lowered towards the table. Sophia grabbed Nadia's left hand and turned it palm up. "Look," she said. "Look what those bastards did to my sister. They branded her like she was an animal."

Charlotte examined Nadia's wrist. "Oh, darling, that's terrible," she said. "What have the police done about it?"

"The police?" Nadia said. "I can't tell the police. They'll

send me back to Romania."

"But you can't just let them get away with this. You have to tell someone."

"She has told someone," Christina said. "She's told Karl. He's taking care of it. When he finds out who's responsible, he'll—"

"He'll never find out. They're too clever." Sophia said. "The bastards who branded my sister will just go on doing this to other girls, and there's nothing anybody can do to stop them."

85

"What time are they handing over Katya tomorrow?" Paul asked as he entered Karl's office. "Have you arranged for the place to be watched?"

"No, I'm an amateur at this," Karl said. "I thought I'd just roll over and do exactly what they want."

"Sorry," Paul said, flinging himself into a chair. "I'm just worried about the kid."

"We can only do so much until we get her back. We've got away with outsmarting them before."

"Do you think this Flynn bloke will turn up tomorrow?"

"Don't worry about him. We'll catch up with him in Dublin." Karl walked over to the drink's cabinet. "Want one?"

Paul nodded. "From what I've heard," Paul said as he reached for the glass, "this Patrick Flynn seems to be a pretty elusive bloke."

"What do you mean, elusive?"

"Well, nobody seems to know much about him. His neighbours say he's rarely at home. He doesn't mix much. He has a wife, though. They say she's friendly enough."

Karl sat. "Do we know much about her?"

"Not really. Her name's Charlotte. She's a pretty blonde, according to the bloke across the street. I got the impression he fancies her." Paul delved into his pocket and retrieved a photograph. "I managed to get into the house through the kitchen window. I found this photograph of the happy couple on their wedding day." He handed it to Karl. "Anybody look familiar?"

Karl stared at the picture for a few seconds. The colour in his cheeks visibly draining as the veins in his neck pulsated.

"That's the girl who came here to visit Erica for a few days," he said. "That's Charlotte."

Paul smirked. "So, she's not as innocent as she would have you believe. Charlotte and her husband are in this up to their necks. What about him? Do you recognise Patrick?"

Karl shook his head. "No, I never met him. I bet he was

involved when she tried to burn my clubs down."

"What about Joe? Do you think he's involved as well?"

"Joe? What makes you ask that?"

"That's him in the photograph, isn't it? Standing next to Erica?"

Karl nodded but said nothing. Paul studied his employer. "Maybe they're still in touch."

Karl frowned and lit a cigar. "I wouldn't think so. Charlotte lives in Ireland."

"But don't you think it all looks suspicious, Joe running Jonny Dalton's old place just a few hundred yards from the Amethyst? Something's definitely not right."

"Don't worry about Joe," Karl said. "I'll deal with him in good time. There are more important things to be dealt with first."

"Such as?"

"I want you to go over to the Amethyst and have a word with Marco."

"What's Marco been doing?" Paul said. "Don't tell me he's been helping himself to the takings?"

"No, it's nothing like that. I asked him to keep an eye on Alex and let me know what he gets up to."

"You think Alex is hiding something?"

Karl took a sip of his drink. "I hope not, but there's something about that boy I still don't trust. I've felt that since day one."

"You're taking a big chance then, Karl, giving him the Amethyst."

Karl shrugged. "Let's hope he proves me wrong."

Paul walked towards the door. "Do you want me to go over to Manchester now?"

"No, it can wait until tomorrow. You go home and get some kip. You've done enough for one day."

Paul yawned. "Okay, I am feeling whacked."

"I'll see you later." Karl sighed, reached for his bottle of pain killers and a fresh glass of whisky.

86

Alex was about to put down the receiver when he heard Katie's familiar voice.

"Alex?"

"Katie, it's me. Are you okay?"

"Yes, of course. What do you want?"

Alex sighed. "I… I just wanted to say how sorry I was for the other night. I behaved very badly. Too much to drink, I suppose."

"You hurt me."

"I know, and I'm sorry. I promise I'll never do anything like that again. I want to make it up to you. Am I forgiven?"

"I suppose so," she said.

"Can I see you tonight? I thought we could go to the casino. This could be my lucky night."

"What time?"

"I'll pick you up at eleven."

"I'll be waiting. But shouldn't you be working at the Amethyst tonight?"

"Fuck the Amethyst. That's taken care of."

"All right," Katie said quietly. "I'll see you at eleven."

Katie put down the receiver and turned to her companion. "That was Alex," she said. "It looks like we're back on."

"Good. We need to hurry things along. Do you think you can do that?"

"Of course I can. He doesn't need any encouragement from me to spend his dad's cash." She chuckled. "It's like taking candy from a baby."

"Just be careful, Katie. You've seen what a vicious little bastard he can be."

"I'm not scared of him, Joe, not when I've got you to protect me."

Joe smiled. "You'd better hurry up and get ready. He'll be here soon."

She climbed out of bed and walked towards the bathroom.

"Can I come round to yours afterwards?"

"No, I want you to stick with the plan and stay with Alex."

"But, Joe, I—"

"Katie, do as I say," Joe said. "There'll be time for fun when this is all over."

87

Cavendish Cottage was a modest dwelling on the edge of the North Yorkshire Moors. It was nothing like the splendour of Sir Anthony Howard-Cleeve's manor house on the outskirts of Leeds. It was here, at the cottage, that Sir Anthony chose to spend his weekends, and any free time he may have, away from his parliamentary duties. It was here he could submit to his inner demons, his darkest fantasies.

The girl had been brought to him earlier that day. A pretty little thing with an unmistakable flash of defiance in her dark-brown eyes. What pleasure he would get to knock that out of her, to make her submissive to his every whim, he grinned.

Sir Anthony climbed down the stone steps and drew back the heavy bolts securing the cellar door. The girl was lying on the mattress in the corner of the room. On seeing him, she struggled to her feet and tried to distance herself, but the chain around her ankle prevented her from moving more than a couple of feet.

"Calm down." Sir Anthony walked towards her. "I'm not going to hurt you, not if you're a good girl and do exactly what I tell you to do."

"Let me go," she whimpered. "Please, I'm begging you." Tears ran down her cheeks as her body trembled beneath her thin cotton dress.

Reaching out, he cupped her head in his hands. "No, I'm not going to let you go," he said. "I'm going to take you upstairs and bathe you. If you behave well, I will let you eat at the table. Maybe I'll even give you a little wine. Would you like that?" He ran his fingers through her long, unruly hair. "After that, my dear…" He laughed. "After that, we're going to have a little fun." He bent and tried to kiss her on the mouth. The girl spat at him and attempted to claw at his face.

"Get away from me," she screamed. "Get away."

Sir Anthony brought back his right hand and hit her hard across the face. "We can do this the easy way," he said, "or we can do it the hard way. It's up to you. But you will do as I say.

I can promise you that."

He took out a key from his jacket pocket and unlocked the padlock, releasing the chain. "Now, my dear," he said, "let's go upstairs and make ourselves a little more comfortable."

Standing behind her, Sir Anthony held the girl's upper arms as he forced her up the cellar steps. "Up we go." He grinned and pushed her forward. "That's a good girl." She slowly ascended the steps. "By the way, what's your name? I wasn't told."

The girl remained silent.

"I asked you a question." Sir Anthony increased the pressure on the girl's arms. "I don't want to have to repeat myself."

"Katya," she said meekly. "My name is Katya."

88

Joe arrived at the casino at ten-thirty. He was surprised to see Sarah drinking alone at the bar. "Hi," he greeted. "This is a nice surprise. It's good to see you again."

She smiled and swung her revolving seat around to face him. "I fancied a drink," she said. "Would you care to join me?"

"I'll do better than that. Why don't you come upstairs to my private quarters and we can get something to eat?"

Sarah shook her head. "No thanks," she said. "I'm not hungry."

"Of course you are. I'll get some Chinese or Italian food brought up. What do you say?"

She shrugged as she drank the remainder of the vodka. "All right, I suppose so." She slid off the chair and grabbed Joe's arm for support.

"How much have you had to drink?" Joe asked.

She giggled. "I've just had a couple."

"Come on, let's go up to my flat. I'll make you some strong coffee."

"I don't want coffee. I want vodka."

Joe put his arm firmly around her waist and guided her towards the staircase leading to his private apartment.

"This is nice," she said once Joe had deposited her on the couch. "You've got good taste, or was it your wife who chose the furnishings?"

"No, it was all me," Joe said as he took out the menu for the local Chinese takeaway. "What do you fancy to eat?" he asked, scrutinising the menu. There was silence. "Sarah, I said…" Joe turned to see Sarah fast asleep. He lifted her legs gently onto to couch and covered her with a throw. "That's right," he whispered as he kissed her lightly on the cheek. "You stay here and sleep."

Alex and Katie got to the casino shortly after eleven o'clock. Alex cashed a cheque for one thousand pounds and took his chips straight over to the roulette table. "A kiss for luck," he said, pulling Katie towards him. "What's your lucky number, babe?"

Katie shrugged. "I don't really have one."

"Come on, Katie, surely you have a lucky number. Everyone does."

"What's yours? I'll have the same as you."

"Really? Then I'll put all the chips on number eleven. That rarely lets me down."

Five people were at the roulette table as the croupier spun the wheel and released the ball. After a few seconds, the wheel came to a halt.

"The winning number is thirty. There are no winners." The croupier expertly removed all the chips from the table.

"Fuck," Alex spat. "That's just next door."

"What do you mean, next door? Number thirty is near the bottom of the table."

"It's next door on the wheel, you stupid bitch," Alex said. "Wait here. I'll get more chips."

He walked over to the cash booth and spoke to the man behind the screen. A few minutes later, he was back at the table, a broad grin on his face and a large pile of chips in his hand.

"You've got more chips?" Katie asked.

"I've got another three thousand."

"But, Alex, don't you think—?"

He grinned. "Don't worry about it. I can win back everything I've lost in just one spin of the wheel."

By one o'clock, Alex had made two further visits to the cash booth. His losses were mounting.

"I'm sorry, sir," the cashier said, "I'm not able to extend your credit any further this evening. The management would like to speak with you."

"What the fuck's going on?" Alex said. "What do you mean, you can't extend my credit?"

"If you'll come with me, sir."

Alex reluctantly followed the cashier up the side stairs to

the office. Matthew Glendenning was behind the large oak desk. "Good evening," Matthew said. "Would you like a drink, Mr Maddox?"

Alex glared at him as he flounced into one of the two large chairs in front of the desk and took out a cigarette. "Whisky," he said. "Make it a large one." Matthew nodded to the cashier, who promptly poured the drink and handed it to Alex.

"Your debt to this casino seems to be rising, Mr Maddox," Matthew said, studying the paperwork in front of him. "According to my records, you are thirty thousand pounds in the red."

Alex flung back his head and downed the whisky. "Don't worry, mate, you'll get your money."

"I know that," Matthew said, "but when will I get my money, that's what I want to know?"

"Soon. You'll get your money soon. You know I'm good for it."

Matthew stared at Alex. "I know nothing of the sort."

"I own the Amethyst club. Surely you've heard of that?"

"Yes, of course I've heard of it."

"Well then, I own it, so your money's safe. Right?"

"Not quite, Mr Maddox or do you mind if I call you, Alex? As far as I am aware, the Amethyst is owned by your father, Karl Maddox."

Alex smirked. "Not anymore it isn't. Karl signed the Amethyst over to me."

"Are you saying you are the outright owner of the club?"

"That's exactly what I'm saying."

"In that case," Matthew said, pushing a sheet of paper across the desk towards Alex. "I will need you to sign this document."

"Eh? What sort of document?"

"It's a declaration agreeing to put up the Amethyst as collateral against your gambling debts with this casino."

"Fuck off. I'm not doing that," Alex said. "You can't ask me to do that."

"But I am asking you, Alex. In fact, if you want to extend

your credit, I'm insisting that's what you do."

Alex shrugged. "All right," he said, "if that's what it takes. Now, can I get on with my evening?"

"Yes of course, once you've signed the document."

Alex gave the document a cursory glance before signing it.

89

Joe had been nervous to find Sarah in the casino. He knew Alex and Katie would be arriving shortly, and the last thing he needed was for Sarah to see her husband. He watched over her for a couple of hours as she lay sleeping on the couch. A sweet, beautiful woman, he thought, totally wasted on Alex Maddox. Eventually, satisfied that Sarah was in a deep sleep, he went through to Matthew's office.

"Well?" he asked. "Did you get him to sign?"

"Of course he signed." Matthew grinned, handing the sheet of paper to Joe.

"How much does he owe?"

"Just over thirty thousand."

Joe frowned. "We need to get it higher than that if our plan's going to succeed. Karl paid Jonny Dalton forty grand when Alex got in trouble last time."

"Don't worry. Now that Alex is back with Katie, she'll do her magic."

"I hope so."

"By the way, Joe, Charlotte rang. She seemed upset. She's coming over tomorrow."

"I had lunch with her earlier." Joe frowned. "She was in a bit of a state."

"I wonder what's wrong?"

"I'm worried about her, to be honest. She arranged to meet up with Christina Maddox."

"Why would she do that?"

Joe shrugged. "They'd formed some sort of brief friendship when Christina was working as Bunny."

"I wouldn't have thought Charlotte would have anything in common with Karl's daughter."

"Neither would I. That's why I rang Marion and asked her if anything is bothering Charlotte."

"What did she say?" Matthew said.

"Marion said there was some tension between her and Patrick. He promised they would spend time together, but he's been working most of the time."

Matthew shrugged. "Well, it's none of our business, I suppose. By the way, Joe, who's that pretty redhead I saw you taking up to your flat earlier?"

"That pretty redhead is Sarah Maddox, Alex's wife."

"Shit, you've got to be kidding me."

Joe smiled. "Sarah's all right. She's a nice girl."

"She might be, but she could blow the lid off our operation if she finds out what we're up to."

"Relax, Matthew. That's not going to happen."

"What's not going to happen?"

Both men turned to see Sarah standing in the doorway. She yawned. "I haven't interrupted anything, have I?"

"No... no of course not." Joe walked towards her. "We were just... just talking business."

"Well, it's late. I think it's time I was going home. Alex will be wondering where I am."

"I'll drive you," Joe said. "My car's round the back, or—"
"Or what?"

"You could stay here for the night. It's up to you."

90

Access to Cavendish Cottage was gained down a muddy, overgrown lane. Luke had been to the cottage a couple of times to deliver girls to Sir Anthony. It was almost midnight when Luke parked the van at the top of the lane. Beside him was Ken, a thick-set man of about thirty, and in the back of the van was a teenage girl. She was distressed and crying softly. Her hands were bound with tie wraps, and she had a bag over her head.

"Shut that fucking noise up," Luke said as the two men got out of the van. He turned to Ken. "Grab the girl and follow me."

The three made their way through the undergrowth to the cottage. Luke lifted a plant pot by the door and withdrew a key. "Stupid bastard," he said as he put the key into the lock and entered the small hallway.

Downstairs was in darkness, but Luke could hear noises coming from upstairs. "You stay down here with her," he whispered. "I'll tell you when to bring her up." He made his way quietly up the stairs. There was a light beneath the door at the top and he could hear murmured voices from within. He slowly opened the door.

A large bed with a wrought iron headboard was directly across from the door. Lying face down and spread-eagled on the bed was a young girl. She was naked with her wrists and ankles tied with leather cuffs. The girl was whimpering like an injured animal. A ball gag had been placed in her mouth, preventing her from screaming. Luke could see red, swollen welt marks across her back and buttocks. Standing next to the bed was the naked Sir Anthony Howard-Cleeve, a leather whip in his hand.

He turned to face Luke as he came into the room. His eyes widened. "What the hell? What do you want?"

"I need the girl," Luke said, walking towards the bed.

"No, you can't do that," Sir Anthony said, placing himself between Luke and the girl. "I've paid for her, and she's mine for the week."

"Not anymore she isn't," Luke said as he pushed past Anthony and undid the cuffs. "She has to come with me. Where are her clothes?"

"Clothes?"

"Yes, clothes. I can't take her out looking like this."

"I don't know. She has a dress somewhere."

"Never mind, this will do," Luke said, picking up a white shirt from the floor.

"You can't take that, it's mine."

"Not anymore it isn't."

Luke removed the gag from her mouth before handing her the shirt. "Put this on," he said. He walked onto the landing. "Bring her up," he shouted. He turned to face Sir Anthony. "Don't worry, I've brought you another girl. The boss says you can have her for a couple more days for free." Ken came up the stairs and roughly pushed the girl into the room. "There you go." Luke grinned. "This one's all yours."

Luke grabbed Katya by the arm and steered her towards the stairs. "You're going home," he whispered in her ear. "Aren't you a lucky girl?"

91

It was two o'clock in the morning when Karl got the call.

"Be at the church at the bottom of King Street in one hour," the caller said.

"Let me speak to her," Karl said. "I want to know she's all right."

"One hour," the caller said, "and make sure you bring the right laptop this time."

Karl put down the receiver. "They want to exchange," he said to Peter and Paul who were both lounging in his office. "One hour, outside the church on King Street."

"I know it," Paul said. "Do you want me to go there now, boss, and—?"

Karl shook his head. "No, let's just get her back safely. I think the poor kid's been through enough, don't you?"

Paul shrugged and remained seated.

Peter walked towards the door. "I'll let Dad know," he said. "He'll want to be there."

Karl's eyes narrowed. "No, not yet," he said. "We don't know what those bastards have done to her. She might need—"

"Need what?"

"She might need medical attention. I'll give Alex a call and ask him to come over."

Paul brought his fist crashing down on the table. "If they've hurt her, I'll…"

"Steady on, Paul. Keep calm," Karl said. "There'll be time for that when she's safe."

Peter frowned. "I still think we should tell Dad."

Karl sighed heavily. "We'll tell Victor soon enough, but I'm going to handle this my way."

"But Karl—"

"Make yourself useful and get my pills off the shelf," Karl said.

Paul frowned. "You should go back to the doctor," he said, handing the pills to Karl, along with a glass of whisky. "They should be able to do something to ease the pain."

"They can. They want to operate again."

"So what's the problem?" Paul said. "You can't go on taking pills forever."

Karl swallowed the pills and drank half the whisky. "You're starting to sound like Lisa."

"Seriously, Karl," Paul said, "why not get it seen to properly?"

Karl was silent for a moment. "It's my heart," he said. "Any operation can be risky with my heart condition."

Paul frowned. "I thought that was fixed."

"I have a pacemaker, but that doesn't fix the problem," Karl said. "It just makes it more manageable."

"Well, if you ask me, I think it's worth taking the risk if it means being pain-free."

Karl drained the whisky from his glass. "I'm going to hang on a bit longer until I get this business sorted," he said. "Then I'll think about having the operation." He got up from his chair and headed towards the door, carrying the computer under his arm. "I'd better be going. I don't want to keep that smarmy little bastard waiting."

"Are you sure you don't want Peter or me to come with you?" Paul said.

Karl shook his head. "All they want is this laptop, and all I want is Katya. It should be straightforward."

Paul frowned. "Ok, Karl, but be careful. You don't know what they could have planned."

92

King Street was deserted when Karl pulled up outside the church. He had been there less than five minutes when a white van drew up on the other side of the road. The driver climbed out and walked towards Karl's vehicle.

Karl lowered his window. "Where's the girl?" he said.

"She's here," Luke said. "Where's the laptop?"

Karl reached over to the front passenger seat and picked it up. "Bring me the girl," he said.

Luke signalled and within seconds, the side door was slid open. Ken jumped out and pulled Katya onto the street. Holding her firmly by the arm, he steered her towards Karl's vehicle.

Karl climbed out of his car, holding the laptop. He handed it to Luke while reaching out and taking Katya's hand.

"It'd better be the right one this time," Luke said. "No funny business like before."

He placed the laptop on the bonnet of Karl's Mercedes and tapped in the password. The computer immediately sprang into life. "Well, it seems all right," he said, "but if we find it's been tampered with in any way…"

"It's just as I found it," Karl said. "Now, I think our business is done."

Karl helped Katya into the back of the vehicle. Her face was pale and streaked with tears, and her long black hair was tangled. Luke walked towards the van and then stopped and turned to face Karl. "Nice doing business with you," he said. "Maybe I'll see you again sometime."

"You can count on that," Karl said as his Mercedes sprang into life. "And a lot sooner than you think."

93

Alex had been annoyed to receive the call from Paul. He was feeling confident as he began to recoup some of his losses at the roulette table.

"Oh, you can't go yet, Alex," Katie said when he told her he had to leave. "Your luck has just started to come back, babe."

Alex grinned and kissed her lightly on the cheek. "There's only one way to find out," he said, placing all of his chips on the black. "If black comes up, we're back in the money."

The croupier spun the wheel. The ball clattered from one section of the wheel to the other. "Thirty-six red," she said, scooping all of Alex's chips away.

Alex sighed heavily. "I knew I should have backed red."

"Never mind, darling," Katie said, nuzzling his ear. "There's always another night."

Alex frowned. "I suppose so," he said. "I'd better go. The old man requires my presence."

"Did he say what was wrong?"

Alex shrugged. "Karl, confide in me? Don't make me laugh. He trusts those two goons that hang around him more than he trusts his own son."

"I'm sure that's not true, Alex, but I suppose you'd better get over to Leeds. You don't want to keep him waiting."

"Get your coat, and I'll drop you off on the way."

"I was thinking of staying on here a little longer," Katie said. "Have a couple more drinks, maybe."

Alex grabbed her arm. "No, I don't think that's a good idea," he said.

Katie whimpered as she struggled to release his grip. "Alex, you're hurting me."

Alex let go of her arm immediately. "Sorry, Katie," he said. "I didn't mean to. I..."

"Okay, I'll leave if it makes you happy, but I really don't like it when you get jealous."

"Jealous? I'm not jealous," Alex said. "I'm just concerned,

that's all. You're too trusting, and there are some shady characters in here. I don't want you to come to any harm, that's all."

"That's very sweet," Katie said as she kissed him lightly on the cheek. "But I'm a big girl now. I can take care of myself."

"I'd still prefer it if you left with me."

"All right, if that's what you want."

"It is."

94

Karl was back at the Emerald by half-past three that morning. Peter and Paul were waiting anxiously in the car park. They both rushed forward as Karl's Mercedes came to a halt. Peter opened the rear door and picked Katya up in his arms, kissing her lightly on the cheek.

"You're safe now, Katya," he said. "Nobody can hurt you again." The girl smiled weakly but said nothing as tears rolled down her cheeks.

"Let's get her inside," Paul said. "Alex is waiting in the office."

All three men ascended the private staircase leading to Karl's office, with Peter gently carrying Katya in his arms.

"Put her on the couch," Alex said. "Then, you can all leave while I examine my patient."

Karl and Paul were in the deserted VIP lounge when Alex joined them twenty minutes later.

"Well?" Paul said. "How is she?"

Alex poured himself a large whisky before he answered. "She's traumatised," he said. "She's been abused for days by those bastards."

"Will she be all right?"

Alex shrugged. "Physically, I suppose, but mentally, who knows?"

Paul moved forward. "Can I see her?" he said. "Can I talk to her?"

"I've given her something to make her sleep," Alex said. "She'll be out for a few hours."

Paul sat back on the couch, his head in his hands. "Peter's gone to fetch Dad," he said. "He can take her back to his house. She can rest there."

"We need to talk to her first," Karl said. "We must find out where she was being held."

Paul sat bolt upright. "No," he said. "Katya's been through enough. She needs to forget about what's happened."

Karl banged his fist on the table. "She can forget her own bloody name as far as I'm concerned." Karl turned angrily to face Paul. "After she tells me all she knows about these bastards."

Paul shook his head. "We can find them without involving Katya."

"Are you prepared to let what's happened to your cousin go unpunished?" Karl said. "Is that the sort of son Victor raised?"

"No, it is not," boomed a voice from the open doorway. Startled, everyone turned to see Victor, a thunderous look on his face, standing in the aperture. "Where is she?" he said. "Where is my Katya?"

Karl walked towards his friend and shook his hand. "She's through here," he said leading the way to the office.

Katya was lying on the couch, covered by a woollen throw. Her breathing was shallow and even, with just a hint of colour in her cheeks.

"The kid's had a rough time," Karl whispered, "but Alex says there's no permanent damage as far as he can tell."

Victor walked over to the sleeping girl and knelt down at the side of the couch. "She looks a lot like her mother when she was young," he said as he gently pushed strands of hair from her face. "I begged my sister to come to England with her brothers and me, but she wouldn't. She was in love with Katya's father and wanted to stay with him in Romania."

"Let's go through to the lounge and have a drink," Karl said. "I'll fill you in on what I know about these bastards."

Victor followed Karl into the VIP lounge, leaving Paul keeping vigil at Katya's side.

"Anything I can do, Karl?" Victor said when Karl had finished relaying the events of the last couple of days. "Jan and Erik are ready to help too. Just tell us what you want us to do."

"Nothing for now," Karl said, "but we'll make our move soon, Victor. Just make sure you and your brothers are ready."

"Don't worry," Victor said. He smiled. "It will be like old

times, eh, Karl?"

"Yes, my friend," Karl said. "Just like old times."

95

Karl woke with a start. He had fallen asleep on one of the couches in the VIP lounge, as had Victor and Peter. It was a few seconds before he realised it was the shrill ringing of his mobile that had woken him. He sat up and reached for his phone.

Yawning, he answered. "Yeah?" he said.

"Karl, it's Lisa."

"What do you want, Lisa? I'm busy."

"Harry's here at the house."

Karl sat upright in his chair. "Delaney? Put him on."

"I think you'd better come here. Harry's really scared. He thinks he's being followed."

"Okay, tell him I'll be there in about twenty minutes," Karl said. "Make sure to lock the doors." Karl ended the call and shook Peter. "Wake up, mate," he whispered. "Come on, I've got a job for you."

Peter rubbed his eyes and yawned. "What time is it?"

"Half-five," Karl said. "We have to get over to my house quick."

Paul, who had been watching Katya in the office, walked into the room. "What's up?" he said.

"I have to get over to mine," Karl said. "Harry Delaney's there. He thinks he's been followed."

Paul frowned. "Do you want me to come with you?"

"No, I'm taking Peter. You stay with Katya and your dad. I should be back soon."

"Okay," Paul said. "Be careful with this Delaney bloke. We don't know that much about him. He could be a nutcase for all we know."

Karl reached for his coat. "Is Alex still here?"

Paul nodded. "Yeah, he's sleeping in the night watchman's office."

"Well, get him up and check on Katya," Karl said. "Peter and I will be back soon."

Half an hour later, Karl pulled onto the drive of Maddox

Mansion. He turned to Peter. "You wait in the car," he said. "This won't take long." He walked up to the front door, but it was locked. He fumbled in his coat pocket for the key when the door was opened from the inside by Lisa.

"Thank goodness you're here," she said.

"Where is he?" Karl said as he pushed past her.

"He's in the kitchen. I've just made some coffee."

Karl rushed into the kitchen. "Well?" he said. "What have you got to tell me?"

Harry Delaney was a handsome man in his early forties with an expensive tan and sun-bleached hair. It was obvious that he paid more than a frequent visit to the gym as his upper arms strained against his crisp white shirt. "I… I think I was followed," Harry said. "Two men in a white van."

Karl walked over to the window and pushed the blinds to one side. "There's no white van out there," he said. "Are you sure you're not imagining it?"

Harry paced nervously around the kitchen. "I know what I saw. I was being followed. I'm telling you."

"If you were, they've gone now," Karl said.

Harry adjusted and readjusted his tie. "You've got to believe me," he said. "I had no idea what my lorries were being used for. I only—"

"I'm not interested in what you don't know," Karl said and moved closer to him. "I want to know everything you do know. Do you hear me?"

Harry backed away towards the sink.

"You're shaking," Lisa said, handing Harry a mug. "I've made you a coffee. Drink it, and you'll feel better."

"He hasn't got time to drink fucking coffee," Karl said.

"Karl, Harry's upset, you can see that."

Harry took the mug and began to sip the contents.

"I'm waiting," Karl said. "I don't have all day."

Harry took a deep breath. When he spoke, his voice was shaky. "It all started about four years ago. That's when I first met him."

"Met who?"

"The Irishman. One of my drivers, Albi Kolkovsky, introduced us."

"What was the Irishman's name?"

Harry shrugged. "I don't know his proper name. He said to call him Paddy."

Karl scowled. "Paddy?"

"Paddy said he would guarantee a thousand pounds every trip if I let him have access to my vehicles the night before they left to go across the Channel."

"What were they hiding in your vehicles?"

Harry shrugged. "You know, booze, fags, the usual stuff. Everybody's doing it, so I thought, why not me? It was easy money." Harry took a sip of his coffee. "My lorries made at least one trip a week, sometimes two."

"Did you ever see this contraband?"

Harry shook his head. "No. The stuff was put in the vehicles while they were in Calais, and he always paid me the cash up front."

"What do you know about Paddy?"

"He lives in Ireland. Dublin, I think. We got talking one night over a few beers."

"But surely he's got a place in England?" Karl said.

Harry shook his head. "If he has, he never took me there."

"You must have met him somewhere?"

"You mean the warehouse?"

Karl grabbed Harry by the shoulders. "Of course I mean the fucking warehouse," he said. "Where is it?"

Harry attempted to move away from Karl. "It's in Leeds," he said, "but it's abandoned now. It was ready for demolition the last time I was there."

"What was kept in this warehouse?" Karl said.

"What do you mean?"

"Well, was it booze and fags, or was it girls?"

"I didn't see any girls. I've told you that. I'm as shocked about that as you are."

"So, there were just boxes of fags and booze?"

Harry frowned. "I didn't see any boxes either. There was

just the van. I assumed that's what he used to transport the contraband after my vehicles brought them over the Channel."

"Where exactly is this warehouse?" Karl said. "I need to see it."

"It's in Chapeltown," Harry said, "but it was in a bad state. The roof was leaking and—"

"Show me," Karl said. "Take me there now."

Harry shrugged. "Okay," he said, "but you're wasting your time if you think you'll find Paddy there."

"It's my time to waste," Karl said as he walked towards the door. "Come on, hurry up, we don't have all day."

96

Karl scowled as he pulled the car up outside an old warehouse in Chapeltown. "Is this it?" he said. "It looks abandoned."

"I told you it was," Harry said. "There's a door round the side."

Karl and Peter climbed out of the car. "Come on, Delaney," Karl said. "You too."

Reluctantly, Harry got out of the car and led the way to the side entrance. Karl shook the heavy padlock on the door. "Peter, fetch the bolt cutters," he said. "We should be able to get this open without much trouble."

Peter returned a few seconds later with bolt cutters. It took just a few seconds for the padlock to be released.

"After you," Karl said to Harry.

The inside of the building was just as Harry had described. The slate roof was in a bad state of repair and pigeons were roosting in the eaves.

"Like I told you," Harry said. "There's nothing here."

Karl frowned. "Then why did Paddy meet you here? There must have been something important about this place."

"He probably used it as a garage for the van."

Karl shrugged. "Maybe," he said, "or maybe there's something here that we're not seeing."

Karl walked cautiously around the building, stepping over piles of rubbish as he did so.

"Bit of a wild goose chase, don't you think, boss?" Peter said. "Whatever was here is long gone."

"Then why the need for a padlock when there's nothing here to protect?" Karl walked over to a pile of cardboard boxes neatly stacked along the far wall of the building. "Peter, come here a minute and give me a hand," he said and pushed the boxes away.

"Christ, Karl, I don't believe it," Peter said. "It looks like a trap door."

Karl tugged on the ring in the centre of the steel plate. Slowly the plate opened up revealing a stone staircase. "You stay here," Karl said. "I'll see what the bastards have been hiding."

Karl descended the staircase into the gloom. The air smelt damp and acrid. There was no light source, so he took out his phone and turned on the torch. "Fucking hell," he said, looking around the room. "Peter, come and look at this."

Peter joined Karl. Six bare mattresses were piled up, and a series of chains were fastened to the walls. A small plastic table with two benches sat in the centre of the room, and a couple of buckets that had been used as toilets were in the far corner.

"It looks like we've found where they kept the girls destined for Leeds," Karl said. "But there's no sign of the bastards responsible."

"Do you think this is where Katya was held?"

Karl shrugged. "Probably," he said as he walked back to the stairs, followed closely by Peter.

Back in the warehouse, Karl looked around and frowned. "Where's Delaney?" he said. "Don't say the stupid bastard's made a run for it?"

Peter rushed over to the far side of the building. "Over here, Karl," he said. "It's Delaney."

Harry Delaney lay in a crumpled heap on top of a pile of garbage, blood was pouring from a gaping wound to his neck.

"So, the poor bastard was right," Karl said as he joined Peter. "He was being followed."

Peter rushed over to the door and looked out. The street was deserted. "Whoever it was, they've gone now," he said. "What are we going to do with him?"

Karl stared at the lifeless body of Harry Delaney. "Leave him," Karl said. "There's nothing anyone can do for him now."

Peter shrugged. "Okay, but we have to get out of here, Karl."

They had been driving for a few minutes in silence before Peter spoke. "What are you going to tell Lisa? She'll ask after Delaney."

Karl frowned. "Don't worry about her. Lisa knows when to keep her mouth shut."

"Okay, Karl, if you say so. Do you want me to take you home?"

"No, I'll go over to the Emerald first. Katya should be awake by now. I need to speak with her."

97

Charlotte arrived at the casino just before noon. Matthew and Joe were in Joe's flat when she arrived.

Matthew walked over to her and kissed her lightly on the cheek. "Hi, Charlotte," he said. "I'm sorry I missed you yesterday."

She smiled. "How was your mother? Do you know when she'll be coming home?"

Matthew shrugged as he helped Charlotte take off her coat. "The doctors say it will just take time. I just have to be patient."

Joe came over to Charlotte and hugged her. "Are you feeling any better? You didn't seem yourself yesterday," he said.

Charlotte looked away. "I'm sorry about that, Joe. I was a bit of a cow, wasn't I?"

Joe put his arm protectively around her shoulder as he guided her to the couch. "Are you ready to tell me what's upset you so much?" he said. "I can't believe Patrick's unfaithful. He seemed totally devoted to you."

Charlotte sat on the couch and sighed. "I don't know what to think," she said. "All I know is he's definitely up to something."

Matthew raised an eyebrow. "What makes you say that?"

"It's hard to explain really," she said. "It's lots of little things."

"Such as?"

"A couple of days before we left Ireland there was a message left on the answerphone. The message had been meant for Patrick. It was from a bank in Switzerland, apologising for the network being temporarily down and confirming that the money had been received."

"What did Patrick say about it?" Joe said. "I presume you did ask him?"

Charlotte shook her head. "No," she said. "I deleted the message so he wouldn't know I'd heard it."

"Did you know Patrick had an account in Switzerland?"

"No. Patrick never discusses finances with me."

Joe lit a cigarette. "You said there were other things?"

"Yes. A couple of weeks ago he told me he had been in France with a client."

Joe frowned. "And you don't believe him?"

"It was when I was getting his suit ready to go to the dry-cleaners I found a restaurant receipt for the time he was away," she said. "The restaurant was in Bulgaria."

"Bulgaria?" Matthew said. "Are you sure?"

She nodded. "Yes, of course I'm sure."

"I don't suppose you still have the receipt?" Matthew said and poured three glasses of wine.

"No. I threw it away."

Matthew handed Joe and Charlotte a glass. "Do you know any of Patrick's clients?"

Charlotte shook her head. "No. Patrick insists on keeping business out of the home. He always has."

"You've never seen him in the company of anyone who looked... suspicious or who made you feel uneasy?"

"No, I don't think so. Oh, there was one man who came to the house a few weeks ago. I didn't care for him much. Patrick didn't seem pleased to see him either and took him straight into his study."

"Can you remember the man's name or what he looked like?"

She pondered for a few seconds. "I think... no I'm certain his name was Luke."

Matthew frowned. "His name was definitely Luke?"

"Yes. I remember thinking at the time he would have been quite good looking, but there was something sinister about him that made me feel uneasy."

"Did you say anything to Patrick?"

"No. It was late when Luke came to the house, so I went to bed and left them alone. The next morning Patrick left early, so Luke was never mentioned."

"Did he—?"

"Matthew, for goodness sake, you're not a policeman now," Joe said. "You sound like you're conducting an interview."

Matthew shrugged, smiling. "Sorry," he said. "Asking questions is a habit, I guess."

"By the way," Joe said, "did you meet Christina last night?"

Charlotte nodded, smiling. "Yes, it was lovely to see her again. We went to that new bistro that's opened up. Some of her staff from the salon came too."

Matthew grinned. "So, it was a girls' night out, eh? That must have been fun?"

"Well, sort of I suppose," Charlotte said, "but one of the girls claimed she'd been trafficked from Romania. Can you believe that?"

Matthew sat bolt upright in his chair. "Are you sure about that, Charlotte?"

"Of course I'm sure. Her name was Nadia. She said she had managed to escape and make her way to Leeds to be with her sister Sophia. Sophia works in Christina's salon."

Matthew frowned. "Did you believe her?"

"Of course I believed her," Charlotte said. "Nadia had a green tattoo on the back of her wrist. She said the traffickers had put the same mark on all of the girls."

"What sort of green mark?"

"Christina said it was a three-leaf clover, but it wasn't a clover at all. It was definitely a shamrock."

98

Katya and Victor sat on the couch, drinking coffee, as Karl got back to the Emerald, and walked into his office. "How are you feeling?" he asked. He could see by her pale complexion and dark shadows underneath her eyes that she was far from well.

She smiled weakly. "I'm all right," she said. "Thank you for helping to get me away from those men."

"Oh, you're very welcome," Karl said, sitting on the couch next to the girl. "Now, Katya, I want to ask you some questions about—"

Victor clasped his hands tightly. "Can't this wait until she's feeling better?" he said. "Don't you think the poor kid's been through enough?"

Karl shook his head. "No, Victor. I'm afraid it can't wait."

"It's all right, Uncle Victor," Katya said. "I want to help find them."

"Good girl," Karl said. "I need you to tell me everything you can remember, from the time you left Romania to when you were rescued. Do you think you can do that?"

She nodded and gripped Victor's hand tightly. "I remember Ivan offering me a coffee from his flask. I must have passed out because the next thing I remember was being in a cellar with other girls." She leant over and put the coffee cup onto the table.

"Go on," Karl said. "What happened next?"

"We were drugged and put into a lorry. The next thing I remember was being taken out of the lorry and pushed into the back of a van. One of the girls said we were in England." She trembled as tears rolled down her cheeks.

"That's enough," Victor said, placing his arms protectively around the girl's shoulders.

Karl ignored Victor's protest. "What happened to the other girls in the van?" he said. "Do you know where they went?"

"Nadia managed to get away. She was very brave."

"Yes, I know about Nadia. What about the others?"

"Three of the girls were taken out of the cellar by Luke. He said they were going to work in a house. I think he meant a brothel."

"What about you and the other girl that was left?"

"Anna? Luke said we were going to work in a club. Anna said it would be easy to escape from a club."

"What happened?"

"Luke came back to the cellar and said I was going to a special customer for a week. Then I would be going to the club to join Anna."

Karl frowned. "Do you know the name of the club Anna was taken to?"

Katya shook her head. "Only that it was in Manchester," she said.

"And you were taken to this special customer?"

She nodded. "Luke took me to a house, and I was locked in a cellar. Then the man who had bought me came and…"

"Take your time," Karl said. "Do you know who this man was that bought you?"

"I heard Luke call him Sir Anthony."

"Sir Anthony? Are you sure about that?"

She nodded. "Oh yes. I remember every detail. Everything that was said, everything that that pig did to me."

"I don't suppose you know where the house was?"

Katya frowned. "It was a small house in the country. I could see through the window that there were lots of trees."

"Is there anything else you can remember?"

"When Luke came to the house to collect me, he had another girl with him. He said Sir Anthony could keep her for a week instead of me."

"Who was the girl?" Karl asked.

"I don't know. I'd never seen her before."

"Could you identify this Sir Anthony if you saw him again?"

She nodded. "Oh, yes. I could pick him out of a line-up of a hundred men."

Victor stood up and helped Katya to her feet. "I'm taking her to my house now," he said. "She can be properly looked after there."

Karl nodded. "Okay, Victor. You take good care of her and don't worry, I'll find this Sir Anthony, whoever he is, and when I do…"

Victor glared at Karl and shook his head. "No, my friend," he said. "When you do, you tell me. I'll deal with him myself."

99

"Are you thinking what I'm thinking?" Joe said when Charlotte had left.

"I've never met Charlotte's husband. What's he like?"

"I've only met him a couple of times, but he seemed all right."

"You never thought he'd be mixed up in anything... dodgy?"

"For Christ's sake, Matthew, he's a solicitor. Of course he would."

Matthew grinned. "You don't have a very high opinion of the law, do you?"

"With good reason," Joe said. "Anyway, what are we going to do about Charlotte? If her husband's up to what we think he is, she could be in danger."

Matthew frowned. "I don't see what we can do. We don't really know anything for certain."

Joe drummed his fingers on the table. "She said the funeral is on Thursday, didn't she? I think I'll take a trip to Ireland and see for myself."

"Do you want me to come with you?" Matthew asked.

Joe shook his head. "No, it's best you stay here and deal with Alex. It's about time we started tightening the screw on him, don't you think?"

Matthew sighed. "Well, he's certainly running up quite a bill."

"Next time he comes in, start to come down heavy."

"Okay, if you think so. He owes nearly a hundred grand at the moment."

"Good. Katie's bringing him over tonight. We need to get his debt up to the two hundred grand before we can move forward."

Matthew grinned. "She's doing a good job, young Katie. I think she deserves a bonus."

"Not until she gets the job done."

"What's going on between you two anyway? She seems

smitten to me."

Joe laughed. "Katie's just a bit of fun, nothing serious."

Matthew shrugged. "Okay, if you say so. By the way, Joe, I've been going over the books. We've made a fantastic profit since we opened, much more than I expected."

"Even covering Alex's losses?"

"Yes. We've just about covered our start-up fees. I'm beginning to think this casino business isn't such a bad idea after all."

"Don't tell me you want to continue after we fleece Karl?"

"I couldn't get this return on my money with any other investment. What do you think? Are you in?"

"It wasn't in my five-year plan to run a casino," Joe said, "but I'll think about it."

100

Karl scanned the computer screen. "Sir Anthony Howard-Cleeve," he said. "Here's his profile. The bastard lives in North Yorkshire. Can you believe that?"

Paul frowned. "Are you absolutely sure he's the right bloke? You know what Dad's going to do when he catches up with him? We can't get it wrong."

"He's the right bloke," Karl said. "The description fits perfectly with what Katya gave. Send this through to Victor's computer for Katya to confirm."

Paul studied the screen. "He looks old," he said. "Old and tired."

"Not too old to abuse a young girl for days," Karl said. "This is the pervert who took Katya. He deserves everything that's coming to him." Karl poured himself a whisky before turning back to the screen. "I'm just sorry that I won't be there to see it. I think this is something Victor needs to handle on his own."

"Dad won't be on his own. There'll be me and Peter as well as Uncle Erik and Uncle Jan."

"Surely it's not going to take five of you to take out one fucking pervert?" Karl smirked.

"It's a matter of family honour. This man defiled Katya."

Karl frowned. "Remind me not to mess with your family," he said.

"That would be wise," Paul said. "That would be very wise."

It was a warm evening as Sir Anthony Howard-Cleeve stepped out into the street. He was looking forward to the short walk to his home from Beaumont House, the private gentlemen's club where he spent most evenings when he was in the City. The streets were almost deserted as he approached the crossing. He didn't notice the dark-blue people carrier parked across the street. He didn't notice it being driven slowly behind him, nor did he notice when it overtook him and came to a halt a few yards ahead.

Victor wound down the driver's window. "Excuse me," he said. "Could you direct me to Melrose Avenue, please?"

"Melrose Avenue?" Sir Anthony said as he stopped and leant towards the open car window. "I'm sorry, I haven't heard of it, I'm afraid."

"I was told it was in this area." Victor smiled. "Are you sure you…?"

Peter and Paul swiftly jumped out of the vehicle and grabbed hold of Sir Anthony. Paul placed a plastic carrier bag over his head and helped Peter haul him into the back of the vehicle. Sir Anthony struggled to get free as he began kicking out at his two assailants and wriggling violently. Paul sat on top of him as Peter bound his wrists with the tie wraps he had brought. Jan and Erik, who had been sitting up front with Victor, watched the proceedings in silence.

"Drive," Paul said. "Hurry up and get out of here."

It was early the next morning when the body of Sir Anthony Howard-Cleeve was found underneath a motorway bridge. Later, the pathologist would conclude that almost every bone in the old man's body had been broken.

101

Joe arrived at St Bede's Church just minutes before the coffin, carrying the body of Shamus Phelan Flynn, arrived. The church was almost full to capacity. Joe managed to get a seat towards the back. He caught a fleeting glance of Charlotte who was sitting with Patrick and Marion in a pew at the front of the church.

Halfway through the service, the priest called upon Patrick to say a few words about his father. Joe watched as the handsome twenty-something climbed into the pulpit and began his eulogy. Joe studied him closely. Patrick was articulate in his address as he spoke fondly of his father, Shamus. He frowned, wondering if such a man could really be involved with sex trafficking? He was Charlotte's husband, after all. Could she be in love with a man capable of such things?

The service drew to a close, and the coffin was carried up the aisle of the church. Patrick and Charlotte, together with Marion, walked directly behind the coffin. Behind them, he assumed by their appearance, had been Shamus' work colleagues. Slowly the mourners began to file out of the church. Joe's posture stiffened, and his hands formed into fists. Walking up the aisle amidst the mourners was Luke. Joe recognised him immediately from Charlotte's description.

Joe joined the throng as they assembled around the graveside, and the service continued. He saw Luke give a slight nod of acknowledgement to Patrick. Charlotte smiled at Joe, signalling him to join them at the graveside.

Joe walked over to her. "Are you all right, Charlotte?" he said.

Charlotte smiled weakly and placed her hand on Joe's arm. "Thank you for coming to the funeral," she said. "It was very kind."

Patrick walked over to his wife and placed his arm protectively around her shoulders. "Nice to see you again, Joe," he said. "It's been a long time. You'll be coming back to

273

the house for a drink and a bite to eat?"

"I'd like that," Joe said.

"Good." He kissed Charlotte lightly on the cheek. "If you wouldn't mind giving Charlotte and Marion a lift?" he said. "I'll join you at the house shortly. I have some business to attend to first."

Joe nodded. "Of course. My car's just outside the cemetery gates."

Joe walked towards the car, followed closely by Charlotte and Marion. He glanced back to see Patrick deeply engrossed in conversation with Luke.

It was almost an hour later when Patrick arrived at the house. The wake was in full swing with stories about old Shamus being relayed around the room, much to people's amusement.

"I remember him as a boy," said an elderly, yet distinguished gentleman sitting by the fireside. "Shamus was always a keen scholar. He would choose a book over a bicycle any day." He began to chuckle. "That's why he became such a good lawyer, I suppose. Don't you think so, Dermot?"

Dermot nodded. "I'm proud to have called him a friend as well as a colleague," he said. "He's going to be missed by all that knew him, that he will." Dermot drained his glass before turning to Patrick. "You'll be joining the practice now, will you Patrick? I know that's what Shamus wanted."

Patrick shook his head. "No, I don't think so. Tax and probate aren't my thing."

Dermot frowned. "What branch of the law is it you deal in? Shamus was a bit vague when I asked him."

Patrick refilled Dermot's glass with whisky. "Overseas investments mostly," he said.

Dermot raised an eyebrow. "Is that right? What's so fascinating about that to make you turn your back on your father's practice?"

Patrick shrugged. "The travel, I suppose," he said. "I enjoy travelling, in fact, I'm leaving for Poland first thing in the morning."

"So, you definitely won't be joining the practice?" Dermot shook his head. "That is a shame. Poor Deidre was hoping to stay on and be your secretary. She'd worked for your father for over twenty years."

Patrick frowned. "I deal with my own admin," he said. "Maybe she can work for the new solicitor you appoint."

"Maybe she will," he said. "It'll be a terrible shame if we have to let her go, so it will. Your father thought the world of her."

Patrick shrugged his indifference.

Dermot took a sip of the whisky, a mischievous glint in his shrewd-blue eyes. "By the way, Patrick," he said, "did you know Shamus had me draw up his Will last month?"

Patrick frowned, banged his glass on the table, and turned sharply to face Dermot. "What do you mean? He made a Will four years ago. I drew it up for him myself."

"Shamus made that Will before you got married," Dermot said. "He became very fond of Charlotte."

Patrick scowled. "What's in the new Will?"

Dermot frowned and shook his head. "I'm not really supposed to say," he said and drained his glass. "Not until the official reading."

"I think we can dispense with formalities, don't you?" he said scowling. "Tell me."

Dermot took a deep breath as he sat back into his chair. "Well, put very simply, Shamus has left everything to Charlotte," he said.

"Everything?"

Dermot nodded. "The house, his share of the practice, and his money and investments, of course. Shamus had quite a sizeable amount put away, as you well know."

Patrick stared at the old man. The veins on his neck pulsating. "Are you saying Charlotte is to inherit the entire estate?" he said, banging his fist on the table. "That's not right. I will oppose it."

Dermot shook his head and pointed a bony finger. "It's

perfectly legal, Patrick. Shamus is entitled to leave his estate to whoever he chooses, and I'm afraid he didn't choose you."

On hearing the commotion, Charlotte rushed over to her husband. "Is everything all right, darling?" she asked.

Patrick grabbed her by the shoulders and shook her. "Did you know about this, you scheming bitch?" he asked, his face contorted with anger.

Charlotte tried to stand back from her husband. "Patrick, what's wrong?"

Patrick moved forward and grabbed hold of her, pinning her against the wall. "Don't pretend you don't know," he said. "Visiting Shamus at the hospital pretending to care about him, when all the time you were plotting to steal my inheritance."

Tears ran down Charlotte's cheeks. "Patrick, please stop. You're hurting me," she said. "I have no idea what you're talking about."

Patrick grabbed Charlotte around the throat. "You won't get away with it," he said. "Do you hear me, Charlotte? No whore's daughter is going to take what's mine."

Joe rushed over to Charlotte and pushed Patrick aside. "Get your hands off her," he said, placing himself between them. "Touch her again, mate, and you're dead."

"Mind your own fucking business," Patrick said. "She's my wife, and I'll do what I want."

"I don't think so, pal," Joe said. He turned to face Charlotte. "Get your things together. I think it's best if you come back to England with Marion and me."

Patrick sneered. "Yeah, you take her back to England. I'm sure Karl Maddox will love to make her acquaintance again, eh, Charlotte?"

Charlotte sobbed uncontrollably. "Patrick, I… I swear I didn't know anything about this," she said.

Patrick pushed past her and headed for the door. "I don't believe you. You'll not get away with this, Charlotte, do you hear me? I'll make sure you don't get one penny of Shamus' money."

102

Alex's taxi picked Katie up outside her apartment. She smiled as she climbed into the vehicle beside him.

"Hi, babe," she said, planting a kiss on Alex's cheek. "Feeling lucky tonight?"

"I'm always feeling lucky," he said. "I'm a very lucky guy."

Katie laughed. "Who's covering the Amethyst? I thought Marco was on holiday."

Alex shrugged. "He is, but there is plenty of staff to manage things while I'm away. Anyway, Thursday night is quiet. The club is only half-full."

Katie frowned. "Your dad won't like that," she said. "He expects it bursting at the seams every night."

"Well, he's going to be disappointed then, isn't he? Anyway, he's going over to Dublin first thing tomorrow."

"What for? He's not thinking of opening a club there, is he?"

Alex shrugged. "Who knows? I just know he's going to Ireland with Peter and Paul."

"It sounds like it could be important."

Alex nuzzled Katie's neck. "As long as he keeps his nose out of my business, I don't give a fuck."

Alex and Katie arrived at the casino just after midnight. He made his way straight to the cashier's window and wrote a cheque for two thousand pounds.

"Let's have a drink first," Katie suggested as she walked towards the bar. "What do you fancy?"

"Whisky," Alex said as he took his seat at the roulette table. "Make it a large one."

Two hours later, Alex was a further twenty thousand pounds down.

Katie yawned. "Maybe it's time to call it a night," she said. "It's getting late."

Alex ignored her. "Fourteen red," he said, placing the last

of his chips on the table.

The croupier spun the wheel. Mesmerised, Alex watched as the wheel spun round and round. "Eighteen red," she said as she expertly removed Alex's bet and paid out to the young couple sitting at the end of the table.

Katie put her arm around Alex's neck. "Come on, babe," she said. "It's time we were—"

Alex roughly pushed her away. "Leave me alone," he said as he headed towards the bar. "I'll go when I'm ready and not before."

"Alex, please, you—"

He roughly grabbed hold of her and shook her. "I said, shut your stupid mouth. I need another drink."

A security guard who had witnessed the incident came over to Katie. "Is everything all right, miss?" he said. Katie nodded but said nothing.

"What the fuck has it got to do with you anyway?" Alex slurred. "It's none of your business. You're just the hired help."

The guard grabbed Alex by the arm. "I think it's time you were leaving, sir, don't you?" he said.

Another security guard joined his colleague. "Put the lady in a taxi," the first guard said. "Make sure she gets home safely." He turned to face Alex. "I think it's time to call it a night, don't you, sir?" he said.

Alex pushed past him and headed towards the bar. "I need a drink," he slurred. "After all the money you've made out of me tonight, I think you owe me that much."

The guard took a firm grip on Alex's arm. "I'm sorry, sir," he said. "I must ask you to leave."

Alex struggled to free himself. "Get the fuck off me," he said. "Do you know who I am?"

"Yes, sir, I do. I also know you are very drunk and you must leave the premises."

A second guard took hold of Alex's other arm, and together they bundled him towards the exit.

Matthew approached the group. "Is everything all right?"

he asked.

"Yes, boss. This gentleman is just leaving."

Alex turned to Matthew. "Are you going to let these goons get away with treating me like this?" he said. "They're a disgrace. A fucking disgrace."

Matthew indicated for the two men to release their hold on Alex. "There's a taxi rank outside, Mr Maddox," he said. "I think it best if you go home."

Katie was standing in the doorway. "Alex," she said. "Do you want to come back to mine? There's a taxi waiting."

Alex walked over to Katie. "All right, let's get out of here," he said. "Who needs a fucking casino anyway?"

"You do, Mr Maddox," Matthew said softly as Alex climbed into the taxi. "You do."

103

It was raining heavily when Karl, together with Peter and Paul Borowicz, arrived at St Bede's Church in Dublin at eleven o'clock on Friday morning.

Karl frowned as he pulled up his coat collar against the cold wind. "The place looks deserted," he said. "Are you sure this is the place?"

"That's what the old bird in the solicitor's office told me," Paul said. "Friday, eleven o'clock, at St Bede's."

"There's a bloke over there in the cemetery," Peter said. "Let's go and ask him."

The three men walked over to the old man who was pushing a wheelbarrow full of weeds.

Paul smiled as he approached him. "Good morning," he said. "It's cold this morning, isn't it?"

The old man grinned. "It's always cold here," he said. "I like it cold."

"We've come to pay our respects to Mr Flynn," Paul said. "His funeral's taking place here today."

The old man frowned. "Flynn? You mean old Shamus Flynn?"

"Yes, that's right," Paul said. "Shamus Flynn, the solicitor."

"Oh dear," he said, slowly shaking his head, "you've come a day too late, I'm afraid. Old Shamus was buried yesterday. That's his grave over there." The man pointed to the fresh mound of earth covered with wreaths and bouquets. "Very popular in Dublin was Shamus," he said. "He'll be missed, that's for sure."

Karl snorted and stared angrily at Paul. "You mean we've come all this way for nothing?"

Paul shrugged. "The woman said Friday. There's nothing wrong with my hearing or my memory."

Cursing, Karl headed towards the car, followed by Peter, leaving Paul with the old man.

"Was it a big funeral?" Paul asked. "Were there lots of

people?"

The old man grinned. "Oh, yes, half the town were in the church," he said. "Mind you, only the select few went up to the house for the wake."

"I don't suppose you were invited?"

The old man chuckled. "Me? No, I wasn't, but the wife and daughter were."

"Really?"

"They did the catering," he said. "By all accounts, I missed a good party. The wife said sparks were flying good and proper."

Paul frowned. "Why, what happened?"

The old man leant on his spade. "The wife said young Mr Flynn was furious when he learnt that Shamus had left everything to Charlotte, his daughter-in-law. Shamus had cut Patrick off without a shilling."

Paul tutted. "Patrick wouldn't have liked that."

The old man chuckled again, clearly enjoying spreading the gossip. "No, he did not." He looked over his shoulder before continuing in a hushed tone. "Of course, there are those who think it was terrible the way Patrick treated his father over the years. He never offered him any help when he took bad."

Paul shook his head. "Still, it doesn't seem right, does it, Charlotte not being of his blood?"

The old man shrugged. "Maybe not," he said, "but Charlotte is a lovely girl. Very kind she was when my wife was taken poorly last year. She offered to do her shopping, and she helped my daughter with the business. Nothing was too much trouble for her."

"Is Charlotte still at the house? I'd like to call and pay my respects."

The old man shook his head. "No, that's the thing. After the bust-up, Patrick flounced out and said he never wanted to see Charlotte again. The poor girl was distraught. It was a good job her gran and that nice black chap were there to take care of her."

"What did they do?"

"They took her over to England with them."

Paul frowned. "What about Patrick? Where's he?"

The old man put the spade into the wheelbarrow and picked up its handles. "The wife said she heard him say he was going to Poland," he said. "Anyway, I can't stand here chatting. There's work to be done. This new priest is keen as mustard to keep the cemetery tidy."

Paul turned and headed towards the car. Karl and Peter were already inside.

"What did he have to say that was so interesting?" Karl asked. "Haven't we wasted enough time here already?"

Paul grinned and climbed into the car. "On the contrary," he said. "I've just learnt something very interesting about Patrick Flynn and his wife. Something very interesting indeed."

104

It was late evening when Karl arrived back at the Emerald. "Peter, I want you to stay in the club," he said. "It looks busy tonight. Paul, you come with me."

Karl and Paul went up to the office. "We need to find out where Charlotte is," Karl said. "We'll start with the casino. See if she's with Joe."

Paul frowned. "She's more likely to be with Marion. Do we know where she lives?"

Karl shrugged. "I haven't a clue. I'll leave that to you to find out."

Paul yawned. "I'll ask around tomorrow," he said. "Right now, I need some sleep. I think we both do."

Karl banged his fist hard on the desk. "We can sleep when we've found the bastard who took Christina and killed one of my girls," he said. "If word gets out I've done nothing, I'll be finished."

Paul frowned. "Patrick is evasive, and he's clever," he said. "We don't have the manpower to flush him out."

"Then hire some. I want Patrick Flynn found."

Paul leant back in his chair and pursed his lips. "Perhaps I could have a word with Joe," he said. "See if he knows where Patrick is. I can go to the casino tomorrow."

Karl shook his head. "Joe wouldn't piss on me if I was on fire."

"He would if he thought Charlotte was in danger. From what that bloke at the cemetery said, Patrick threatened her in front of everyone."

Karl shrugged. "It's worth a try I suppose, but I'm not holding out much hope."

"What are you going to do if you do catch up with him? You can't just—"

Karl's eyes narrowed. "No? You leave that bastard to me."

The telephone on the desk rang. "Yeah?" Karl said.

"Karl, it's me, Lisa. What's going on? I've been trying to get in touch with you all day. Alex said you'd gone to Ireland."

"What's up?"

"It's just been on the news. Harry Delaney, he's... he's been found dead."

Karl shrugged. "What's that got to do with me?"

"You were with him a couple of days ago. I just thought—"

"Thought what?" Karl's posture stiffened. "The last time I saw Delaney, he was fine. Now get off the line, I have some calls to make."

"Okay. What time will you be home?"

"Late."

Lisa sighed. "Oh, no. Not you too. Christina's not home yet, either. I can't get hold of her."

"Where did she go?"

"She said she was meeting a friend for dinner."

"I don't suppose you know which friend?"

"No."

"Then what the fuck do you expect me to do?"

"There's no need for that, Karl. I was only saying—"

"Go to bed, Lisa. I'll see you when I get back."

He hung up and turned to Paul. "Pass me my pills mate. This bloody leg..."

105

Patrick anxiously paced the floor in Luke's stylish Manchester apartment. "I don't believe that stupid old bastard would disinherit me," he said. "I'm going to get him declared insane."

Luke frowned. "Can you do that? He was surrounded by solicitors. Surely they would know if your dad was off his trolley?"

"Maybe they were all in it together. None of the partners liked me in that firm. They probably conspired."

"I can't see them doing that," Luke said. "Your best bet is Charlotte. Talk to her and make her see sense."

"Do you seriously think she would give up everything Shamus left her? Her friend Joe will see to that."

Luke lit a cigarette. "That bloke at the funeral — he wasn't the one that came poking around your dad's office, was he?"

Patrick shook his head. "No. Deidre said he was white and his name was Paul."

"Do you think it was him that was sniffing around the warehouse with Karl and Delaney?"

Patrick shrugged. "Probably. It's a pity you had to kill Delaney. It's not going to be easy finding another haulier."

"I didn't have much choice," Luke said. "The stupid idiot took Maddox straight to the warehouse. We won't be able to hold girls in there again. What I don't understand is how Delaney knew about the warehouse."

"I met him there once to do business," Patrick said. "But he didn't know what the warehouse was being used for. He thought it was where we held the booze and fags."

"Well it didn't take Karl long to get onto him and find the warehouse, did it? How did he even know about Delaney's involvement?"

Patrick shrugged. "How the hell do I know?"

A faint smile came over Luke's face. "We really pissed Karl off, taking his daughter like that."

Patrick shook his head. "Don't worry about Maddox. He

was pretty smart pulling the stunt with the briefcase, I'll give you that, but he can't hurt us. We have the laptop, and he's got his daughter and that other girl back. That's all he was interested in."

"Let's hope you're right," Luke said. "Anyway, have you decided what you're going to do about Charlotte?"

"She'll most likely be with Marion in Leeds. I'll turn on the Irish charm. I'm sure with a little grovelling on my part, she'll be putty in my hands."

"After the way you spoke to her at the wake? I think you're going to have your work cut out. You were pretty cruel."

Patrick grinned. "Leave Charlotte to me. I can win her round. I always have in the past."

"Do you want me to go with you, just in case there's trouble?"

"Yeah, it might be best. Joe might be there. From what Charlotte told me about him, he's a hard bastard, not one to be messed with."

Luke grinned and pulled out a gun from his jacket pocket. "He might be tough," he said, "but he's not tougher than this."

Patrick reached over and snatched the gun from Luke. "No. Put that away. I need Charlotte to come back to Ireland with me willingly."

"Don't tell me you're going to play happy families?"

"I've told you, leave Charlotte to me," Patrick said. "Once I've persuaded her away from family and friends, she'll do whatever I ask."

"You really think she'll give everything back to you?"

Patrick smiled. "I think she'll make a Will to that effect," he said. "In fact I'll draw it up myself."

"And then what?"

"Well, it will all be very sad, but Charlotte will meet with a fatal accident. Her car brakes failing perhaps, or maybe a fall down the stairs. I haven't decided yet."

Luke grinned. "You really are an evil bastard, aren't you, Patrick."

"It takes one to know one," Patrick said smiling. "Now let's get over to Leeds."

106

Joe yawned. "How is she this morning?" he said, stretching his arms and legs.

"Charlotte's still sleeping," Marion said. "How was your night? It can't have been comfortable on that couch."

He grinned. "I'm fine," he said. "I wouldn't mind a coffee though."

"I'll make it, and then we need to have a serious talk with Charlotte."

Marion busied herself making the drinks in Joe's kitchen. "I must say, this apartment is very smart. Are you planning on staying here?"

"Maybe," he said. "I haven't really decided yet. Matthew wants me to stay on at the casino with him indefinitely."

"What about you? Is it what you want?"

Joe shrugged. "Like I said, I haven't made my mind up about what I'm going to do long-term. We have some business to deal with and after that... well, we'll have to see."

Marion walked back into the room. Her brow furrowed. "What is it you two are up to? I know there's something going on."

Joe frowned. "It's best you don't know," he said. "Now, what are we going to do about Charlotte?"

"Did I hear my name mentioned?"

Marion smiled. "Oh, you're up," she said. "I'll get you some juice."

"Thanks, Gran."

Joe sat on the couch and patted the cushion next to him. "Come and sit down," he said. "Marion and I need to talk with you."

Charlotte's eyes darted from one to the other. "You think Patrick is involved in trafficking, don't you?"

Joe nodded. "It certainly looks that way. It explains all the mysterious trips away."

"We don't really have any proof," Charlotte said. "The shamrock tattoo on Nadia's wrist isn't enough."

Joe reached out and gently took hold of Charlotte's hand. "Charlotte, Marion and I think it's best if you go away until this mess is sorted out."

"Go where? You heard what Patrick said at the wake."

Marion sighed as she handed the orange juice to her granddaughter. "Didn't Shamus give you any indication that he was leaving his estate to you?"

Charlotte shook her head. "No. I'm as surprised as anyone." She sipped at her drink. "Maybe Patrick's right," she said. "Maybe everything Shamus left me does belong to him."

Joe scowled and squeezed her hand. "Absolutely not," he said. "That inheritance is your security. If Shamus wanted Patrick to inherit, he wouldn't have left everything to you."

"Joe's right," Marion said. "I think Shamus knew his son was rotten. He left you the money so you could get away."

Charlotte sighed and shook her head again. "I don't know what to think," she said. "I can't believe I've been so stupid as to trust him."

"I'm going to… oh, who's that ringing at this time?" Joe said. "Hello…?" Joe took the phone through to the kitchen. He was frowning when he came back into the lounge a few minutes later. "Guess who that was?" he said.

"Patrick?"

"No. It was Paul. Karl Maddox's man. He wants to meet."

Marion frowned. "I wonder what he wants?"

"We'll soon find out," Paul said. "He'll be here in half an hour."

Marion and Charlotte were upstairs in the flat when Paul arrived. Joe showed him into one of the casino's booths. "I take it Karl knows you're here?" he said.

Paul nodded and looked straight at Joe. "I know you and Karl have your differences," he said, "but I think you both want the same thing."

"Really? And what's that?"

"To find Patrick Flynn and put a stop to his operation."

Joe shook his head. "I don't know where Patrick is."

Paul's eyes narrowed. "Maybe you don't, but his wife might. I take it Charlotte's here with you?"

Joe clenched his hands into fists. "That's none of your business," he said. "Charlotte has nothing to do with any of this."

"I'm not suggesting she's involved, but she might know where to find him."

"She doesn't. Anyway, what's Karl's interest in Flynn?"

"The bastard took his daughter and threatened to kill her."

Joe leant into Paul. "Karl shouldn't have tried to keep the laptop, should he?"

Paul was momentarily taken aback. "How did...?" Paul gained his composure. "Flynn's a ruthless bastard," he said. "We both know that. After the threats he made at the funeral, I don't think Charlotte's going to be safe until he's stopped, do you?"

Joe frowned. "How did you know about that? You weren't at the funeral."

Paul sighed. "It seems that one way or another, you've both been dragged into Flynn's dirty business. Don't you think it's time for you to join forces and put an end to it?"

Joe snorted and leaned back in his chair. "Work with Karl Maddox?" he said. "Never!"

"I shouldn't be saying this," Paul said, "but Karl has proof of what Flynn's been up to."

Joe raised an eyebrow. "If he has proof, he should let the police know."

Paul shook his head slowly. "We both know that's not going to happen. Karl prefers to do things his way."

"Patrick Flynn is not only dangerous, but he's clever and resourceful," Joe said. "He won't get caught by me or Karl. The only hope of stopping him is by getting the police involved."

"So that's your final word?"

"It is."

107

Luke scowled. "She's not here," he said. "The neighbour says Marion hasn't been to the flat in days." He climbed into the car and turned to Patrick. "What the hell do we do now?"

"She must be with Joe at the casino," Patrick said. "Let's get over there."

Luke frowned. "Are you sure you want to go there? Joe looked like he was going to kill you at the wake. If you show up at the casino, he might just do it."

"I don't have much choice," Patrick said. "I have to get to her before Joe and that old woman fill her head with poison about me."

Luke sighed and started the car's engine. "Okay, if you're sure," he said. "Back to Manchester it is."

"I have to work tonight," Joe said. "Will you two be all right in the flat?"

Charlotte grinned. "Stop fussing," she said. "Gran and I will be absolutely fine."

"She's right," Marion said. "You've got work to do downstairs. We'll be perfectly safe up here."

"All right," he said, "but make sure you keep the door locked and shout if you need anything, okay?"

"Bye, Joe," both women chorused.

At about nine o'clock, Joe was tending to a problem with one of the fruit machines at the far side of the casino. He didn't see Patrick and Luke enter, nor did he notice as they made their way through the door marked *Private*. Behind the door was the staircase leading up to Joe's flat.

The two men quickly ascended the stairs.

"You stay on the landing and keep watch," Patrick whispered. "I'll go inside and speak with her."

Luke frowned. "Okay, but hurry up," he said. "Joe could come back at any time."

Patrick gave a sharp rap on the door.

"That'll be Joe," Charlotte said, turning the key and unlocking the door. "Joe, I... Oh, Patrick, it's you." She stepped back quickly into the room. "What do you want?"

Patrick pushed his way into the flat. "Charlotte, we have to talk," he said. "Please, darling, let me apologise for the other day. I don't know why I said those horrible things to you. I was upset and—"

"Get away from her," Marion screamed, running towards him, flaying her arms. "Leave her alone and get out of here."

Patrick put up his arm to defend himself. "That's enough, Marion," he said as she reigned down blows. "Stop that before you get hurt." He pushed her, causing her to fall back against the wall and bang her head.

Charlotte ran over to Marion and knelt beside her. "You've hurt her. You've hurt Gran."

Patrick raised both arms. "I'm sorry. It was an accident," he said. "I didn't mean to do that. I just wanted to talk to you."

Charlotte cradled Marion's head, glaring defiantly at her husband. "I don't want anything to do with you," she said. "Joe's told me what you've been doing. I think you're evil."

Patrick scowled. "You shouldn't believe what he tells you," he said, grabbing Charlotte by the arm and attempting to get her to her feet. "We can work this out, Charlotte, I know we can. I can explain everything."

Charlotte pulled away from him as tears trickled down her cheeks. "If you don't get out of here now, I'll shout for Joe."

There was a commotion on the landing. The door burst open and Joe and Luke came tumbling into the room. Luke had his hands tightly around Joe's neck. Joe struggled to free his grasp while kicking out at Luke at the same time. Matthew came running from his office and threw himself at Patrick bringing him crashing to the ground.

Charlotte put her hands up to her face and screamed. "Stop it. All of you stop it," she said. "Marion's hurt." She turned to Patrick. "I want you to leave. Get out," she sobbed.

Patrick moved towards her. "Not without you," he said. "You're my wife and—"

Joe placed himself between Patrick and Charlotte. "You've got one minute to get out of here," he said, "before I give Karl Maddox a ring."

Patrick's eyes narrowed. "Karl Maddox? I thought you two were—?"

"Enemies?" Joe said. "We are until it comes to getting rid of scum like you."

Patrick shrugged and walked to the door. "Your last chance," he said, turning to Charlotte. "Come with me now, and there's a chance to save our marriage."

Charlotte carefully helped Marion to her feet. "Go to hell," she said. "I don't want you in my life anymore."

"No, but you want Shamus's money in your life, don't you? Money that is mine by rights."

She turned to face Patrick. "Is that why you came here? For the money?"

"Why else?"

Joe stepped forward and grabbed Patrick by the arm. "I think you'd better make yourself scarce, mate," he said. "Don't let me see you around here again, or next time you won't get off so easily."

Patrick scowled and pulled his arm free of Joe's hold. "I'm going," he said, "but this isn't over. Not by a long way."

108

It had been two weeks since Shamus Flynn's funeral. Despite his best efforts, Karl had been unable to locate the whereabouts of Patrick and Luke.

"At least we've stopped the bastard's operation," Paul said as he poured Karl and himself a whisky. "Sending that memory stick and George's notebook to the cops was a stroke of genius."

Karl merely grunted in response.

"It was on the news last night that the police have traced over twenty girls. It's a pity you sent the information anonymously though. You should be given a medal."

Karl shrugged. "I didn't do it for a medal. I wanted to flush the bastards out."

"Don't worry, the police will find Patrick and Luke. They can't get far without money and a passport. I heard they've had their bank accounts frozen."

Paul frowned as he watched Karl take two painkillers with the whisky. "Now things have quietened down a bit, why don't you see about getting your leg fixed properly?" he said.

Karl shook his head. "I've told you why. Having the operation can be risky."

"Taking risks has never stopped you before," Paul said. "I think you should get it seen to and—"

Karl thumped his fist on the desk. "And I think you should mind your own fucking business," he said. "I'll deal with it when I'm ready, okay?"

"Sure, you're the boss."

Karl closed his eyes briefly and sighed. "How's Katya doing?" he said. "Is Victor taking care of her?"

Paul nodded. "She's getting better. She wants to go back to Romania as soon as she can."

"Did the police catch the bastard responsible over there?"

"Ivan? Yes, he's in custody," Paul said. "He won't be drugging any more young girls." Paul drained his glass and walked towards the door. "It's almost time to open up," he said. "Are you coming down? You don't seem to spend much time in the club these days."

Karl shrugged. "There's not much for me to do. You and Peter seem to have the Emerald running like clockwork."

"We try, but I think the punters would like it if you made an appearance occasionally."

Karl sighed. "Okay, I'll be down about nine, but don't have the music on too loud."

Paul grinned. "You're starting to sound like an old man."

"I'm starting to feel like one. I think it's these bloody pills."

"Well, in that case, Karl, you know what you have to do," Paul said. "See you downstairs."

109

Joe drove to the airport with Marion and Charlotte.

"I can't believe you've talked me into cruising," Charlotte said. "The Caribbean sounds wonderful."

"It'll do you a world of good," Marion said. "Three months on a ship and you'll feel a new woman."

Charlotte smiled. "Yes, I suppose you're right," she said. "By the way, I was speaking to the police yesterday. They've still no idea where Patrick is."

Marion shrugged. "Well, don't you worry about Patrick, he can't hide forever," she said. "By the time we get back from our cruise, he and the rest of those evil men will be behind bars."

"I hope so. I can't bear to think what those poor girls went through."

"Well, it's all over now, darling, so stop fretting. Most of the girls have been rescued, and the evil network Patrick and Luke set up has been crushed."

"Right, ladies," Joe said as he pulled up outside the airport. "This is as far as I go."

Charlotte kissed him on the cheek. "Thanks, Joe," she said. "Thanks for everything. I don't know what I'd have done if you hadn't stopped Patrick from…"

"That's enough, Charlotte. No more talk of Patrick Flynn. From now on, you're a free woman. Enjoy yourself."

"You will say goodbye to Matthew for me, won't you?"

"Sure. He's sorry he couldn't be here to see you off, but he had to visit his mother at the nursing home."

"I hope he gets her home soon."

"I'm sure he will," Joe said. "Now, don't forget, Matthew and I want to hear from you regularly." Joe smiled as he took the suitcases out of the car boot.

"Of course, and you make sure you let me know what happens with Alex."

Joe winked. "That's going to be dealt with soon. Everything's in place."

Marion raised an eyebrow. "What's this?" she said. "Is it Alex Maddox you're talking about?"

Charlotte smiled. "I'll tell you all about it on the plane, Gran," she said. "Now, let's hurry up and check-in. We don't want to be late."

Marion smiled broadly as she walked towards the check-in with her granddaughter. "Next stop, Barbados," she said.

110

The ferry was packed with holidaymakers, all eager to get over the Channel to begin their summer holiday. Nobody noticed the two men sitting quietly in the corner of the bar.

"What's the plan when we get to France?" Luke said. "We can't start up again straight away, it'll be too dangerous."

Patrick frowned. "Tell me something I don't know. We'll just lie low for a while and wait."

"Wait? Wait for what? The police have all your contacts from the computer. Christ knows how Maddox managed to find them."

"It would take a genius to get through the security and work out the password," Patrick said. "I don't think Maddox could do that."

Luke shook his head. "Probably not, but I bet he knew someone who could."

"I'll deal with Maddox later," Patrick said. "Right now, I have more important things to think about than petty revenge."

"You're not going to let him get away with ruining our operation?"

Patrick lit a cigarette. "Luke, shut up," he said. "I'm trying to think."

"Well, you'd better think fast because the way I see it, we're fucked."

"We still have some contacts left," Patrick said. "I didn't put everything on the computer."

"The police raided every address in the UK where the girls were being held. How did they know about them?"

Patrick raised his hands. "How the fuck do I know?" he said. "You kept the UK records, didn't you? Maybe the police got hold of them somehow."

"How? I had them on my phone, and I destroyed that."

Patrick sighed. "Well, there's no point in worrying about it now," he said. "Anyway, all is not lost. I managed to get us new passports, didn't I?"

Luke shook his head. "What? A couple of dodgy passports that got us on this shitty ferry. That's only because they weren't inspected closely."

"Don't worry about the passports. They'll get us where we need to go."

"And where's that exactly?" Luke said. "I haven't heard your master plan yet. You do have one I suppose?"

Patrick grinned. "Yes, I have a plan," he said.

"Are you going to share it?"

Patrick moved closer to Luke and lowered his voice. "First we get to Switzerland," he said.

Luke scoffed. "Switzerland? Don't tell me we're going skiing?"

"Don't be a twat. Switzerland is where the bulk of the money is."

"Both our bank accounts have been frozen."

Patrick grinned. "In England, yes, but they can't touch the Swiss accounts."

"Are you sure about that?" Luke said. "I thought—"

"Luke, let me do the thinking, eh?"

Luke scowled. "It's a pity you didn't think a bit more carefully when you left the briefcase with the laptop inside at that hotel," he said. "We wouldn't have been in this bloody mess if—"

"Yes, that was careless, I admit that," Patrick said.

"Careless? It was bloody catastrophic."

Patrick narrowed his eyes and stared at Luke. "What's done is done," he said. "We can't change what happened."

"And what about Charlotte? She took your dad's cash from right under your nose. You didn't see that coming, did you?" he said. "Maybe you're not the mastermind you'd like to think you are."

Patrick was silent for a moment. The muscles in his face tightened as his eyes narrowed. "Believe me," he said. "I'll make sure Charlotte doesn't get to enjoy that money."

"Why, what are you going to do?"

"Wait and see," he said. "I have more important things to

deal with first, but when I'm ready, I'll make that scheming bitch pay."

"So, you really think we can start up again?"

Patrick nodded. "I have a few ideas. I just have to work out the details."

Luke shrugged and picked up the two empty glasses from the table. "I think we've just about time for another drink before we dock," he said. "Same again?"

111

Karl was preparing to go down to the club when the telephone rang. "Yeah?" he grunted.

"Is that Mr Maddox?" said a female voice. "Mr Karl Maddox?"

"Who are you?"

"Mr Maddox, my name is Frankie. I'm one of the dancers at the Amethyst."

"Why are you ringing me? Alex runs the Amethyst now, not me."

"Well, that's just it. Alex isn't here. The club should be open, but it isn't."

"Where's Marco? Isn't he there?"

"Marco has tried to get the doors open, but the locks have been changed."

"What the fuck are you talking about? Who's changed the locks?"

"I don't know. Like I said, I'm just a dancer. And another thing, Mr Maddox, my wages didn't go into the bank yesterday. Neither did any of the other girls."

"Put the phone down, and I'll ring Alex," Karl said. "There's been a cock-up somewhere."

Karl dialled his son's number. It went straight to answerphone. He rang the landline at his flat and again there was no reply. "What the fuck's going on?" he said as he raced down the stairs into the club. "Paul, we have to get over to the Amethyst fast."

"What's up?"

Karl shook his head. "I'm not sure what's going on. I'll explain on the way."

Both men left the club and were soon driving at speed in the direction of Manchester. Karl relayed the conversation he had had earlier with Frankie. "What do you think?" he said.

Paul shrugged. "Maybe Alex just fancied a few nights off and forgot to tell anyone."

"Then why change the locks? No, something serious is

going on there. I knew it was a mistake to give Alex the club. The stupid bastard's a liability."

"Calm down," Paul said. "It's no good making assumptions until we know the facts. Try ringing his number again."

Fifty minutes later, Karl arrived at the Amethyst. The club was in darkness, and a large group of people were standing around in the car park. On sight of Karl's vehicle, they rushed forward. The cacophony was almost deafening as Karl stepped out of the car. "Where's Marco?" Karl said. "Has anybody seen Marco?"

"I'm here," Marco said as he walked towards Karl.

"What the fuck's going on? Where's Alex?"

Marco shrugged and handed Karl a piece of paper.

"What's this?" he asked, struggling to read it in the dim light.

"It's a foreclosure notice," Marco said. "It was pinned on the door when I arrived. It says the club has been repossessed."

"Repossessed by whom?"

"By the new owners."

"What new owners? Alex owns the club."

Marco shrugged. "Not according to this," he said. "The new owners are the proprietors of the Lady Luck Casino. That's Jonny Dalton's old place."

Karl shook his head. "I don't understand. What's been going on?"

"Your son has been in the casino almost every night for the last few months," Marco said. "I've heard he owes them thousands. It looks like he's used the Amethyst as collateral for his debts."

Karl threw his hands up. "No, I don't believe this. Alex wouldn't be so stupid."

"Maybe you should get over to the casino and take it up with them."

Karl's face contorted with anger. "This will be Joe's

doing," he said. "If that bastard thinks he's taking the Amethyst—"

"There are two of them who own the casino," Marco said. "Joe is one, the other is a bloke called Matthew Glendenning."

Karl scowled. "Glendenning? That little runt who threatened me years ago? I don't believe this."

"I don't know anything about that," Marco said. "I just know Matthew's the one with the big bucks."

Karl grabbed Marco by the shoulder and put his face close to his. "Why didn't you tell me about Alex gambling?" he said. "I asked you to keep an eye on him."

"Alex isn't my responsibility," Marco said. "You should have watched him more closely instead of chasing after sex traffickers. You're the one who took his eye off the ball."

Karl shook with rage as he brought back his fist. Paul grabbed his arm. "Not now, Karl," he said. "We have to get over to the casino and sort this shit out."

Karl got back in his car.

"By the way, did you know the staff haven't been paid this month?" Marco said. "I don't think the utilities have been paid either." He smiled. "Your son's done you over good and proper, mate."

112

The Lady Luck Casino had been closed to the public that night. Joe and Matthew sat in the bar drinking whisky.

"He should be arriving any time," Joe said. "I can't believe it's finally coming to an end."

"You do still want to go ahead with the plan? It's not too late to walk away."

"Matthew, we've both got our initial investment back so what is there to lose? We go ahead like we agreed."

Matthew smiled. "Okay, just making sure you're still up for it," he said.

Joe whistled softly. "Two hundred and twenty-two thousand pounds," he said. "That's the final tally of what Alex owes."

"No wonder he left. He couldn't bear to face the music," Matthew said. "And Sarah has no idea where he's gone?"

Joe shook his head. "No. She got up this morning to find he'd packed and ran for the hills. It seems he took whatever monies were in the Amethyst account with him."

"Where's Sarah now?"

"I've put her in a hotel in town. I'm going to meet her after we've finished here."

"So, it's serious between you two?"

Joe smiled. "It's early days, but yes, I think Sarah could be what's missing in my life."

"You certainly like to live dangerously, Joe," Matthew said. "That's two of the Maddox women you've taken."

Joe grinned. "What about you? Are you still seeing Christina?"

Matthew shrugged. "It's complicated. We had dinner the other evening, but she has no idea about the casino or what Alex has been up to. I don't know how she'll react when I tell her what's been going on."

"I hope it works," Joe said. "She certainly seems to make you happy."

"I haven't told you the best bit, have I?" Matthew said,

smiling. "My mother's coming out of the nursing home next week. The doctors feel she's strong enough to cope."

"That's great news. I'm sure she'll soon be back to her old self."

Matthew frowned. "God, I hope not. A little mellower would be nice."

There was a sharp screeching of brakes, followed by the slamming of car doors.

Matthew winked at Joe. "It sounds like we have company," he said.

The casino's main door flew open, and Karl and Paul came striding into the room. "What the fuck's going on?" Karl said. "Where's my son?"

Joe walked over to Karl. "Good evening, Karl," he said. "It's good to see you looking well after all this time."

"Fuck you," Karl said, throwing the foreclosure notice down on the bar. "What the fuck is this all about?"

"It is what it says," Joe said. "It's a Foreclosure Notice on the Amethyst."

"Are you mad? I own the Amethyst."

Joe shook his head. "Not according to the document Alex produced," Joe said. "It stated quite clearly that he was the owner. Because of that document, Alex was allowed to use the Amethyst as collateral against his gambling debts."

"I don't believe you. He wouldn't—"

Matthew walked over and stood at Joe's side. "Alex has been in here most nights," he said. "In fact, he's probably our best customer."

Karl's eyes narrowed. "How much?"

Joe laid the chits out on the bar. "These are copies of the chits he signed," he said. "I have the originals."

Karl gave a cursory glance at the documents and then swept the pieces of paper to the floor. "This is madness," he said. "This can't be right."

"I assure you it is perfectly legal," Joe said. "Your son owes this casino two hundred and twenty-two thousand pounds."

Matthew folded his arms and sighed. "It seems that rather

than honour his debts, Alex has chosen to do a runner instead. As the Amethyst is not going to come anywhere near covering his debt, we will be taking legal action to recover the remainder of the money owed from his other assets."

"You just try and I'll—"

"We understand Alex also owns a share in three other clubs," Matthew said. "The Emerald, the Topaz and the Sapphire. Perhaps possession of the Emerald would cover the remainder of the debt. What do you think, Joe?"

Karl stepped forward, pointing a finger at Joe. "You won't get away with this," he said. "You might have stolen Erica from me, but you won't take my businesses as well."

Joe smirked. "That's exactly what I will do, Karl, and there's not a thing you can do to stop me."

Paul came over to Karl. "Let's go," he said. "We'll get Beauchamp to look this document over."

Karl lunged towards Joe. "I'm not going anywhere until I knock the smug look off that bastard's face," he said.

Skilfully, Joe stepped to the side. "I'm not fighting you, Karl, I don't have to. What's happened here is perfectly legal. This Beauchamp bloke will tell you that."

"This isn't over," Karl said. "Nobody makes a fool of Karl Maddox. Nobody, do you hear me?"

"Karl, there is one way we could settle this amicably," Matthew said.

"What do you mean?"

"Are you prepared to gamble?"

"What do you mean, gamble?"

Matthew smiled and walked towards the roulette table. "I suggest we sort this out with a spin of the wheel."

Karl scowled. "Are you fucking crazy?"

"No, I'm not crazy," Matthew said. "Joe and I are prepared to stake the casino and the whole of Alex's debt against all of your clubs. Winner takes all." He raised an eyebrow. "Well, Karl, what do you say? Are you in?"

Paul grabbed Karl's arm. "Don't do it, boss," he said. "We can sort this out another way."

Karl pushed Paul's arm away. "Let me get this straight," he said. "You'll put up this place, and the money Alex owes, against my businesses. Is that right?"

Matthew nodded. "That's exactly right," he said.

Karl licked his lips. "Well, I'll say one thing for you, you've more balls than your old man had."

Matthew frowned. "Leave him out of this," he said. "This is between you and me."

Karl laughed. "And it's to be decided with one spin of the wheel?"

Matthew nodded. "That's right. Red or black? You choose."

Karl frowned. "What do you think, Paul? Do you think I should gamble?"

Paul shook his head. "No, boss," he said. "I think you should walk away and leave it to Beauchamp."

"But you were only telling me earlier to take a risk. Don't tell me you've changed your mind?"

"Karl, this is crazy. Don't do it."

Karl walked slowly over to the roulette wheel. He was silent for a moment. The pulse on his neck throbbed and beads of sweat appeared on his forehead. "All right," he said. "Let's do it."

Matthew and Joe joined Karl at the roulette table.

"Well?" Matthew said. "What's it to be? Red or black?"

Karl stared at the wheel for a few seconds. "Black," he said. "I bet everything on black."

Matthew spun the wheel and carefully released the ball. It clattered noisily as it bounced from one compartment to another. The wheel rotated again and again before it slowed down and eventually came to a shuddering halt...

About the Author

Eva Carmichael followed her dream to live by the sea when, along with her husband and miniature schnauzer, she moved to Redcar in 2016.

Eva comes from a legal background, working first as a shorthand/typist for the West Yorkshire Police and then as a Special Constable. More recently, Eva worked as a legal PA in Leeds.

Although she has always enjoyed writing fiction, it wasn't until she came to live in Redcar that Eva took her writing seriously. She became a member of the U3A in Saltburn and joined the novel writing group, then joined the Scriveners Writing Group in Guisborough, where she was encouraged to pursue her dream of writing a book.

Eva's first novel, '*Bad Blood Rising*' was published towards the end of 2019. Her current book, '*More Bad Blood*' follows the same gritty path, delving into the seedy underbelly of the sex industry in the north of England.

Other Books by This Author

Bad Blood Rising – A Northern City... Money... Girls... Crime... Murder... And Bad Men

When a young prostitute is murdered by her pimp, Karl Maddox, he thinks the terrible secret she had threatened to expose is buried with her.

But when the murdered prostitute's daughter arrives in Leeds eighteen years later, she is seeking answers.

Slowly but surely, Karl's life as the wealthy, powerful kingpin of his clubland empire begins to unravel as loyalty is replaced by treachery, and friendship is replaced with hatred.

Is Karl about to find out that no secret can remain buried forever?

An exciting romp through the criminal underworld.

Printed in Great Britain
by Amazon